Daruss

Dragon Skull MC Daddies

April Kelley

Hard Rose Publishing

Cover by Miblart

Edited by No Stone Unturned

Contents

Daruss

One is his enemy. The other is his fated mate. As leader of his dragon shifter MC family, Daruss has never had so much to fight for.

Dragon shifter Daruss Oyen has everything to lose. After a rival club starts a war over territory, Daruss is there to fight for the family he's found. But everything changes after he falls in love with a snarky human named Jude, who happens to be the rival club's spy.

While he's determined to keep Dragon Skull MC together and somehow get his boy back, he meets his fated mate along the way. Daruss wonders if a sweet and innocent college graduate could ever go for bad boy biker like him.

But when Jude and Raylee are threatened, Daruss and the Dragon Skulls will have to win the fight if they're going to make it out alive.

Daruss is the first novel in the ***Dragon Skulls MC Daddies***. This steamy Paranormal Romance features a dragon shifter Daddy who's even more dangerous with his biker family by his side, a sassy human who's lived a hard life and will do anything to protect a sweet guy like his Daddy's fated mate, and an innocent college grad who know nothing about bad boys and Daddies. If you like a lot of sexy time between a Daddy and his boys with a happily ever after and danger thrown in, then you'll love this spicy romance.

Buy ***Daruss*** to find out how a Daddy handles two mates at once.

Trigger Warning: Violence (Not between the MCs), physical abuse (Not between the MCs), human trafficking.

Prologue

Darkness had settled into the room a few hours ago and hadn't left yet. The sun would rise in about an hour. Light from the moon streamed through the window and the television cast a soft glow. The local news was the only thing on so early in the morning. The newscaster regurgitated each story every hour. Jude had heard it twice.

The house was quiet. Jude lay on the couch trying to get tired enough to sleep. Memories of a party hung in the air in the form of marijuana smoke and the sour smell of spilled alcohol. No one had bothered to clean it up.

Feet pounded on the stairs. More than one set came down. Jude was startled when something, or rather someone, banged against the wall. They must have fallen into it because there was a feminine giggle right after.

"Watch your step, honey." The deep voice of Terrell, the Chained Devils MC leader penetrated the darkness.

Jude stiffened and sat up, scooting to the furthest end of the couch, getting as far away from Terrell as possible. He didn't want to draw attention to himself. Jude had learned the hard way how much Terrell didn't like him. As far as Terrell was concerned, Jude was a necessary part of keeping Mitch, Jude's older brother, on his payroll.

It didn't take much for someone to make Terrell angry. And it took even less time for Jude to set him off. Mitch kept Terrell from giving Jude a beat down. He would kill Terrell if he laid a finger on Jude.

Jude knew they were close to leaving the Chained Devils. The money Terrell gave Mitch to steal for him wasn't worth dealing with Terrell's volatile nature. Terrell had been throwing Mitch under the bus anyway. In the few months Mitch had decided to ride with the Chained Devils the level of danger for each job had increased. The last one had given Mitch a reputation because it had made the national news. The story ran on the news program Jude was watching. The evidence was stored in Terrell's garage in long crates containing rifles. Mitch would go to prison or worse, get killed, if he didn't get out from under Terrell soon.

Terrell came around the corner with the woman he'd gone upstairs with three hours ago. The woman's mascara was smudged. She swayed when she walked. Terrell had to hold her around the waist to keep her upright.

She smiled at Jude and tried to close the distance, but Terrell held onto her, keeping her from moving closer. She scowled at Terrell. "He's pretty. He'd make money."

Terrell sneered. "Who would buy him? He's just a little shit who's always fucking here." The last part Terrell said to Jude as if Terrell hadn't agreed to Mitch's terms when they'd negotiated all those months ago. Jude and Mitch were a package deal. Everyone who knew them knew that.

"Let me know. I'll add him to the auction list." And with that she stumbled her way to the front door. She even turned and waved at Jude as if they were best friends saying goodbye.

Terrell still stood in the living room, staring at Jude as if seeing him for the first time.

Jude might not have understood everything about what was going on but he picked up on the basics. He knew the woman sold humans. Knowing Terrell, he was probably trying to get a piece of the pie somehow. For all Jude knew, Terrell might even have people locked up and waiting to be sold to the highest bidder.

Disgust took over. He couldn't hide it. "Fuck you, Terrell. That's sick."

Terrell took a step in his direction, but Mitch came around the corner into the room. He carried a dufflebag. It was the one they used whenever they moved.

Jude knew his brother almost as well as he knew himself. He could tell by Mitch's expression that he'd heard the conversation. Terrell and the woman hadn't kept their volume down. But Mitch had been ready to leave before that, which meant he'd known what line of work the woman was in and what Terrell intended for the club. One more criminal enterprise to add to Terrell's list of sins.

Mitch was fully dressed. He even wore boots and his leather jacket.

He punched Terrell in the mouth, splitting his lip. Terrell stumbled. Mitch grabbed him by his shirt. "Jude is off-limits."

Jude could tell Terrell wanted to lash out but wouldn't with Mitch. He knew Mitch was the better fighter. Mitch was accustomed to street fighting and had even done it to support them at one point. Everyone knew Mitch's reputation. His size went a long way toward fueling the fear as well.

Terrell backed off, holding up his hands. He smirked. "Take him and don't come back, Mitch."

Mitch picked up the dufflebag he'd dropped and met Jude's gaze. "Let's go."

They were out of the door within seconds. Jude's heartbeat quickened. They bypassed Mitch's bike and took the car they shared instead.

Neither of them spoke until they were miles away. Mitch explained, "That woman...she's a human trafficker. I met her at one of the underground fights. She sells fighters to people looking to profit off them."

Jude shuddered. "Against their will?"

Mitch nodded. "She's bad news, baby bro. Terrell's looking to capitalize. I don't know how. But that isn't what we're about."

"Where are we going to go?"

"I know about some people. They aren't far away. They'll keep you safe while I figure out how to get those guns out of Terrell's possession. They're too high profile. He'll do something stupid, and I'll take the heat. I have to do something before that happens." Mitch made it sound too much like they would be separated. That wouldn't go well if they weren't together.

"What are you going to do?" Jude didn't want him to get hurt.

"I don't know. I'll figure something out." Mitch glanced at him.

Jude's stomach knotted. He wouldn't be able to talk Mitch out of it, so he didn't try. All he could do was let Mitch know where he stood. "I think we should stay together."

"I'm a liability to you at this point, baby bro." Mitch's name was in the mouths of a lot of people, so he was right in that way. Jude would be guilty by association, even though he didn't have anything to do with the crime Mitch was most noted for. He knew about them. That would be enough to put him in jail.

Jude sighed. “Just be careful. And promise you’ll come get me as soon as you can.”

“We won’t be separated for that long.” It wasn’t the promise Jude had wanted but it was as good as he would get.

Chapter One

The club was always packed on the weekends. More than just members were allowed to party. Non-members paid for their drinks as well as for other things if someone wanted to take part.

They were getting enough outsiders for Daruss to consider charging for entry. He'd have to bring it up with the guys to see what they thought. They had enough income streams and made a good enough living that every member got a piece of the pie. Charging for entry would put even more money in their pockets.

Skippy was on bouncer duty. There was always one asshole who put his hands on one of the boys. Everyone knew the Dragon Skulls didn't allow unwanted touches, looks, or anything else for that matter. But a newbie would come along and mess up. Skippy was spoiling for a fight on a normal day. Whenever it was his turn to watch over everyone the cops were called. It had gotten so bad the sheriff called Daruss once a month to get the schedule.

For the time being everyone was having a good time though.

Casper, their resident bartender, had one of the other members help on the weekend. They split the tips and the cash Daruss gave them after the night was over.

Most of the time, whoever helped did so because they needed the money. But Jonik was the one behind the bar with Casper. Daruss knew money didn't factor in for him.

Jonik had met his mate not long ago. The bonding was fresh. The little guy had a lot of trauma to work through. Part of the process was reacclimating back into society. But the Dragon Skulls clubhouse wasn't a normal place to be. Still, Jonik's mate, Wren, sat on a stool behind the bar and watched every move Jonik made as if he thought he would disappear if Wren didn't keep an eye on him.

Jonik set him up at the music thing they had in the corner. It wasn't DJ equipment so much as someone's cellphone hooked up to Bluetooth playing music through the speakers. It worked well enough. Wren did a fantastic job of picking the right tunes for the vibe of the room.

Even Daruss's boy was dancing. Jude didn't always. He preferred to drive Daruss crazy with lust by sitting on his lap and grinding against him. Of course, Jude's idea of dancing was to shimmy and shake as he bent at the waist. Daruss had a front row seat to bare ass cheeks jiggling like they meant business.

Daruss was five seconds away from kicking out whoever was in the club bedroom and having his way with him—that was Jude's goal.

When Jude danced his way to a standing position again and turned, Daruss crooked his finger and patted his thigh, inviting Jude to come sit on his lap.

Jude grinned and started to close the distance between them. He hadn't quite made it off the dance floor when an outsider grabbed his arm. Jude's smile stayed in place for about a second and then he scowled. He said something, pointing to Daruss.

When Jude tried to pull his arm out of the guy's grasp Daruss was up and out of his seat. Daruss had the man by the throat before he knew what was happening.

People moved out of the way when Daruss lifted him off his feet and carried him to the door. Several of the outsiders' eyes were wide. There were a lot of humans in the crowd. More than on a normal night. They didn't know about dragon shifters, so they hadn't expected that level of strength from Daruss. Especially not with such a big person.

As soon as Daruss was outside, he dropped the guy and then crouched in front of him, letting his eyes and hands shift. "No means no inside the club."

The man touched his neck when he regained the ability to breathe, but he scrambled away from Daruss.

Daruss stood, shifting back again. He watched as the human ran to a bike at the far end of the parking lot.

Daruss turned to go back inside when he caught a glimpse of a shadowy figure stumbling in the dark. He had to shift his eyes again. His vision enhanced with his dragon eyes. He saw a woman, bloody and beaten, stagger toward him. She wore a leather jacket and held her side.

Daruss went back inside for a second. Skippy stood by the door. "We got an emergency. Get Ronin."

Daruss didn't stick around long enough to find out how Skippy carried out his order.

The woman must have recognized him as the Alpha of the Dragon Skulls. She was a dragon shifter too, although Daruss didn't remember having met her. They must have been in the same room at some point because she sighed as if relieved when she saw him.

Daruss put an arm around her, holding her up. "Can you make it inside?"

She smirked but it came off as more of a grimace because of her fat lip and swollen cheek. She held her left arm close to her body as if it pained her to move it. "If I can't, we'll both know it."

Daruss lifted her into his arms.

By the time he made it inside, the music had stopped, and Ronin made his way into the main room from the back.

Daruss turned to Skippy. "Make all the non-members leave."

"If you ain't a Skull, get the fuck out." Skippy's booming voice carried across the room.

Daruss laid the woman on the couch.

Jude had put on his pants, which was a shame. Daruss liked it better when he was naked. Nothing but the pretty red thongs against his creamy skin came a close second.

Not that he had time to think about fucking Jude anymore. He had a very real problem on his hands, and he needed to focus.

Daruss met Ronin's gaze. "She's one of your runners, right?"

Ronin nodded. He pulled out his phone and typed. Something in the woman's coat pocket chirped like a bird. Daruss figured it was her phone, so he fished it out for her.

While he brought up the screen, he started giving the orders. "Jude, come here."

Jude closed the distance, sitting on the floor beside her. He gave her a concerned smile before meeting Daruss's gaze. "How can I help, Daddy?"

Daruss pulled his phone out of his pocket and handed it to Jude. "And stay with her."

No one would leave the woman alone to fend for herself. Someone would always be with her, which meant his boy would be safe too.

Daruss met the woman's gaze. "Password."

"Three four nine two." The woman closed her eyes but she kept wincing.

As soon as Daruss saw the words *Dragon Skull*, he knew it was Ronin. He brought up the texts and then read it to her. 'Was it the Chained Devils?'

She nodded. "A guy named Stan and one other asshole. The same two who got Gregory last week."

Ronin put his phone into his pocket. He scowled when he signed to Daruss. "What do you want to do?"

Daruss had to think about it. "Seryn and Avit, follow me to the back room."

Daruss didn't wait for them to follow instructions. He knew they would. They were two of his most ruthless members. They had skills beyond that of a normal person. Avit was a dragon shifter, but he could blend in with the best of them. He had a bit of a baby face, so he always took people by surprise whenever he went in for an attack.

Seryn was something else entirely. Even Daruss wasn't sure what he was. All he did know was that he was a warlock. But that wasn't all. He grew claws and fangs on occasion. He'd never met anyone who had abilities like those and was also a warlock until they'd rescued Seryn.

How Daruss had ended up with two rare paranormals was anyone's guess. Maybe it was the work of the gods.

Landry sat alone, drawing in his sketchpad. He wasn't much for partying and didn't like crowds. He was one of the best artists Daruss had ever met and a great tattoo artist too. Daruss didn't let anyone else touch his skin but Landry.

Landry met his gaze. "Do you need me to leave?"

"You can stay."

Landry raised his eyebrows when Seryn and Avit entered the back room. "Is there anything I can do?"

Daruss contemplated that for a moment. "Yeah, babysit Ronin's runner and my boy for the rest of the night."

Landry nodded and stood. He closed his sketchpad but took it and his pencils with him.

Daruss met Seryn and Avit's gazes. "Infiltrate the Chained Devils. Cause a little trouble while you're there."

Avit nodded but it was Seryn who smiled and said, "One by one, they fall like dominos."

He said the weirdest shit sometimes. And he spoke in a serene tone, even when he talked about killing people. He was aptly named for that reason.

Avit scowled at him. "Creepy little shit."

Seryn chuckled. "I like a good party."

Avit met Daruss' gaze. "Thanks for pairing me with him. You know how much he creeps me out."

Says the guy who kills people for a living. "Stop being so fucking judgmental."

Seryn just smiled as if he thought Avit's reaction was a compliment.

"Can we get started right now?" he said it as if Daruss had given him a gift.

"The sooner the better." Daruss needed to nip the territory war with the Chained Devils in the bud before it turned into something he couldn't control. As it was the frequency of the attacks made him feel as if he were losing his grip on the situation.

Chapter Two

The speed limit went from forty-five miles an hour to twenty-five as he entered downtown Wingspan. The man on the motorcycle either hadn't seen the signs stating what the limit was or he didn't care because he came up fast behind Raylee and zipped past without a thought.

Raylee rolled his eyes. If Raylee had still been in the city, he might have let his road rage fly. But didn't everyone know each other? Especially a dragon shifter town where the residents were also a part of the clan.

A few cars took up the parking spaces. Someone, who seemed to be headed for a grocery store, waved as Raylee drove past. And a man with salt and pepper hair came out of the flower shop carrying a bunch of small sunflowers. The flowers appeared happier than he did. Raylee found the contrast amusing.

Raylee's phone rang. He pulled onto the side of the road before pressing the green phone icon. "I'm almost home."

His older sister, Jazlyn, had always had bad timing when it came to calls. He had the same issue with their mother, so maybe it was a genetic trait. Raylee hadn't inherited the trait, but he was like her in every other way. Jazlyn had a different dad biologically, but Enzo Galloway had adopted his ex-wife's baby. So Raylee, who was human, had grown up with a wonderful dragon shifter father.

"Dad wants to know if you're hungry."

Raylee heard his dad's deep voice in the background.

"That's not what I wanted to ask him. Just give me the phone," Dad said. "I want to know if you've eaten."

Raylee smiled. "Not since leaving my apartment this morning."

Raylee had spent the past three days packing everything he owned into a small trailer. The big move after finishing college shouldn't include working for his sister at her store and moving back in with his father, but it wasn't as if he had a choice. It was only for the summer, just until he figured out where he wanted to live. He had a nursing degree. Since nurses were in demand across the country, he could work anywhere. A bigger city held some appeal. Thanks to his older sister giving him a job and his dad letting him move back home for a while, he didn't have to decide anything right away.

"You drove all day without eating." Dad sighed. The next thing he said, he must have been saying to Jazlyn. "This is why we need to make sure he takes a job around here. We need to make sure he's taking care of himself."

"I've drunk water." And that should count for something. All through nursing school, he'd subsisted on coffee and energy drinks. When Dad had harped on him, he cut back on the caffeine for a while but always fell back onto bad habits. The past week he'd cut out caffeine because he knew Dad would get after him if he didn't. It was rough for the first couple of days but he'd made it through the headaches. Dad should be proud of him, not complaining about his other bad habits.

Did he have to change them all? Some he kind of liked. Like his addiction to chocolate. Loved that. And he liked cookie dough ice cream. He ate that for dinner at least twice a week. And he wanted his coffee back, damn it.

"I'll make your favorite."

Raylee's stomach rumbled with the thought of Dad's macaroni and cheese. "You're the best. You know that, right?"

The affection was clear in Dad's tone. "And you're my favorite child."

"Hey. I'm right here." Jazlyn's protest was loud enough for Raylee to hear. She must have been standing right next to the phone. "The least you could do is say it behind my back."

Dad chuckled. "We'll see you soon, son."

They ended the call and Raylee got the car moving again.

It wasn't long before Raylee was pulling into Dad's long driveway. Trees lined the paved drive. Dad kept the forest tamed but it was still a part of the property, as if it were a protective barrier from the outside world.

Dad had created the perfect retirement oasis for himself. But he had bought the property because of the acreage. He'd renovated and added two separate living spaces, anticipating his babies coming back into the nest at some point.

Dad stood on the front porch but closed the distance when Raylee parked in the drive behind Jazlyn's slick red Camaro.

As soon as he shut off the engine and exited his vehicle he was enveloped in Dad's big arms. Raylee had always felt safe or secure, especially when his dad hugged him.

"Your mother called." Dad leading with that meant Mom had ratted him out about his caffeine consumption.

"I'm no longer addicted to coffee so she can suck it." Raylee shut his eyes and just breathed in the fact the long drive was over. He could relax and let his dad baby him for a while. "And besides that. She doesn't know what I do. She's not even in the states."

Dad chuckled. "You just told me that. Not your mother. You never were good at keeping stuff from me. Or your mom, for that matter."

Raylee groaned. "I always believe you when you lie. That's what it is."

Dad growled in a teasing way. "I didn't lie. She really did call. A couple of hours ago wanting to know if you'd made it. She said you hadn't called her in two days and she's worried about you."

Well, shit. Raylee really had told on himself then. "I've been busy packing."

"Don't tell me. Tell her."

Raylee sighed. "I'll call."

The front door opened and closed right before Jazlyn squealed. Dad let Raylee go so Jazlyn could have a turn.

Jazlyn's hug was almost painful. "Six months is too long to go without seeing you."

Raylee agreed and hugged her back. He'd wanted to make a final push and take classes through the summer, so he hadn't come home.

She'd changed her hair, putting it into long braids. They hung down her back. She was taller than him by a few inches, but she'd always been thin.

Raylee pulled back with a grin, meeting her gaze. "How is it that you get more gorgeous in your advanced age? It's not fair, considering I'm so much younger than you."

Dad snorted.

Jazlyn narrowed her eyes. “I say how much I miss you and you call me old. Mean little shit.”

Raylee chuckled. “Thirty seems ancient. I’m just saying.”

Jazlyn growled and pulled him into a hug again. “I really have missed you.”

Raylee tightened his hold. “Me too. And you seriously have gotten more beautiful. It’s very unfair.”

Jazlyn chuckled. “It’s Dad’s cooking.”

“She treats my refrigerator like a supermarket.” Dad might bitch but he loved taking care of them.

Jazlyn snorted and rolled her eyes. “Says the dragon who has mac and cheese baking in the oven for his ‘favorite kid’.”

Dad winked at Raylee. He had striking green eyes, which Jazlyn had inherited. But Dad’s skin was a darker shade of brown. Jazlyn had inherited her beauty from him.

“Fine. I don’t have favorites, but if I did, you would be my favorite daughter.” Dad headed into the house.

“I’m your only daughter.” Jazlyn held Raylee’s hand as they followed.

“That we know of. I was wild in my youth. How do you think you got here, Jazzy?” He stopped and looked up at the sky as if the memory was projected on a cloud. “That was a fun night, not that I remember all of it.”

Raylee laughed. “Oh my gods, Dad.”

Jazlyn made a face. “You have a twisted sense of humor.”

Dad chuckled. “Where do you think you got it from?”

“Thank you for giving me a job while I figure out what’s next.” He leaned into Jazlyn and bumped shoulders with her. He appreciated his family more than he could ever express.

"No way would I miss a chance to boss you around." She smiled and then sighed. "I need the help if I'm being honest. I hired a part-time person, but I don't think she's going to work out. She's nice and all but she gets a little testy with the customers."

"It's a bookstore. What's not to love about that? That's like saying working with puppies puts her in a bad mood." Raylee didn't understand why someone wouldn't be all smiles around books.

"That's what I said." Jazlyn shook her head. "I just hope I can find someone before you're off to your fancy job in a hospital or wherever."

Raylee chuckled. "I love how you classify helping sick people."

Jazlyn might not have wanted to follow their parents' lead and work in the medical field, but she knew how *"fancy"* it wasn't. She just didn't want to have to hire someone else. In her defense, it probably was difficult to find good help in such a small town like Wingspan.

Raylee headed straight for the kitchen. The aroma of rich cheddar cheese filled the air.

It was good to be home.

Chapter Three

Jude cuddled closer to Daruss, tightening his hold. Daruss always slept on either his back or his side. And he always held Jude the whole night. Jude hadn't felt so safe and protected before.

He was in love, and he suspected Daruss knew it. Both created more problems than Jude was prepared to deal with. He didn't know how to get out of the mess he was in as it was. Being in love complicated everything.

At the moment he had three problems. One was his stay with the Dragon Skulls had always been temporary. He'd have to leave Daruss when Mitch came to get him.

His second and most immediate problem was the fact he was Mitch Burke's brother. Mitch had done a good job of hiding Jude, considering the Dragon Skulls were enemies of the Chained Devils. Everyone who knew anything about the MC gangs around these parts knew it. But Mitch was still associated with the Chained Devils. He hadn't done enough yet to get out from under their shadow. Or if he had, Jude hadn't heard about it.

Daruss would lose his shit all over Jude when he found out who Jude was.

The third problem was one he needed help with. Months had gone by with no word from Mitch. It had been too long. Jude worried Terrell had gotten the better of Mitch somehow. He needed to find his brother. Daruss would be able to help. He had the resources, but Jude didn't think he would. He considered Mitch an enemy. He'd mark Jude as one too. Worse, he'd view him as a traitor once he found out Jude's secret, but what choice did Jude have? He didn't see any other way.

He knew Daruss well enough to know there wasn't an excuse he'd accept. Daruss had an edge hard enough to cut anyone who crossed him.

Jude sent a silent prayer to whatever god cared that Daruss wouldn't be a prick when Jude told him the truth. No doubt, the gods laughed their asses off because even they knew how ridiculous the request was. Daruss wouldn't give Jude a chance to explain himself very easily. If he could find the right thing to say, then maybe Daruss would help him.

Jude rolled away from Daruss. The lack of contact chilled him. Daruss was always like a furnace. Jude pulled the covers up to his chin and stared at the ceiling, trying to talk himself out of doing the hard thing but he didn't have anyone else who would help him.

He would save himself if he stayed quiet. Not that he thought Daruss would hurt him. At least he wouldn't get violent. Daruss would smash his heart into a million pieces, call him a liar and a traitor, and try to lock him up somewhere until he figured out what to do with him. But maybe somewhere in the mess of all that Daruss would hear Jude's words instead of who his brother was.

"Get back here, boy." Daruss's voice was rough and sleepy. Despite that there was still affection in his tone.

Jude smiled. And moved into Daruss's side again.

Daruss ran his hand along Jude's back to his ass. "Go back to sleep."

"I can't." Jude didn't want to say why. It would mark the start of his confession.

Daruss patted Jude's ass cheek. "Straddle my lap."

When Daruss gave an order, Jude's body wanted to obey. It went against his nature not to. "Yes, Daddy."

All thoughts went out of Jude's mind the second he felt Daruss's cock touching his balls. Jude rubbed against Daruss.

He shut his eyes when he did it again.

Daruss, smacking his ass, startled Jude. Jude's cock jumped, wanting another one. "Did I give you permission to take what you want?"

Jude whimpered as he stilled. He bit his lip and met Daruss's gaze. "No, Daddy."

Daruss's gaze heated. "Is this why you couldn't sleep? Did you wake up needing me?"

Jude thought about whether answering in the positive was a lie and decided it wasn't. Jude did need Daruss, although he hadn't been thinking about sex until the moment Daruss's hard length pressed against him.

Jude nodded. "I always need you inside me, Daddy."

What if it was the last time?

Jude stood on a pile of what ifs. They shouted about all the possible consequences he could face. All of them led away from Daruss.

Daruss growled and grabbed a tube from the nightstand. It sat next to Daruss's phone and the lamp. Daruss didn't have an alarm clock in his bedroom. A guy like Daruss didn't wake up to an alarm. He went to bed in the early morning hours and woke up in the afternoon. Any business took place when Daruss wanted it to. Not the other way around.

Daruss squirted lube onto his fingers before reaching behind Jude.

Jude laid on Daruss, giving him room. Jude shivered when he felt Daruss's finger enter him. And then he moaned.

God, he loved getting fucked. There wasn't anything better than having Daruss inside him.

It made him forget everything else. All his stress left his body, and he was left with pure pleasure.

Did that make him an addict? It seemed as if he chased a high. But he wasn't sure if that made him addicted to fucking or addicted to Daruss.

Daruss added another finger. Jude could tell Daruss didn't want to go slow. He wouldn't linger because it wasn't about foreplay. Daruss knew Jude didn't need it.

When Daruss thought Jude was open enough, he pulled his fingers out.

Jude whimpered, wanting Daruss. He didn't like the sudden empty feeling.

"Lube my cock before you take me."

Jude nodded and grabbed the tube, squeezing the lube into the palm of his hand. He moved to free Daruss's cock. It settled against his ass cheeks. Jude reached behind himself for Darruss's cock, coating it in slick.

Daruss moaned and after only a couple of pumps, he growled. "That's enough. Put it inside you, boy."

Jude positioned Daruss's cock at his hole and then sank onto it. It felt familiar and exciting all at the same time.

Daruss held his waist, lifting him when Jude took about half his cock. His strength was amazing. Jude was above average in weight. He didn't have a poor body image. He was comfortable in his own skin.

And Daruss loved Jude's body. He always made Jude feel gorgeous. But Daruss being able to lift him was sexy.

Jude sank down again, taking Daruss's entire length. He braced himself on Daruss's chest and let Daruss move him where he wanted him.

Daruss held him in place, fucking into him. Daruss was never passive or submissive. He wasn't good at letting Jude top from the bottom. It was another thing Jude loved about Daruss because Jude was about as submissive as they came where sex was concerned. They meshed on every level. Sex with Daruss was the best Jude had ever had.

Daruss set a punishing pace.

It didn't take long for Jude too feel his orgasm build in his core. Jude moaned and shut his eyes. "I'm gonna come, Daddy."

"Come. Now." And just like that. The command was all Jude needed to get the rest of the way there. Jude shot streaks of cum onto Daruss's abdomen.

Jude's hole tightened, making Daruss feel even bigger inside him.

Daruss wasn't far behind. Daruss fucked into him harder. Their skin slapped. The strain from chasing the white-hot pleasure was evident in Daruss's expression.

If Jude hadn't been watching Daruss, he might have missed the way Daruss's eyes had turned reptilian as if his dragon had come out. He also had fangs. When Daruss came, he did so while growling, "mine".

Daruss stilled. His muscles relaxed as he came down from the pleasure. He held him when Jude collapsed onto Daruss.

Jude's cum made a wet mess between them.

Jude didn't know what his eyes and fangs meant. It had never happened before. Jude knew Daruss was a dragon shifter, but he'd never seen the dragon part of him. Jude had managed to avoid the violence between the Dragon Skulls. Not that they fought very often but all motorcycle clubs had an initiation ritual which included violence of some kind. He knew from the talk around the club that the Skulls weren't any different from the Chained Devils in that regard.

The sun was bright as it streamed through the gap in the curtains. A streak of light made its way to Daruss as if it sought him out. His light green eyes were human again.

Jude relaxed, laying his cheek on Daruss's chest.

Daruss rubbed his back and then his ass cheeks. His cock was still inside Jude. It wasn't quite soft enough to fall out on its own. "Are you okay?"

"Yeah." Why wouldn't he be? Especially after Daruss fucked him so good.

"Do you have any questions?"

Jude frowned. "About...what?"

Daruss sighed. "I know you saw me shift."

Jude stiffened and tried to move onto the mattress again, but Daruss held him in place.

"I won't hurt you."

Oh god. "You thought about it?"

Daruss swatted Jude on the ass. It startled him because he wasn't expecting it. "I just told you that I wouldn't. I've never lied to you."

He could pretend it hadn't happened. Jude had become very good at pretending Daruss was a normal biker. He'd like to keep the illusion.

"It means that I have affection for you."

Oh god. That hurt Jude's heart.

Jude hadn't expected more than Daruss wanting to scratch an itch before the next boy came along. In some ways Daruss not reciprocating Jude's feelings made Jude's secret easier to tell. It meant maybe Daruss's reaction wouldn't be so harsh when he found out.

Jude spoke in a rush, wanting to get it over with. The sooner Daruss knew the thing, the sooner Jude could work to get him to understand why he'd kept it a secret in the first place. "Mitch Burke is my older brother. He's in trouble. I need your help."

Daruss stiffened and then lifted Jude off him. His cock left Jude's body. Daruss stood and slammed the door to the bathroom.

Jude tried to keep the emotions at bay. He didn't want to cry. That wouldn't help him or Mitch.

He decided to take a shower. As soon as he opened the door, Daruss came out of the bathroom, walking to the nightstand and grabbing his phone. "Don't leave this room."

"I only want to shower." Jude had cum on his stomach and dripping from his ass.

"Don't. Leave. The fucking. Bedroom." Daruss turned, hiding from Jude again. He heard Daruss say, "fucking infiltrator. I should have known" before the door slammed shut again.

Jude sat on the side of the bed, trying to figure out how long he should hold out hope for Daruss to come around. He rubbed his chest when it began to ache and told himself not to think about how Daruss would break his heart before it was all said and done.

Chapter Four

How had Daruss let himself get sucked in by Jude? Daruss had let his dick lead him until Jude had him by the fucking balls. It was the stupidest thing he'd ever done.

Daruss drank dragonshine straight from the bottle. Thank the gods Ronin had made extra, and it was stronger than his last batch. The gang made the most money on dragonshine, so Daruss put eighty percent of their energy into it. It was why the territory war they had going on with the Chained Devils was such a big problem.

Ronin was very good at specialty blends. He experimented with fruit and spices a lot. The batch Daruss drank from was flavored with apples and cinnamon. It was the best one yet, in Daruss's opinion.

Daruss raised the bottle to Ronin, who sat at the bar watching him. Ronin doubted himself a lot. He was always looking to Daruss for reassurance. As the alpha of Dragon Skulls, it was Daruss's job to take care of every member. They were a family. Daruss wanted to build Ronin's confidence, but he wasn't sure how, other than to praise him when he did a good job.

Hell, he'd rescued almost every member in the club. Izzy was the only exception and that was because Izzy had been his ride or die since they were kids.

Ronin smiled and nodded. His hands flew as he talked about sending bodyguards with each runner.

"I didn't think to do that. That's a smart move." Daruss didn't need to raise his voice for Ronin to hear him. Dragon shifters had very good hearing.

Ronin was the best at reading Daruss. Daruss didn't give much away, but he couldn't escape Ronin's scrutiny. No one really could. Ronin lived in a world where people spoke to him, but he couldn't reciprocate the same way a speaking person could. He could hear but his ability to speak had been cut out of him, quite literally.

The scars on his neck went deep. Sometimes Daruss thought they went as deep as Ronin's soul.

Ronin asked him what was wrong and Daruss glanced at Jude, who'd curled into the far corner of the couch. He wore clothing, not just the tiniest thongs he owned. That alone told everyone in the club something wasn't right. The tension between them was palpable. Everyone felt it, even though Daruss hadn't talked about it yet.

Jude couldn't get further from Daruss if he tried, but it seemed as if he wanted to. Daruss couldn't let Jude out of his sight, but he wished he could. For three solid days he'd kept Jude close but at arm's length. He wanted Jude miles away from him, so he didn't have to see him anymore.

He couldn't take Jude's sad blue eyes, making silent accusations as if it were Daruss who'd betrayed him and not the other way around.

Fucking hell.

Daruss had never been in love before. And Jude wasn't his mate, not that it seemed to matter. Daruss had feelings for him anyway. A part of him wanted to kick Jude's sweet ass for that alone. He felt cursed by Jude. As if he had cast a spell.

Ronin didn't ask more questions, which was a good thing. Daruss wasn't ready to talk about it.

Daruss pointed to Jude, telling Ronin to watch him. He grabbed the bottle off the table and stood.

"Stay here."

Jude didn't respond.

Daruss turned to him. "Acknowledge me, Jude. Now."

Jude met Daruss's gaze, but he didn't speak. He hadn't said a word since his little confession three mornings ago. Probably because Daruss was on the edge of anger. Jude knew when to keep his mouth shut. He was a smart boy. He also knew he was a prisoner. Daruss could practically see the cogs turning in Jude's mind, trying to figure out what his next move should be.

But Daruss wanted to reassure him, although having the feeling at all pissed him off, as if he were a traitor to himself.

Daruss leaned down until he was inches from Jude's face. "I won't hurt you. You should know that."

Jude rolled his eyes. "Yeah."

So that wasn't what had Jude's wheels turning. He must want something. That was the only explanation. "What the fuck do you expect from me then?"

Jude averted his gaze. "Help. I need to find my brother. He's in trouble. Please, Daruss."

Daruss shook his head. "Help the little traitor find the enemy."

"No!" There was so much conviction in Jude's expression. "I never betrayed you, and I never will. The only reason I told you was because I think...I think Mitch is in trouble. He's been MIA for too long."

Daruss growled. "Keeping secret was your mistake."

Daruss wanted to believe him, but he needed to know he could trust him first. Jude could be the very thing that would bring Daruss to his knees if he wasn't careful.

Jude shook his head. "You wouldn't have kept me safe if I had told you."

The way he worded that made Daruss pause because he would have kept the secret too, if he were in Jude's shoes. "I would have kicked you out of the club as soon as I found out who you were."

"I know." Jude sighed. "So was I just a piece of ass then? All that eye shifting, and fangs doesn't mean affection, does it?"

"No, it doesn't." Daruss knew the second he lied that he shouldn't have. He was so fucking pissed and he wanted to hurt Jude.

He did a damn fine job of that.

The light went out of Jude's eyes. He averted his gaze. "It was never just that for me, Daruss. Not even our first time."

He squashed the part of him that wanted to hold Jude and apologize. Daruss let him go. "If I knew you'd keep your mouth shut, I'd send you back to your brother."

"I don't know where he is." The words were spoken as if he were dead inside. The confident boy who'd walked into the club all those months ago was gone. In his place was someone resigned to his fate.

Daruss growled and turned. He took the bottle with him when he went outside. He leaned against the building and took a swig.

Thirty bikes were in the lot, parked together. They were similar but unique in their own way. Daruss took them in even as the decision to get drunk took hold of him.

Izzy came out, standing next to Daruss.

Daruss passed the bottle over.

Izzy drank. "Ronin is a fucking artist, man."

That was a good way to describe him. "He's perfected the art of moonshine. No doubt about that."

Izzy handed the bottle back to Daruss. "What's up between you and your boy?"

"Three days ago he told me he was Mitch Burke's brother." It wasn't all Jude had said, but it caused Daruss the most stress. He didn't know what to do about Jude.

"The guy who stole all those guns for Terrell Gibbs?" Izzy lifted his eyebrows.

"One and the same." If there was another Mitch Burke who also was Daruss's enemy, he would have wanted to know who he was.

"Well, shit. That's not good." Izzy had a way of simplifying things and making a big deal into a not so big deal. His response would have made Daruss laugh except for the fact the little traitor inside the club held Daruss's heart in the palm of his hand.

"You think it has something to do with all the attacks on our people?"

"I don't know." It wasn't such a stretch for someone like Mitch. Daruss knew quite a bit about Mitch because he'd done his homework on the guy when word had reached Daruss's ears that Mitch was a damn good thief. One thing about him that stuck out was his fighting record on the underground circuit.

"Maybe you should ask your boy. I bet he'd know." Izzy was serious. He wasn't trying to be an asshole, but the comment made Daruss feel stupid for trusting Jude.

Daruss shook his head. He didn't want to admit his feelings for Jude, but he knew he could trust Izzy to keep his mouth shut. "I'm in love with him."

"That makes it a whole hell of a lot more complicated." Izzy held his hand out for the bottle, so Daruss handed it over again.

Daruss chuckled but shook his head. If he didn't laugh, he might kill someone. Getting shitfaced was a nice alternative. Daruss took the alcohol back and drank. "No one touches him until I know more."

"I figured." Izzy nodded to the bottle. "We'll keep an eye on him."

"Also, find out if Mitch is still with the Chained Devils. Get Seryn to look into it." If he could corroborate Jude's story, then it would go a long way toward regaining trust.

Chapter Five

With so many forests and all the beautiful trees, Wingspan was picturesque, even outside the kitchen window. Or maybe it was especially beautiful from that spot.

The colorful leaves sway in the breeze.

Dad entered the room. "Is your kitchen broken?"

Raylee smiled. His suite had everything, including a full kitchen. Dad had even stocked it with some of Raylee's favorite snacks. "You have the best coffee."

Dad grumbled about mooching kids, but Raylee knew better. He loved that he had both of his chicks back in the nest again. "Don't drink so much of that, son. You tend to go overboard."

"Don't buy fancy machines that make foamy coffee and don't get the peppermint mocha creamer if you don't want us to." Raylee sipped his coffee and watched the sunrise.

Before Dad could respond, Jazlyn entered the house through the back door. "Amen, Little Bro."

Dad kissed Raylee on the temple. "Good morning, Moocher Number Two."

Raylee chuckled. "Good morning."

Dad put a pod in the machine and then a cup under the spout before pressing the button. He wrapped an arm around Jazlyn and pulled her close before kissing her much the same way he had Raylee. "Good morning. Do you want creamer, Moocher Number One?"

Jazlyn nodded and yawned. "Thanks, Dad."

"I'll get it so you don't have to move." Raylee opened the fridge. "Do you want peppermint or raspberry chocolate."

"Raspberry chocolate sounds wonderful." Jazlyn shut her eyes and yawned again. "Why do bookstores have to open so early in the morning?"

Raylee shook his head. "You're the owner. You can open it whenever you want."

"Nope. Doesn't work that way, although I wish it did. Hours are posted and I am just a poor slave to time." Jazlyn opened her eyes and met his gaze. "You are too."

Raylee smirked. "I like mornings."

"Asshole."

Raylee chuckled. He grabbed the creamer and handed it over.

"Be nice to your brother." Dad winked at Raylee and smiled. And then he mouthed "grouch" and glanced at Jazlyn.

Raylee snorted and figured he'd just say the word aloud. She knew how she was anyway, and she called him an asshole. Turnabout was fair play and all that. "Grouch."

"I need coffee first. And then I'll kick your ass."

Raylee rolled his eyes. "Start your morning off right, Jaz."

"Gods. I hate it when you quote Mom." Jazlyn's whining was annoying, but he had to give her props for being so good at it. "Fine."

She put her mug on the counter and walked to the door, exiting. She even shut it behind her. When she opened the door again, she was all smiles. "Good morning, family."

Dad chuckled. "That's Oscar-worthy."

"Thank you but I'm just channeling Raylee."

"You play me better than me." Raylee wasn't so chipper upon first waking. He hated the alarm clock. A shower and a cup of coffee put him in a better mood.

"We should go for a walk amongst the trees. They're so pretty this time of year." Jazlyn's smile was more of a smirk and she aimed it at Raylee.

Raylee couldn't help but laugh at that. "That's exactly what I was thinking. Except I thought maybe we could walk to the bakery in town and get donuts or something."

Dad chimed it. He had a sweet tooth. "Grab a cinnamon roll or four."

Jazlyn lost some of her sarcasm and grouchiness. She hugged Raylee. "Seriously, though. I'm happy you're home. Even if you are sickeningly cheerful in the morning."

Raylee met Dad's gaze. "Will you pick me up after work? We're riding together this morning, but I get off at two o'clock."

"Sure."

Raylee smiled. "Thanks."

Raylee finished his coffee and then went to his bathroom to brush his teeth. When he came out again, Jazlyn was ready to go.

It didn't take them long to get to town. It was about a five-minute drive. Jazlyn parked in the public lot at the end of the row of shops.

"Do we have time for the walk to the bakery?" Raylee wasn't sure how long it would take. He'd only driven by the bakery once and he had a terrible sense of direction.

Jazlyn laced her arm through Raylee's. "Plenty of time."

The public lot wasn't that big, and it just so happened that it was right next to Jazlyn's bookstore. The Dragon's Hoard was in a craftsman-style house that Jazlyn had converted. It had a medieval feel to it, right down to the blue dragon on the wooden sign. She'd even painted the house a dark forest green which seemed to blend into the forested backdrop. It also stood out amongst the rest of the shops too. It was on Main Street past the row of store fronts.

The town had a lot of charm. The shops all had fun window displays. Some of them even included dragons in their décor. Raylee would love to know where they got them.

Raylee pointed to the florist shop that had fall-themed gnomes with their pointy hats and long beards. "I love gnomes."

Jazlyn smiled. "Me too."

"The display is cute. It makes me want to go in. Maybe I can talk Dad into stopping at the end of my shift."

Two men on motorcycles rode by. The sound of their engines drowned out Jazlyn's response. The one in the lead had long dark blond hair and wide shoulders. He made the motorcycle seem dangerous, instead of the other way around. There was something about him that grabbed Raylee's attention. Maybe it was because he was gorgeous. Raylee had seen gorgeous men before and they hadn't held his attention the way the biker did.

He watched them ride past until he couldn't see them anymore.

Jazlyn grabbed his hand and pulled him down the sidewalk. "He's bad news, little brother."

Yeah, that fact was hard to miss.

Chapter Six

Jude didn't have much. He'd found a backpack in the back of the closet in the room Daruss had locked him in. Daruss had already thrown his clothing onto the bed, which made it easier to pack.

It made Jude's chest ache to see everything he owned in disarray, because it signified the end of their relationship. Not that they'd had one as far as Daruss was concerned. But Jude had thought it was. So what if they played around with other people. When the love hit hard, Jude had stopped doing that. He'd thought Daruss had for the same reason but maybe he'd been going along, not wanting to push Jude into anything.

Daruss had a heart of stone and he made sure Jude knew it.

It didn't take much to shove everything he owned inside the bag and then went to the window. He was on the second floor, and it was a pretty good distance from the ground. He had to pray he didn't break a limb or do worse damage.

He had to find Mitch on his own. It was clear Daruss wouldn't help him.

Jude bit his lip and stared at the ground. It wasn't cold, which he was thankful for, but it probably would be soon. The leaves on the trees would change. Jude had to think about what winter would mean if he couldn't find Mitch in time. He'd never been homeless when the snow fell. Him and Mitch had been close to sleeping in the snow before, but Mitch had always managed to pull them out of the deep end right before it became a problem. He'd slept in the streets a time or two. He didn't want to ever again.

It was a long way down. He didn't know if he'd be able to make it. He leaned out of the opening, trying to find something for his foot to grab onto. Maybe the window right below would hold him long enough for him to use it as a step.

Jude was getting ready to climb out and take his chances when he heard someone mess with the lock on his door.

He didn't bother shutting the window or getting rid of the backpack. He was done with secrets and lies. He would have tried to hide his escape if he were in anyone else's home. But he would never lie to Daruss again.

Daruss entered the room, larger than life. He always managed to take up more space than everyone else. It didn't matter that there were a few people who were bigger than him, although not many were. Still, his demeanor demanded attention and obedience.

Jude couldn't help but give Daruss attention, but he didn't have to obey him. He wasn't Daruss's boy anymore. Daruss had made it very clear he wasn't a Dragon Skull but their prisoner. So yeah, Daruss could fuck off if he thought Jude would do what he said.

Jude's bravado shrank to nothing when he saw the guy behind Daruss. Jude recognized Nash because he'd been at the Chained Devils club and at Terrell's house. He even wore the Devils cut.

Daruss didn't seem to be alarmed. In fact, he appeared rather comfortable in Nash's presence.

Nash met Jude's gaze and scowled. "That's Mitch's little brother, boss."

Boss? Did that mean...Nash was a plant. Jude sighed in relief.

"That's what I said on the phone. What I need to know is what the fuck to do with him? Can he go back to Terrell Gibbs? Is he safe there?"

Nash leaned into Daruss, talking in whispers but Jude heard what he said. "He's never been safe, man. Terrell hates that kid."

Daruss nodded as if that were the end of it.

Jude shored up his courage. "I want to go back."

Jude would have anyway. It was the last place he'd seen Mitch. He'd have to ask questions of the right people. Doing so without Terrell spotting him was the tricky part.

Daruss never lost his stoic expression when he met Jude's gaze. "You don't get a say."

Jude narrowed his eyes. "You don't get to tell me what to do anymore, Daruss."

Daruss took a step toward him. His eyes shifted, turning reptilian. "Don't challenge me, boy."

Jude puffed out his chest. "Don't call me 'boy'."

Daruss shook his head. "I don't trust traitors. You'll tell them everything."

Jude stiffened. He hated every time that word came out of Daruss's mouth. "Fine. Keep me a prisoner. But I'll find a way to get away from you, Daruss Oyen. Mark my words."

It was Nash who responded. "You're better off here than with Terrell."

Jude raised his eyebrows. "I know. It's not Terrell I'm worried about."

Nash shook his head. "You should be. He'll make you wish you were dead."

Yeah, Jude already knew that, but it wasn't anyone's concern but his own.

Daruss scowled and turned to Nash. He nodded to the door. "Let's talk in the hall."

Nash left.

Daruss met Jude's gaze and then glanced at the open window. "Shut the window. It's getting cold in here."

Jude flipped Daruss off. Damn the consequences. But all Daruss did was growl and slam the door as he left. Jude heard the lock click into place.

Jude walked over to it and put his ear to the door. He heard Daruss say, "That boy can piss me off quicker than just about anyone."

"Yeah, no shit, boss."

"I need to find out if his story is true."

"All I know, is I haven't seen Mitch around for months. And no one's talking about where he is."

Jude stepped away from the door. Oh god, he'd waited too long to do something. He felt the urgency in his chest. At the same time his stomach clenched.

He grabbed the pack. His hands shook as he threw the bag out of the window.

The sense of urgency took over everything, overshadowing even his broken heart. It wasn't a nice reprieve from the ache, but it was still a break from it. It had been a week since he'd told Daruss and in all that time, he felt as if his heart bled Daruss's name. He'd felt as if he mourned a person who was still living and one who hated him. So maybe the fear wasn't welcome, but it was different.

Jude panicked when he couldn't find the lower window ledge with his foot. He had to look for it, which meant he had to at the very least glance at the ground. It appeared so far away. It was impossible not to imagine himself broken, lying on his back in the grass. Maybe he'd even bleed from somewhere.

He had to protect his head. Everything else would heal well enough.

Jude had a few inches to go before he made it to the ledge. Jude was out of shape and didn't know if he had enough strength to make it. But he had to try.

While his mind worked overtime trying to figure out what his next move would be, his body did the thing he needed it to do. His arms shook but his fingers never slipped from the windowsill. There was a moment when he thought he might fall, but then he felt the ledge.

The rest of the descent seemed to happen without a lot of thought. He let go and jumped, landing on his ass, but the fall was about six feet less than it would have been had he jumped from the second story. He sat there for a second, thanking God he had an ample enough ass to cushion the fall. But gravity was the bitch who stole his breath.

What got the air flowing again was hearing Daruss's growl through the open window.

Jude scrambled to his feet, grabbing his pack, and then ran. He didn't care where he went as long as he got away.

Daruss's roar spurred him on. Fear crashed into him again, making him feel nothing but panic. His flight instinct took over.

Jude made a beeline for the forest, hoping he could hide from a dragon amongst the trees. Daruss's outside light left him too exposed. Not even the moon and stars seemed to penetrate the dense forest.

He plunged into the darkness as if it were his best friend, and fell when something grabbed his ankle. It took him a second to realize he'd landed on someone and that they held him from behind. The bag had somehow fallen from his hand during the fall.

He tried to scream but a hand covered his mouth.

They pinned his arms to his sides. He still had control of his feet and legs so he kicked as hard as he could.

The person grunted when a kick landed.

He didn't expect his assailant to punch him in the stomach. It knocked the air from his lungs. The pain stunned him enough for the person to push him away.

And then they hauled him to his feet.

As soon as he saw Stan Garrett, he knew his life was over.

"You have a lot to answer for, Jude. So does your brother." Stan was the smartest person in the Chained Devils gang. He used all of his intelligence to get Terrell and the others out of the trouble.

"Mitch doesn't have anything to do with it." Jude wheezed every word. He had a feeling the pain would only get worse.

It might be too late to save Mitch. He was in as much trouble as Jude.

Chapter Seven

Daruss roared and tore out of the house after Jude. He could feel that little troublemaker getting further from his grasp. As soon as he was outside, he partially shifted, tracking Jude's scent.

Daruss hadn't thought Jude would climb out of the window. The room was on the second floor and Jude was human. He could have broken his neck.

Nash followed him out. Jonik fell in step behind Nash. Or would have had his mate not protested.

Jonik cupped Wren's cheek and kissed him. "You have to stay here. It could be dangerous."

Wren nodded without a word, but his expression spoke for him. It said he didn't like being left behind.

Daruss followed Jude's scent trail across the yard and then the little troublemaker veered toward the forest.

Nash stopped Daruss with a hand on his shoulder. "I smell a human. Not your boy."

Daruss had been so focused on Jude, he hadn't noticed anything else. As soon as Nash pointed it out, the smell was there though. It was faint at first but as soon as they stepped into the tree line, the scent was strong. It mixed with Jude's.

Jonik had shifted into his fox. He sniffed, getting Jude's scent. Jude and Jonik had been good friends and sometimes fuck buddies. The three of them had played a lot up to the point when Jonik had met Wren and Jonik had put a halt to fucking around. Daruss and Jude had been exclusive after that, although the agreement had been more of a silent one.

Jonik sat and met their gazes. The ground seemed as if it had been trampled on. The wet soil was exposed in places where fallen leaves should have been. The vegetation was smashed.

Nash sniffed the air and growled. "Smells like rum, soda, and pachouli. That's particular to Terrell's righthand man. His name is Stanley Garrett. He's a drunk but a high-functioning one. He's also the guy who keeps everyone out of trouble."

Daruss nodded. He'd heard the name before. He had a file in his office with Stanley Garrett's name on it. "He's a psychopath according to his hospital records. And he has one of the Skull boys."

Jonik shifted. His lanky, naked form was in stark contrast to the surroundings. Daruss couldn't figure out why it bothered him until he realized Jonik was far too clean to be traipsing through the damp forest. "Jude's a Skull boy again?"

Daruss raised his eyebrows. "Are you asking or saying you have a problem with that?"

"Asking." Jonik was a bold person when he thought it was necessary. He'd been trained to fight by one of the most notorious gangsters to ever exist. Jonik's father was retired and reclusive, but he'd taught his son everything he knew before he had disappeared.

Jonik nodded toward the west. "The human went that way. The kidnapper probably parked on the road and made his way to this spot. He's likely drove off with Jude by now."

Nash nodded and sighed. "I'm sure Stan saw me enter your house. My cover is blown."

Daruss followed Jude's scent, so Nash and Jonik did as well.

"I know someone who will help," Jonik said.

"Not your father." The last thing Daruss needed was Isaak Raynard coming out of hiding. There was no way he would be able to control him.

"No. Not him. Not for this, at any rate. Gods forbid if we pull him away from his books." Jonik sounded as if he were a cross between exasperation—as if the sheer number of books his father owned was overwhelming—and affection. "I know someone else."

"Who? Don't tell me he's a part of your little mob."

Jonik glanced at him in surprise. "What do you know?"

"Enough to know you're not here to screw us over. Though I don't know what you want." Daruss had people who could get information on just about anyone. He always looked into the new guys. Jude was the only one who had ever fallen under this radar. "We'll discuss it later. For now tell me who it is."

"A warlock. He's...special."

"Special like you?"

"Not like me. He has certain abilities. Very helpful in certain situations." Jonik waved off the question. "Our boss planted him with the Chained Devils because he suspects them of talking to known traffickers."

They got to the road and sure enough, there were tire tracks in the dirt and Jude's scent disappeared.

Daruss growled. "Call your guy, Jon." Daruss wanted to know everyone he needed to kill for laying a finger on Jude. "Tell Avit and Seryn we have someone else on it too. Make sure they don't get in each other's way."

Nash nodded and pulled out his phone. He started back to the house.

Jonik and Daruss followed him. When Jonik spoke, he kept his voice down. "Mitchell Burke probably put Jude here because he knew you wouldn't hurt him. At least not physically. I don't think it crossed his mind that Jude would fall in love with the Skulls' alpha."

"Fuck off, Jonik." He didn't want to hear it. It just made him crazier than he already was.

Jonik patted Daruss's arm. "I hope we find Jude alive. I really do."

Daruss hadn't considered the fact Jude could die until Jonik pointed it out. "Is that supposed to make me feel better?"

Jonik was Isaak Raynard's son. No doubt about that. "Yeah."

Daruss shook his head. "Thanks, I guess."

They found Nash making a fire in the pit. It had really gotten going by the time Jonik and Daruss closed the distance. Wren held Jonik's clothes. He ran to him when he saw them.

Jonik took Wren into his arms and whispered to him. "Are you okay, baby?"

Wren nodded.

Daruss wanted what they had. He hadn't realized it until that moment but he couldn't deny it to himself any longer.

Nash took off the Devils cut and threw it in the firepit. "Fucking glad to get that off. Finally."

"It's good to have you back." Nash had been the best at blending in with others. He was likeable and made friends easier than most. That was why Daruss had sent him to the Devils. He also had a mind like a steel trap. "We'll debrief in the morning."

Nash nodded. "Main thing is Terrell is trafficking people. Different people for different things. Not sure where his victims are going. I was close to finding out before this happened. I told Avit to take up the torch. And Seryn is still going after Mitch. But me not being there is a setback."

"I don't think it will be one for long. Whoever Jon is working for knows more than we do. I got a feeling Jon's people are trying to rope us into helping them take out the trafficking problem we have around here."

"Are you gonna do it?" Nash sprayed lighter fluid on the cut and then lit it on fire.

Daruss didn't answer right away. Instead, he watched the cut burn. "I don't know enough about Jonik's people to make that decision. I won't do anything until I have Jude back anyway. He's the priority."

Daruss wouldn't sleep until he knew Jude was safe.

Chapter Eight

Raylee liked Wingspan. It was a pretty but small town surrounded by forests. He could see himself becoming a permanent resident. Not that he'd tell Dad that. He wouldn't want to get his hopes up.

"We should get some pastries for dessert tonight. Like we did with the cinnamon rolls last time. Those strawberry cupcakes looked really good."

"It's nearly closing time and it's a slow day. Let's close early." Jazlyn started on the closing procedure.

"What happened to being a slave to time?" Raylee teased but he started to clean up as well.

"Shut up and give me a break. I practically live here as it is." She worked long hours. And although she seemed to love it, it would take a toll if she didn't find decent help soon. She needed balance.

With both of them doing the closing chores, it didn't take long to finish. Ten minutes later, they locked up and headed out.

They'd made it to the grocery store when that same motorcycle guy from the other day rode through. Three others followed him on their bikes. Unlike before, the sexy blond man met Raylee's gaze and held it as he came closer.

Raylee smiled. There was something about the attention he really liked but it made his face heat.

The lead biker sniffed the air as if he were a bloodhound catching a scent. And then he pulled into a parking spot. The three others parked beside him.

Jazlyn grabbed Raylee's arm, pulling him down the sidewalk, away from the one person Raylee wanted to know more about.

"Wait." Raylee tried to free himself, but she held on.

"I told you before. Those guys aren't people you want to know, Raylee," Jazlyn whispered under her breath.

The gorgeous guy was heading right for them. He took up so much space on the sidewalk it was as if he owned it.

The other bikers were behind him. They all wore leather and denim. And not one of them wore a helmet.

"Wait, Jaz. I think he wants to talk to us." Raylee couldn't take his eyes off him. There was something mesmerizing about him. His sex appeal was off the charts.

The closer the guy came the faster Jazlyn walked. Raylee was almost running behind her, still trying to break free from her hold. When she figured out she wouldn't outrun the bikers, she finally stopped and released Raylee.

Jazlyn cursed and took her phone from her pocket. "I'm calling Dad."

Raylee smiled as he closed the distance. He'd always been awkward around guys he liked. Maybe he had an inferiority complex, as if he thought everyone was out of his league. Maybe it had been true some of the time, but it was ridiculous to think it was every time. But it was accurate with the hot biker.

The guy was a dragon shifter. His size gave him away. Dragon shifters were bigger in almost every way. His eyes were also reptilian, and he had fangs.

Raylee should have listened to Jazlyn and run in the opposite direction. The partial shift could be a sign of aggression. For that reason, he stopped and stiffened, freezing in place. His fight or flight response was broken.

Jazlyn put herself in front of him. She had her phone in her hand and whispered, "Dad's on his way."

Raylee sighed. "Gods."

As soon as the guy was close enough, he sniffed Jazlyn.

"Thank fuck you're not it." He had a deep, rumbly voice. "Move out of my fucking way."

There was something about him. Maybe it was the frown lines on his forehead or the way his lips were pinched. Raylee wanted to comfort him. The urge was so strong he didn't think about his next move—damn the danger. Self-preservation went out of his mind. In its place was the instinctive realization that the sexy dangerous biker was his mate.

He stepped around Jazlyn. As soon as he did, the guy pulled Raylee into his arms. Raylee hadn't been expecting it, so he stumbled, face planting into a wide chest.

Strong arms came around him before he lifted Raylee off his feet. "I've got you, mate."

Raylee hadn't been carried like a child since he was one. He wasn't sure if he liked it. To decide, he settled into it.

Jazlyn cursed again. "Put my brother down. Right now."

Of course, he didn't listen. Instead, he held Raylee closer. "Do you know what a mate is, boy?"

Raylee hadn't been a boy in a few years, but it still hadn't been that long ago. And he knew he looked his age. To a dragon shifter, who lived a lot longer than was humanly possible, he probably did seem young. But in case the guy was fishing to see how old he was, to make sure he was over the age of eighteen, they might as well have a conversation about it. "Yes, I know everything about mates. And I'm twenty-three. My birthday was last month."

The guy smiled with his eyes, but the rest of his face seemed tired and worried. "You're young."

"Not that young." Raylee cupped the guy's cheek. "Can I help with whatever's wrong?"

The guy raised his eyebrows. "You can tell? Already. When we haven't bonded yet?"

Raylee nodded. He'd always been a bit of an empath. He wasn't sure why he picked up on other people's emotions so easily, but he'd learned not to run from the gift. He wanted to be helpful to others. "My name is Raylee. I just finished nursing school, so if it's something medical, I might be able to help."

"Raylee. That's a nice name. It fits you."

"Raymond Leon Galloway, at your service." Raylee smiled.

"At my service? Be careful what you give away. I'll take it all." That sounded less like a threat and more like a promise. It also sounded dangerous enough to make Raylee shiver. And maybe he grew hard because of it too.

"How about I just offer my help with whatever is making you worry?" He chickened out when he should have come on to the guy a little harder.

"I might take you up on that." The guy sighed and ran a finger down Raylee's cheek. "You're soft. Innocent."

"Yes. He is. Way too innocent for the likes of you. So leave him alone." Jazlyn stood with her hands on her hips. She had claws and her green eyes turned reptilian. She also growled on a near constant basis, even when she spoke.

Raylee smiled and rolled his eyes. "My sister's protective."

"She should be. She knows my reputation." And what sort of reputation was that? "My name is Daruss Oyen. I'm the alpha for the Dragon Skulls."

"What's a Dragon Skull?" But he sort of knew from the motorcycles and all the leather. He'd never met someone from a motorcycle gang before.

Daruss put him on his feet and then he pressed his lips to Raylee's forehead. "Do your homework before you commit to me, boy."

Raylee wasn't ready to let Daruss go when he turned toward his bike again. "I want to see you again."

"I'll find you." Daruss got the bike started and roared away without a second glance. The other bikers followed him.

That was when Dad pulled into the spot they'd vacated.

Raylee was the one who closed the distance between them. As soon as Dad got out of the truck, Raylee went in for a hug.

"Daruss Oyen is my mate and he just left." It felt like a rejection even though that was not what Daruss had said.

Dad rubbed his back, not saying a word.

"It's good he left," Jazlyn said. "Daruss is a criminal. You heard him say he was alpha of that biker gang."

"Daruss Oyen also has standards, and he keeps his guys in line. Wingspan's Alpha is a part of that gang and he's not a criminal." Dad met Raylee's gaze. "He does bad stuff. Sells drugs and shifter hooch.

Rumor has it, he's sold guns some of the time too. But he won't hurt you. You can count on that."

Jazlyn narrowed her gaze. "I don't like this. I think we should go to Wingspan's alpha."

"And tell him what, Jaz?" Dad shook his head. "It's not up to anyone but Raylee." He hugged Raylee again. "Trust your instincts, son. Listen to what they're telling you."

Raylee nodded. "I'll try."

There wasn't anything for Raylee to do. He thought meeting his mate would mean a lot of nakedness for a long time. And then they'd talk. That was the way it should have been. Most mated pairings didn't wait to mate. They shouldn't have started off with Daruss leaving five minutes after they met.

Chapter Nine

The bass made the floorboards bump, although that was all he could make out of the actual song. Terrell and the rest of the guys had always played heavy rock music. That habit probably hadn't changed in the time Jude had been gone.

9396 August Street was the place to sin, depending on someone's favorite poison. Drugs, alcohol, sex, buying stolen guns and sex slaves—Terrell had it all.

Everyone within a fifty-mile radius knew most of what went on there. Even the cops. But no one stopped it.

The Chained Devils' headquarters, aka Terrell's house, was located in the seedy part of Litchford. The town was about twice the size of Wingspan, which still made it small. Jude suspected almost everyone who didn't want to contribute to Terrell's criminal enterprise drove past the two-story clubhouse with some sort of disdain or fear. Only the stupid and desperate stopped.

Litchford wasn't a rich town. There was no industry to speak of unless the Chained Devils' criminal income streams counted. Most of the working-class people commuted to the city, which was twenty minutes away. They pretended the poverty-stricken parts of the small town didn't exist. Most people even went out of their way to avoid it. Maybe they were afraid poverty would catch up with them if they did.

Some people weren't far from poverty. One wrong move was all it took. A single father working construction could support his two boys so long as he didn't get lung cancer. In the nine months it took for his body to give over to the disease he'd racked up a mass amount of medical debt. While he had insurance, it wasn't the good kind that paid for everything. The debt ate up his savings and his life insurance policy, all of which he intended to leave to Mitch and Jude. Not that Jude's father had intended to die at the young age of forty-two. Like most people, he thought he'd make it into old age.

Jude and Mitch had gone into foster care for a while. Thankfully, they'd stayed together, and Mitch had been almost eighteen anyway. When he left the system, he'd taken Jude with him.

Jude had gone from living in a middle-class Litchford neighborhood to the poverty-stricken one in less time than it took for grass to grow over his father's grave. The neighborhood sucked people in, ate them, and never spit them back out again. Jude and Mitch hadn't been an exception.

Jude had had a glimpse of a better future. Or so he'd thought. Daruss was different than a typical criminal. Maybe poverty had sucked him in too and that was why he did what he did. But he wouldn't do just anything for money.

Jude was right back where he'd started. The slums of Litchford hadn't changed. The only thing that had was Jude's perception of them. He'd been sucked back in again. And worse he was a prisoner locked in a room in Terrell's house. A cell within the town he couldn't seem to escape from no matter what he did.

And he had no idea where Mitch was.

Jude sighed and shut his eyes, trying to ignore the pain in his stomach and head. It was severe enough Jude stopped considering ways to leave. Jumping from a window wasn't an option this time. For one, they were nailed shut from the outside. And Terrell's beating had taken the option off the table even if they hadn't been.

He needed to rest. Didn't sleep help with healing? The pain kept him from it regardless.

The door handle jiggled. Someone fumbled with the lock.

Jude stiffened and lay still when he heard Terrell's deep voice. A higher-pitched, feminine-sounding person spoke next. He couldn't make out what was said.

When the door opened, Terrell entered. The hall light took him out of the shadows but then he flicked on the bedroom light. Jude's eye had been beaten shut days ago. The swelling hadn't gone down much. He could see through it a little, but his vision was still limited. The brightness hurt so he shut his eyes.

It wasn't until a woman spoke that he cracked his good one open. It was the woman from before. The one Mitch had wanted him to stay away from. "I can't sell him in his current condition. You needed to keep him pristine, Terrell."

She dressed in black leather, as if she'd ridden there for the sole purpose of getting a look at Jude. Mitch had said she sold people as if they were cattle. And she had talked about an auction before. So maybe she had come for Jude.

She'd cut her hair since the last time Jude had seen her. The short style suited her, making her appear younger than she'd seemed all those months ago, as if she aged in reverse. Or maybe it was because she wasn't drunk off her ass.

He hadn't realized it the first time he met her because he hadn't known about paranormals before meeting Daruss, but he was almost positive she wasn't human. He wasn't sure what she was, although she wore her club's cut. One of the patches was of a wolf. The writing underneath said *Grave Wolves*. She also wore a patch that indicated she was of a higher rank. Maybe she was the alpha.

He should care about being sold but he'd lost hope. A little had left him each time Terrell had hit him. He didn't have much left anymore. Besides that, at least he knew she wanted him in good health, which meant she wouldn't do anything to leave a mark.

"He'll heal." Terrell walked over to him and pulled back the covers. "You can see he's a lot of people's type."

Jude's T-shirt had ridden up so she could see the bruising around his middle.

She shook her head and turned from the room. "I can't make money on him like he is, Terrell. You should have called me before you beat the shit out of him."

"He pissed me off." Terrell whined every word as if she were his mother and he needed to explain his bad behavior.

To her credit, she didn't engage with his childishness. She shrugged and left the room.

Terrell's expression turned to stone and after she walked out, he shut the door behind her.

Jude panicked when Terrell balled his hands into fists. He shrank away from Terrell as much as he could.

He covered his head with his arms and waited for the blows to come. He didn't have to wait long.

Chapter Ten

Daruss sat in Gavin's office trying not to panic.

Gavin was the voice of reason and one of Daruss's best friends. Because he was Wingspan's alpha, he was also a guiding force in Daruss's life. Gavin was part of the Dragon Skulls gang as well, but he didn't wear his cut all the time like the other guys did. He also had boundaries and he made sure Daruss, as leader of the gang, knew what those were. Gavin stayed away from almost everything illegal, but he had fought for the club when it became necessary. He turned out to be a damn good fighter.

Daruss needed a sounding board and Gavin was the best there was at that too. Gavin was just one of two guys in the gang who he would trust to give mating advice simply because they had mates. MacIver was the other one.

Gavin held his mate, Easton, on his lap as if he were the most precious person in the world.

"I have two problems. And when they collide, I'm not sure what will happen." Wasn't that the understatement of the century.

"One of them has to do with Jude, I assume. Have you found him yet?"

They sat in Gavin's office. Gavin had served him coffee. A very sensible drink that did nothing for Daruss's stress level. Dragonshine would take the edge off but he needed all his wits about him for when Jonik's guy came through for Jude.

"Not yet. My gut tells me it won't be long." The fact Jude had slipped out of Daruss's grasp was embarrassing, and Daruss had sort of known he would too. Jude was a normal human. He shouldn't have been able to escape from a second-story window. And he shouldn't have been able to dupe a dragon shifter. Daruss still wasn't convinced Jude hadn't been trying to get one over on him right from the start, though.

Gavin raised his eyebrows. "Are you sure he's in trouble?"

"When we followed his trail, there was evidence of a scuffle."

"Did someone meet him?"

"I don't think so. I think Terrell sent someone and they've been watching for a long time. Jude fell into their trap." Daruss wanted to give Gavin evidence, instead of basing everything on his feelings. But the evidence of a struggle was all he really had.

"It certainly suggests Jude hadn't wanted to go with this person. The question is *when* did he decide not to leave. Was it right away or did something change Jude's mind." Gavin missed his calling. He should have been a cop.

"Between Nash and I leaving Jude's room and discovering him missing, maybe two minutes had passed. So there wasn't a lot of time for Jude to have a conversation with the guy and then change his mind. And the scuffle happened about ten feet into the tree line. If Jude had someone waiting it makes more sense to get as far away as possible first before talking or whatever."

"So he wasn't planted by the Devils?"

"He said his brother sent him to us to keep him safe. I don't know if I believe that." Daruss wanted to trust Jude but didn't know if he should. "He knows a lot about us. If he tells Terrell or even his brother, we might be screwed."

"But that's not why you want him back, is it?" Gavin saw a lot. It was what made him so good at being alpha of the Wingspan clan.

Daruss sighed. "I'm in love with him."

"That's the first issue, right? Not the rescue mission."

"I have that underway. There's no more I can do right now."

"So what's the second issue then?"

Daruss nodded. "I met my mate."

Gavin raised his eyebrows.

"He's a human. The brother of the bookstore owner. He's young and probably just as innocent as he looks." Raylee was way more innocent than Daruss had a right to corrupt. He was the exact opposite of Jude in that regard too.

"Have you...spent romantic time with him?" Gavin couldn't even call it sex. It would have been laughable if Daruss wasn't a little desperate.

"I met him for five minutes and had to leave to track down Jude. He probably thinks I rejected him." Daruss winced. "I don't know what the hell I'm doing, man. I've never been in love before. I didn't really even recognize it until Jude finally told me who he was. And now I meet my mate. I feel like I have ninety-nine problems and no solutions. You know what I mean?"

"I understand. You know Easton and I met under difficult circumstances too."

Daruss ran a hand through his hair. "What the hell do I tell my mate, man?"

"How about the truth?" Gavin raised his eyebrows again.

"That I'm in love with someone else?" How would Raylee take that?

"It's not like you have a choice, Dar. You love who you love. Starting off a relationship with either one of them by lying won't work long term. I don't know Jude well, but I know he's a smart kid. You're not going to get much over on him." Gavin shrugged. "You've managed two boys at the same time before. You're good at it. I say lean into loving both of them. See where it gets you."

Daruss was good at lying when he had to. No doubt about that, but he'd always been up-front about his expectations with the people he was fucking. Of course, he'd never been in love with any of them except for Jude. He hadn't ever had a mate before either.

"So I should go talk to my mate?"

"The sooner the better."

For the first time since they'd been talking, Easton chimed in. "Make sure they know how you feel. Communication is key. Especially with Jude."

Maybe Easton was right. He should have told Jude how he felt instead of pushing him away with hurtful words. When he got him back, if Jude was still alive, Daruss might consider telling Jude his true feelings.

Daruss rubbed his chest. Not that he wanted to think about Jude getting hurt or dying. He would prefer to think of him living it up with his brother, telling every Dragon Skull secret he knew. He might have his doubts about Jude, but he still had to make sure he was safe. He wouldn't leave him in the hands of someone who would hurt him.

Chapter Eleven

Jude came to with his flight instinct intact. It took him a full minute to realize he was alone and Terrell was no longer there. He'd probably left soon after Jude had blacked out.

He relaxed a little. His bladder protested not moving for so long, so he tried to sit up. He cried out when it felt as if knives were stuck inside his gut, but he fought through it. He told himself feeling it was a good thing because it meant he was still alive.

Jude tried to get enough gumption to go into the bathroom. He had to pee, but he knew it would hurt. He'd been pissing blood for a couple of days. His back hurt where Terrell had kicked him. Who knew how much more damage he had from the latest beating.

He breathed deep and held it before getting to his feet. He clutched his stomach as he made his way to the attached bathroom. He'd searched everywhere for some type of pain medication. Even something basic used for headaches and minor pain would take the edge off. But every drawer and cabinet was empty except for soap and towels.

He pushed his sweatpants down far enough to sit on the toilet rather than stand, since he was a bit more comfortable that way. It hurt to pee. The pain was bad enough for tears to spill down his cheeks. He bit his lip and tried to remember to breathe.

He sat there long after he'd finished, leaning against the side of the vanity and shutting his eyes.

His mind drifted. He thought about being somewhere else. He pictured a tropical beach. Sunning himself on the sand. That sounded nice until he grew sticky with sweat and bugs tried to land on him.

Okay, so he wasn't that much of a beach person.

The last place he'd been comfortable and felt safe was at Daruss's house. He wished he could go back there. Maybe he would lock Daruss out of the house since he was such an asshole.

Jude must have fallen asleep on the toilet. He wasn't sure. He was startled when something or someone hit the wall in the hall outside his room. It sounded as if someone had fallen. Their giggle was barely audible.

He groaned when he stood and pulled up his pants before washing his hands. He couldn't stand upright but he managed to shuffle into the bedroom again, covering himself with the blankets.

Jude shut his eyes and had almost drifted off to sleep when the door handle jiggled again. He started to cry. Terrell coming back so soon made him panic. He didn't want to get beaten anymore.

But it wasn't Terrell. Instead, a pretty black man entered the room as if the door hadn't been locked. He wore thong underwear. The rest of his body was bare and beautiful. His skin appeared smooth. He was taller than Jude by at least a head and had lean muscles.

The guy carried a tray piled with food.

Jude hadn't eaten in a couple of days. It wasn't a problem since he was pretty sure he wouldn't be able to anyway.

Jude had never seen the stranger before. Not even when he'd hung around before Mitch sent him off to Daruss.

He smiled and set the tray on top of the dresser. He shut the door behind him and then seemed to chant something. He spoke in a murmur and in a language that wasn't English.

When he turned to Jude again, he stood by the door with his hands behind his back. "No one can get in. No even with a key."

Whoever the guy was, he knew magic and he either intended to hurt Jude or help him. Jude wasn't sure which yet.

Jude decided not to respond, which was easy since he didn't know what to say anyway.

"My name is Samson Fade. I'm a warlock. I'm here to rescue you." That sounded like a whole lot of bullshit.

He didn't trust anyone, least of all a guy in a thong who told Jude he was locked inside the room he'd been locked in for the past three days.

Except what if he really was there to save him.

"Did Mitch send you? Is he all right?" Jude tried to sit, but the pain was too much.

When Samson got closer, Jude stiffened. It must have been noticeable because Samson stopped and held up his hands. "I'm here to help you."

Jude figured Samson probably only wanted to help him sit up. He wouldn't have stopped getting closer if he didn't. Jude nodded.

Samson lifted Jude into a sitting position. He sat beside him with an arm around his waist as if to keep him up right. "I was sent by Jonik."

"Jonik?" Why Jonik? Jonik had been his friend and sometimes fuck buddy, but he was a Dragon Skull. He didn't have a vested interest in Jude anymore.

"Yes. I'm an associate of his father's." That information meant nothing to Jude. He didn't know who Jonik's father was. They'd never talked about their families. But it seemed he was important enough to have associates. Samson being one of them.

Jude suspected Samson was far older than he appeared. It was all in the way he spoke and the way he carried himself.

"Just trust me. Okay?"

Like hell he would. "I don't trust anyone except for my brother."

Samson's gaze was filled with empathy. "You don't have a choice, hon."

Probably not but he didn't see how he'd get out from under Terrell anyway. "Is Mitch dead? Did Terrell kill him?"

"I don't know. I'll help you find out. But first, we have to get you to safety."

Jude's head felt fuzzy. His vision blurred. "Don't know where that is."

"Where what is?"

"Safety." Jude saw the floor coming at him. He thought for sure he'd face-plant. Maybe Samson would be a figment of his imagination. His brain's last-ditch effort to keep hope alive.

But he found himself floating.

Did Samson carry him? He was far too heavy for that.

Samson seemed to be talking to someone. It took a moment for Jude to figure out that it was him. "I've got you. Just a little longer and Daruss will be here."

What did Daruss have to do with anything?

Chapter Twelve

The bookstore was quirky, playing on what humans had thought dragon shifters were way back when dragons flew free of secrets. The store promised magic and medieval lore if a buyer was brave enough to crack open a book.

A small bell announced his entrance, which seemed inadequate. Most of the time, Daruss came with sirens, not a gentle chime.

He also hadn't earned the grin Raylee had for him. Or the way Raylee put a marker in his book and closed it as if he found Daruss more important than following the main character to the end of their journey.

Raylee stood behind a counter. A tablet-type computer sat on top of what was probably a cash box. Raylee came around. His eagerness was clear and very sweet.

Daruss would never be good enough for Raylee. For the first time in his life he wanted to try to be better for another person.

His sister came out of nowhere, standing between them as if she were a knight protecting her brother from the dragon. She had some very firm thoughts about Daruss. That much was clear. "No."

But Raylee didn't like her stepping in. His eye-roll said as much.

"I won't hurt him." Daruss couldn't even if he wanted to. They were mates. It was impossible for them to hurt each other. At least that was true physically. But Daruss could in other ways. Daruss was corruption personified. Two out of three of them knew it.

"You'll get him involved in your criminal shit." She folded her arms over her chest.

Raylee's sigh held frustration. "I'm taking my break now."

"No, you're not." The sister didn't take her eyes off Daruss.

Raylee shook his head and came around the counter, taking Daruss's hand, pulling him toward the door. "Fire me if you don't like it."

Daruss raised his eyebrows. Raylee's sassiness came as a surprise but a pleasant one. At least Daruss knew Raylee would stand up for himself.

"Of course, I'm not firing you." The sister glared at Daruss and pointed at him as if in warning.

Daruss grinned. He knew it came off as menacing. "I'll try very hard not to make Raylee a criminal. I promise."

Raylee lifted his eyebrows. "You couldn't even if you wanted to."

The sister smirked at Daruss. "Fuck off, Daruss Oyen."

Daruss flipped her off.

She went behind the counter and picked up Raylee's book. "Are you buying this book, Ray?"

"Yes." Raylee tried to pull him toward the door.

Daruss stopped him. "Stay there."

He grabbed his wallet from his back pocket and took out a hundred-dollar bill, putting it on the counter. "For whatever he wants."

Raylee shook his head. "You don't have to do that."

Daruss winked at Raylee. "I want to."

"Thank you." Raylee had a smile that could warm the sun. What was Fate thinking when they paired them?

"Drug money?" She didn't lose her smirk. Her gaze grew knowing.

"Jazlyn! Stop being rude." No one had ever stuck up for him. He made Daruss's heart swell.

"Thanks, boy." He met Jazlyn's gaze and answered her question with complete honesty. "Selling dragonshine but not in recent times."

"Does the sheriff know?" She grabbed a gift card from the stack on the counter and did something with the register.

"That I bought something for Raylee? I doubt it." Daruss pulled out his cell phone. "Should I call and tell him?"

Jazlyn narrowed his eyes. "You're a smart ass. As much as I don't like you, you'll fit in to our family well."

That was about as good as it was going to get in terms of her accepting him as her brother's mate. "You won't fit in with my family."

"Thank the gods for that." She handed the card to Raylee and smiled. "You'll still get the employee discount."

Raylee took it, thanking her, but his gaze was on Daruss. "What's your family like?"

Jazlyn shook her head and then gestured to Raylee. "This is what I mean. He's naïve."

Raylee narrowed his eyes. "I am not."

She chuckled. "Right."

Daruss wrapped an arm around Raylee's waist and then leaned into him. "We're a bunch of misfits, bikers, and misfit bikers."

"What's your definition of a misfit?" The question made Daruss rethink Raylee's naivete. Maybe the sister was wrong.

"The Dragon Skulls have rescued most of our members. Some have sustained permanent damage. Physically and psychologically." Daruss sniffed Raylee's hair. His scent was so alluring. It made Daruss want to get even closer. He also made him confess things he shouldn't have. "Everyone deserves to feel safe and secure. Over the years, I've learned that it comes at a cost. I'd rather pay the price than let an innocent get victimized."

Every one of his guys, bikers and boys alike, had needed him in some way. Some still did.

Jazlyn's gaze softened. She pointed to the back. "You can use the back room, Ray."

Raylee grabbed his hand and pulled Daruss along. They went through what appeared to be the storage part of the business. Toward the back was a kitchen with a table in the center.

Raylee gestured to a chair. "Would you like some coffee or a pastry from the bakery?"

Daruss pulled the chair away from the table and sat. "I can't stay very long. I'm expecting a call. But I need to talk to you before the call comes in."

As soon as Jonik's guy had Jude in his sights, they were supposed to call Daruss. Him and a few guys would facilitate the rescue.

Daruss gestured to his lap.

Raylee hesitated and then shook his head. He pulled out a chair and then took Daruss's hand as if attempting to soften the rejection. "I don't know what you want from me yet. For now, let's just keep it to hugs and handholding."

Daruss let it go, which was something he rarely did. He was used to getting his way. He hadn't expected Raylee to challenge him, but it was a welcome surprise. Raylee wasn't scared of him. He wouldn't just go along with whatever Daruss wanted, even if he might not want to. He wanted his boys to stand their ground when necessary. And besides that, what Daruss had to tell Raylee might be a dealbreaker anyway.

Daruss sat forward and took Raylee's other hand. "The call I'm waiting for is a possible rescue mission."

Raylee frowned. "Will you be gone for a while? Is that what this is about?"

"Not exactly. It's about the person I'm rescuing." Daruss took a deep breath. "I have history with him."

Raylee let his hands go and sat back in his chair. He studied Daruss as if he were dissecting the meaning behind the words. "Romantic history?"

Daruss nodded.

Raylee crossed his arms over his chest. "You're already in a relationship?"

Daruss wasn't sure if Raylee's body language suggested he was jealous or if he thought Daruss would deny it. "Yes."

"Where does that leave me?" That was a good question.

"That's up to you." Daruss sighed. "My relationship with Jude is complicated. There's a lot I don't know about Jude's current situation."

"His name is Jude?" When Daruss nodded, Raylee continued. "What do you mean 'his situation'?"

"I don't know if Jude even needs to be rescued. If he does, then he's likely in rough shape."

Raylee's expression was one of confusion.

"We've been through a lot. Jude and I aren't on good terms." That was putting it mildly. "But I'm open to seeing where it goes with both of you. Whatever happens, happens."

Raylee unfolded himself and sat forward again. "So you're saying you want to mate with him *and* me. Am I getting that right?"

"I'm saying I'm open to that. Yes."

"I'm not sure I am if I'm being honest. There's a lot to consider. But if it turns out he's in a bad way, I'll do what I can to help."

"What's your number?"

Raylee held out his hand, so Daruss pulled out his phone, turning it on before giving it to Raylee. Raylee typed on it and then handed it back.

Before Daruss could put it in his pocket again, it rang. He met Raylee's gaze. "This is it. I have to go."

Raylee frowned again. "I hope he's all right."

Daruss did too.

He answered the call. After kissing Raylee on the forehead, he made his way out of the store. Jazlyn watched him leave as he exited.

She probably headed into the back to make sure Raylee was all right. At least Daruss hoped she had.

"We've got him." It was all Jonik said before ending their conversation.

He put his phone into his pocket and was heading to the parking lot, when Raylee called his name.

Daruss stopped and met Raylee's gaze.

"Keep me informed."

Daruss nodded. "Thanks, boy."

"Be careful." Raylee didn't know him well enough to know Daruss was never careful.

"I want you for my mate. Just so we're clear." Daruss needed to say it one more time. He didn't want any confusion.

He didn't know what to expect. He could be walking into a trap for all he knew. Not that it would stop him from going. Nothing would.

Not even knowing Jude was a traitor who could be setting him up. But he wanted Raylee to know where he stood in case something bad happened. He never wanted Raylee to wonder.

Chapter Thirteen

Jude was so fatigued it was as if his injuries infected the rest of his body, injecting him with something that made him want to lie down on the bed again. But Samson wouldn't let him.

"He'll be here. Anytime now. You'll have to be able to walk out of here. Stay awake just a little longer." Wouldn't someone notice a beat-up twink on his last legs? And if Terrell saw them they were definitely screwed. It wouldn't be just Jude either. Samson would pay a heavy price for helping him.

"If Terrell sees you with me, he'll probably kill you. Either that or he'll make you wish for death." Jude knew about being in so much pain he didn't mind disappearing. He felt it in every fiber of his being. He wasn't to the point of wanting to die. But if that was what took the pain away, he'd take what he could get.

Samson smiled and stood, going to the window. He moved the curtain, glancing out into the night as if he could see in the dark. "No one will see us. Especially not Terrell."

Samson seemed to be waiting for something. Jude didn't have the mental capacity to guess what, and he didn't know if he cared. All he wanted was to lie down and go to sleep.

Jude sat on the bed. He hadn't moved in hours. It had been so long, day had turned to night again. All he had to do was curl onto his side. The pillow seemed like a reasonable place to land.

Samson moved from the window, kneeling in front of Jude. He took Jude's hand. "I'm afraid you're concussed. I heard people with head trauma shouldn't sleep. And I can't get you out if you can't walk. I'm not strong enough to carry you."

"I'm stuck here." He wasn't deluded the same way Samson seemed to be. "Do you know who Terrell is? You need to be careful. Get out of here while you can. Don't let Terrell see you leave the room. If he does, go to the Dragon Skulls. They'll protect you."

Samson smiled as if he were indulging Jude. "Do you remember what I told you when I first came into your room?"

"No." Jude didn't remember anything beyond the pain. Maybe Samson was right, and Jude hadn't protected his head well enough. Maybe Terrell had scrambled his brains.

Samson frowned. "We'll get you out, hon. I promise. It won't be long now."

Jude shut his eyes but then opened them again when Samson shook him awake. "No sleeping, remember."

How could Jude forget. That was all Samson had talked about.

When Samson went to the window again, Jude closed his eyes.

He knew he slept. He wasn't sure for how long.

Samson shook him awake again.

When Jude opened his eyes the second time, it was to see Samson clothed. He wore all black with a long dark coat. It was the kind of thing a highwayman would wear in those old-time movies. Or maybe a New Age wizard.

Was there such a thing?

"There is, although I prefer the term warlock. Most of us do." Samson wrapped his arms around Jude and helped him into a sitting position. Jude's shoes were on the floor beside him.

Samson put them on his feet and tied them. "Can you stand, hon?"

Jude shrugged. His head still felt fuzzy.

He wasn't sure why Samson had woken him.

Samson held him around the waist and helped him stand. He guided him toward the door. Jude stiffened, which made the pain worse. His vision blurred, making him fight off passing out.

Samson's hold tightened as if he sensed Jude was about to fall into blackness. "Hold on. Just a little longer."

"Can't go out." Terrell would know. He'd take it out on Jude. Jude couldn't take many more beatings.

Samson chanted something under his breath. When he finished, he turned the knob. "Be very quiet and don't let go of me."

Jude felt like a passenger in an out-of-control car. Samson guided him toward destruction. Jude started crying when they were in the hall. He couldn't stop the tears or the sobbing.

Samson whispered in his ear. "Shh. I'll protect you with my life. I promise."

Jude had stopped trusting people a long time ago. Samson was certainly no exception. He didn't know where Samson was leading him, but he had his doubts that it was toward freedom.

Jude couldn't bring himself to protest. The pain made it impossible to pull away. Even when someone came down the hall toward them, Jude still couldn't move from Samson. Fear made his stomach clench. Dread set in as if it were another open wound.

He didn't know he whimpered until Sampson put a hand over his mouth.

The guy swayed, leaning against the wall, using it for support. His eyes were half-lidded, and he appeared as if he could have fallen asleep standing up if he could only get his body to stop moving. The man had taken something. Maybe whatever Terrell sold. He didn't pay them any mind.

He didn't even glance at them.

Jude sighed in relief.

Samson whispered again. "He can't see us. Magic."

Jude nodded but he didn't know if he believed Samson. Not that it mattered what he believed. The fact was they'd managed to not get noticed by someone so inebriated he couldn't stand. They probably hadn't needed magic to slip past him.

When they took the stairs to the main level and one of the Devils took the stairs without even glancing their way, he knew Samson hadn't been lying.

The party hadn't slowed even a little. Heavy rock music made the floor vibrate. It drowned out any sound he might have made.

They had to go through the kitchen where bottles of liquor covered the counters. Jars of moonshine were scattered amongst them. Terrell had a jar in his hand. He listened as the Grave Wolves woman spoke.

Terrell seemed to stare right through Jude and Samson without seeing them. Samson guided them to the front door.

Terrell would notice them leaving. How could Samson avoid it?

Jude held his breath when Samson started counting with his fingers and mouthing one, two... When he counted to three, he turned the knob, pulling the door open.

Samson guided Jude outside. The air felt nice. He hadn't been outside since Stan had brought him inside Terrell's house. That seemed so long ago.

He couldn't enjoy the fresh air because they were taking the steps. Jude had to concentrate on where he put his feet. He tripped on the last one, pulling out of Samson's arms. He landed on the grass. Knives of pain jabbed every wound he had. It stole his breath.

Jude fought tears when he heard Terrell curse. "What the fuck? Was the door not latched?"

He sounded way too close for Jude's health. Jude knew what was coming. Maybe Terrell would beat him to death. Maybe twenty-four years was all he'd get. Would he get another life after he left the one he was in?

Jude's tears started again.

Samson acted so quickly, Jude didn't know what had happened until he felt him covering his body as though he were a blanket. He chanted again. Jude wasn't sure if it was the same words, but he spoke in a hurried voice.

"That was fucking weird," Terrell said and then the door closed.

Samson sighed and slid off Jude. "Are you okay?"

The trust fell into place all at once. "Thank you."

Samson put his arms around Jude and lifted him with a strength someone as thin as him shouldn't have had. He guided Jude across the lawn and into the neighbor's backyard. A small stand of trees separated the properties.

Jude's vision grayed at the edges. "Gonna pass out."

"Almost there. Just a few more steps." The encouragement didn't help.

The gray turned black. He lost his sight. It wouldn't be long before he lost consciousness.

Voices came to him as if he were in a tunnel. One of them sounded like Daruss.

Someone lifted him into their arms. The pain of being cradled made him finally fall into the abyss.

Chapter Fourteen

Daruss sat on the backseat of Gavin's truck, cradling Jude against him. He wanted to go back to the house and burn it to the fucking ground. The plan had been to do just that, but Jude's situation was an emergency. Anyone could see that. Getting him help was the priority. Everything else would have to wait.

The guy who'd been with Jude sat next the Daruss. He was a warlock and a damn powerful one. Daruss appreciated him for helping to get Jude out of there. Daruss hadn't been sure if it would be a rescue mission or a kidnapping. But it was clear which one Daruss had done. But one thing didn't bode well.

"You better have a good explanation for not getting him out sooner." Daruss had a short fuse. He wanted blood. In particular, he wanted Terrell's and every one of the Chained Devils. He'd kill the warlock if he didn't like his answer. It would satisfy him, at least for a moment. Daruss was always one for instant gratification.

Jude moaned again. Tears wet his lashes and cheeks.

"I've got you, boy. You're safe now." Daruss kissed his forehead.

Daruss was halfway toward full-on shifting. His eyes were reptilian, and his fangs had dropped. He couldn't change them back. He'd never been so close to going feral in his life. His protective instinct was off the chart. And it was all because of Jude.

"I may have blown my cover for him." The warlock said it in a nonchalant way as if it was what it was if he did. And that was true. He couldn't change anything. All he could do was see if he had. It meant he might find out the hard way.

"So fucking what? His life doesn't matter as much as your fucking mission?" Daruss didn't even know him or the person who hired him to spy on the Chained Devils, but he'd been there for a good reason. One Daruss would get behind.

"He's exactly the reason why my employer wanted me there in the first place. And others like him." For someone who was talking to one of the most notorious biker gang leaders in the region, he was very calm, which meant two things. He was confident when it came to his magical abilities and his boss was probably a very powerful person.

Daruss wanted to ask who his employer was, but he didn't know if he cared. His priority was getting Jude medical attention. He'd think about everything else after he knew Jude was out of danger. "So what then? Why'd you wait so long?"

The guy frowned. "I didn't know he was there until Jonik called, asking for help. They kept him upstairs, locked in one of the bedrooms. When Terrell posted guards at the bottom of the staircase, I knew he was up to something."

Daruss decided to give the warlock a break. It was a good explanation and one he didn't have to give.

"If Terrell has more victims, the Skulls will help."

He raised his eyebrows. "Because it benefits you?"

"No." Although it did. The Devils had encroached into their territory with the shine. And Daruss also didn't like the Devils having a shipment of guns. Especially not one so large. Daruss wasn't sure what to do about the guns yet, but he had a handle on the encroachment. The Devils just didn't know it yet. They would as soon as Daruss knew Jude was okay. "The Skulls have a policy about helping abuse victims as well as others. We don't participate and we don't let that shit slide for those who do."

"We're ten minutes from the hospital, Dar." Gavin met his gaze through the rearview mirror but didn't hold it, focusing on the road and driving.

Daruss whispered in Jude's ear. "I'll make the doctors give you the good drugs, baby. I promise."

The guy smiled.

"What's your name?"

"Samson." He smirked. "And no. I'm not telling you who I work for. Just know, we have a very similar stance on protecting those who need it. It's why Jude is still alive."

"Just don't cross me or get in my way when I take Terrell down."

Samson's smile widened. "Why would I do either of those things? I'm the enemy of your enemy. That makes us friends. Doesn't it?"

"No. But it does make us on the same side." And that was good enough for Daruss.

****

When they first stepped into the emergency room, there was a flurry of activity. A man in scrubs led them to a room sectioned off by curtains. Someone else, presumably the nurse, came in as well. The nurse went to a computer attached to the wall. Whatever he did made the screen come to life.

And then he put on gloves.

"Put him on the bed." The doctor washed her hands before gloving up.

Daruss growled and held Jude tighter. When Jude groaned as if Daruss had hurt him, he did what the doctor said.

The nurse hooked Jude up to a machine that would monitor his pulse and blood pressure.

When Gavin came into the room, Daruss lost some of the tension.

Gavin took one look at Daruss's dragon eyes and nodded, taking over. When the nurse asked questions, Gavin answered. The nurse typed into the computer. A lot of it had to do with how Jude had been injured. Gavin answered with honesty.

Daruss understood the cops had to be called. There would be an investigation, which would probably piss Terrell off but who fucking cared. Not Daruss, that was for sure.

Daruss stood by Jude's side, holding his hand.

"How long has he been out?"

Daruss answered that one. "About twenty-five minutes. But I think he might have come to a couple of times. The pain is bad. He makes noises and cries."

The doctor nodded. "Is he allergic to anything?"

Daruss wanted to say Jude had developed an allergy to taking orders lately, but he just shook his head. "I don't really know. Can you give him pain meds?"

The doctor made a noncommittal noise and lifted Jude's shirt, poking around his belly.

Jude groaned but he didn't open his eyes.

Daruss met her gaze and growled, not caring about her seeing him partially shifted. "Pain meds. Now!"

The doctor blinked and she paled. "Let's start an IV, Reagan."

The nurse nodded and finished on the computer. Daruss had to move so the nurse could have access to Jude's arm.

Gavin stood in the corner with his arms folded across his chest. "Will Jude have to spend the night?"

"I can't answer definitely. Given he hasn't gained consciousness, I would say yes."

Daruss pulled out his phone and pulled up Raylee's number. Raylee had put his name as *Fated mate*. It warmed Daruss a bit to see it. He typed a message. *Hospital ER.*

The little text bubbles formed, indicating Raylee was typing and then the message popped up. *Can I come?*

Yeah. Daruss's dragon liked the thought of having his boys in the same place.

He stood next to Gavin. "My mate is coming."

Gavin raised his eyebrows. "You talked to him?"

Daruss made an affirmative sound in his throat. "He's innocent. Somewhat naïve. And a little apprehensive."

"And Jude is only one of those things, I take it?" Gavin had a way of asking one thing when he meant another. It was always designed to make Daruss think.

"They're opposites." Daruss wasn't sure if he knew how Raylee would react to Jude. And vice versa. If Jude ever woke up.

Gods, Daruss prayed Jude's injuries weren't serious. No matter what Jude did or didn't do, he never deserved a beating.

Chapter Fifteen

Daruss watched as Raylee moved around Jude as if he were a firefly wanting to give his wings a break. It came from a place of caring. Raylee was a nurturer—that much was obvious. Anyone could have been lying in the hospital bed and Raylee would have reacted the same way. Daruss had wanted to include Raylee but the logistics of doing so were problematic at best. It was good to know Daruss had made the right choice when he called.

"He's sleeping." Daruss patted his lap. "Come here and sit with me."

Raylee smiled and came over. Instead of sitting on Daruss, he leaned against the windowsill. The chair Daruss sat in was turned toward Jude, but Daruss could still see outside if he wanted. The window took up most of the back wall and the view was nice, but Raylee made a prettier picture.

"We're still not ready for lap-sitting." Raylee softened the blow by smiling.

"I think we are." Daruss was ready for anything. But despite the way he'd teased, he'd follow Raylee's lead.

Raylee was still smiling when he shook his head. "You're incorrigible."

Daruss grinned. "I've been called worse."

Raylee chuckled. "I have no doubt."

Daruss was about to ask what he'd have to do to get a kiss, although he already knew the answer. Before he had a chance, Jules groaned.

His expression pinched and he tried to turn onto his side but seemed to give up. It was clear the movement hurt him.

Daruss growled. He didn't like to see Jude in pain, but he didn't know how to help.

Raylee did though. He was at Jude's side as quick as a blink, pressing the button to call the nurse. He watched the screen, taking note of Jude's vitals. "His blood pressure's up. His pain level may be high."

Daruss stood, ready to take Jude into his arms if Raylee thought it would help.

Jude popped his eyes open. His expression was pinched but he seemed to focus on Raylee.

Raylee smiled. "Hi. Can I get you anything?"

"Water." Jude winced as if it were painful to speak.

Raylee held a cup to his lips and Jude drank.

"Should we be worried about him not drinking very much?" Daruss was worried about everything where Jude was concerned.

Jude glanced at him. "What are you doing here?"

Raylee answered Daruss's question, which kept Daruss from having to respond to Jude. "He's getting plenty of fluids through the IV."

Jude focused on Raylee. "Are you a nurse?"

"Yes, sort of. Do you know where you are?"

"Hospital." Jude glanced at Daruss again before returning to Raylee. "Can you get him out of my room?"

Daruss growled and sat in the chair again. He folded his arms over his chest and shut his eyes. He couldn't deal with Jude's shit, and he couldn't argue with him either.

The nurse came in. Daruss didn't have to open his eyes to know it was the nurse. He could tell it was her because she'd been in before, checking on Jude. She had a unique scent as if she were mated with a vampire.

"He just woke up. He's in significant pain." Raylee held Jude's hand.

"Let me see what the doctor wants to give him."

Daruss didn't open his eyes when he said, "Make it quick."

"Right." The nurse scurried out of the room.

"Thank you," Jude mumbled.

"I'm glad you're awake," Raylee responded.

"I'm not."

Raylee chuckled. "Right. Well, they'll have pain meds for you soon. You'll fall asleep again."

"Will you stay with me?"

"Not going anywhere. I promise."

"You're really nice. No one's ever nice to me."

Daruss opened his eyes, watching them.

Raylee smiled but there was empathy in his gaze. "You're nice too."

"I'm not a nice person. Dickhead can corroborate it."

Daruss growled. "Watch your mouth, boy."

"Fuck off." Jude turned his gaze away from Daruss.

Raylee sighed. "How about you tell me what your name is?"

When Jude looked at Raylee again, it was with a smile. "It's Jude Burke."

"Would you like to turn onto your side?"

Jude's eyes widened and he nodded. "How did you know?"

"You tried to turn as you came awake." Raylee moved to the other side of the room, grabbing the pillows off the empty bed.

Raylee had been sitting between them, creating a buffer. Him moving seemed to make Jude aware of Daruss again because he couldn't keep his eyes off him. He narrowed them and said, "I don't understand why you're here?"

"Because I fucking care about you, boy."

"Don't call me that."

"You still are, whether you want to be or not." That much was true even if neither of them wanted it. Love was love. It didn't go away because they were on the outs with each other.

"I want to hate you."

"Ditto."

Raylee came back with two pillows. "At least you agree on something."

Jude chuckled and then groaned.

Daruss growled. Knowing Jude was in pain, and he couldn't do anything about it, made him want to rip someone's head off so he could feel as though he was helping somehow. He wanted to take Jude in his arms, but he was afraid to hurt him. He also knew Jude wouldn't welcome the embrace.

He took Jude's hand instead. "Don't do anything to hurt yourself, baby."

Jude shut his eyes and squeezed Daruss's hand. It wasn't hard enough to hurt but it was firm. "I wish you could make the pain go away."

Daruss leaned forward and kissed Jude's cheek. "I would if I could."

Raylee met his gaze and smiled. Daruss didn't see jealousy, but his eyebrows drew together as if he weren't sure where he fit into the mix. While Daruss wanted to reassure him, it was a conversation for another time.

"I'll need you to help me," Raylee said.

Daruss nodded.

"On my say-so, gently roll him toward you." Raylee had the pillows ready.

Daruss leaned into Jude, positioning himself to take all of Jude's weight. In order not to hurt Jude, Daruss's chest was flush with his. "If I hurt you, let me know. I'll stop right away. Okay?"

Jude put his arms around Daruss. The hold was loose, probably because Jude couldn't tighten it with the IV tube coming out of him and stuff. At first Daruss thought Jude was helping with the roll and tuck thing, but then he heard Jude sniffle.

Daruss sat on the bed and tightened his hold as much as he could without worrying about hurting Jude.

Raylee rubbed Jude's arms. "It's okay, honey."

Daruss smiled at him. "You're safe, boy."

"I'm sorry." The words were barely audible. Jude sobbed around each syllable.

"We'll figure it all out when you get better." Raylee made himself part of the equation with that statement. It was a welcome surprise.

"Don't worry about anything right now. Just get better. Okay, baby?" Daruss wanted information but he could wait until Jude was well again.

Jude clung to Daruss's shoulders. He calmed by slow degrees, during which Daruss moved him onto his side. Jude didn't seem to notice until Raylee lined the pillows against his back.

Jude relaxed and shut his eyes. "This is good."

He was out before the nurse administered the pain medication.

Chapter Sixteen

In Jude's dream, he wasn't injured anymore. In fact, he'd never felt healthier. He knew it was a dream because he'd never been to Utah where the landscape was red. He'd seen it on television. He was in his brother's car with the windows rolled down and the radio blasting. Mitch drove and Jude stuck his arm out of the window.

They used to go for drives, taking in the countryside. It was one of Jude's favorite things. The last drive he'd been on was with Daruss. They'd taken his motorcycle. Jude had hugged Daruss from behind. It had been thrilling and beautiful all at once.

The air smelled different. Sterile. With a hint of cinnamon. He hadn't expected Utah to smell like that. He thought it would smell like sun-warmed sand, like the beach but without the fishy scent from the water.

If he focused on sterility, it would pull him out of his dream. He heard beeping and people talking. He couldn't make out words. The cinnamon pulled at him even more. It reminded him of Daruss and the Skulls clubhouse. That had been a safe place.

Jude fought to stay under. He focused on Mitch, smiling at him from the driver's seat. And the scenery that never quite changed from the oddly shaped red rock formation. The same one over and over again and Jude knew why. The picture Jude had seen had been in a commercial on television. He couldn't remember what the advertisement had sold. It might have been a car. A woman held the photo while the camera zoomed in on it. And then a car had shown up in the photo and all of a sudden, the photo became her reality. It had become Jude's too. Sort of.

And then a bruise formed on Mitch's cheek. A cut on his forehead. His eye swelled shut.

With each new injury, Jude panicked. He tried to scream but he couldn't make his voice work. The sound went out of him, sticking in his throat as if time stood still for him. But for Mitch, time sped up, bringing new injuries.

Jude sobbed.

He felt something on his face. A cloth? Maybe.

The beeping became more pronounced, louder. It was all he heard for a while.

"Mitch."

Jude wasn't in pain. Or at least, not much. He knew he should be. Did that mean he was still dreaming?

"You're safe. It's okay if you wake up now." It wasn't Mitch who spoke. Jude didn't know who it was. All he did know was the person spoke in soft tones. His voice was soothing.

"I don't want to." He choked on the words. His throat felt as if he'd gargled with the red Utah dirt and then swallowed it.

Something touched his lips. "Take a drink, honey."

Jude realized the thing on his lips was a straw. He sucked on it. The water felt good on his throat. It went a long way to making his voice work again.

Why was everyone always calling him honey?

When the nurse, or whoever it was, chuckled it sounded just like his dream. At the beginning of it, when Jude had no worries in the world. The windows down so the wind could touch his skin. "I don't know why others do it. But I call a lot of people that. It's just habit. I won't anymore if you don't want me to."

For a moment, Jude forgot what he'd said and then realized he hadn't thought he'd spoken aloud. "Can you read my mind?"

There went the chuckle again. Jude wanted to bottle it and use it every time he felt caged like an animal. "That would be a neat trick. There are a few minds I'd like to read."

"Mine?" Jude finally cracked open his eyes. They felt heavy. He would have closed them again if not for the smiling face he saw. The man had dark hair and big brown eyes that made him appear as if life hadn't touched him yet. His lashes were long.

"Maybe yours." He set a white foam cup on the bedside table. Beside it were papers held together by an ink-pen clip and Daruss's keys. He knew the keys belonged to Daruss because of the skull and wings keychain. The symbol was particular to the Dragon Skulls. It was similar to the one tattooed on Daruss's shoulder.

Jude took in the room and then stiffened when he saw Daruss sleeping in a chair beside him. The chair seemed uncomfortable, but it reclined although not by much. "What the fuck is he doing here?"

The guy frowned. "Do you remember waking up before?"

Jude shook his head. "I've been out of it for a while."

"Well, Daruss saved your life. Do you remember that?" The guy sat on the side of the bed next to Jude. He took Jude's hand.

"No. A guy named Samson did." Jude pulled his hand away and frowned at the guy. He had vague recollections of what had happened. He didn't remember it all and couldn't figure out why his memory was so shitty. But he remembered running from Daruss. Stanley grabbing him. Terrell beating him. After that, he wasn't sure. But he remembered Samson. He remembered leaving the room and feeling scared.

When Daruss spoke, it startled Jude. "Jonik sent Samson. Therefore, I saved you. We're not arguing about it."

"If I want to argue about it then I will. I don't have to do what you say. You're not my daddy anymore." Jude noticed the IV in his arm and the blood pressure cuff around his other arm.

"Fine. Argue then. See how far that gets you." Daruss never opened his eyes.

Jude shook his head. "I'm no longer talking to you."

"Good. Your smart mouth is getting you in trouble anyway." Gods, he was so exasperating.

The pretty guy's eyes widened. "Daruss, his blood pressure is spiking."

"Probably because he's an asshole who makes me crazy." Jude focused on the pretty guy, but he knew he needed to calm down. It was just that Daruss had held him prisoner and it seemed as if Jude was right back where he'd started. Only he was beat near to death and in the damn hospital. So he was worse off than he had been before he'd run from Daruss, and something about that made him angry.

"Are you in pain?" Mr. Pretty took his hand again and smiled.

"What's your name?" Jude decided he liked Mr. Pretty way more than he did Daruss.

Mr. Pretty chuckled again. Like before, it made Jude's heart lighter. "You answer me first."

Jude tried to return the smile, but it hurt his mouth. That was when he noticed the left side of his bottom lip had swollen. He didn't remember getting hit there. "Not much."

"Do you have a headache?"

"No."

"What's your name?"

Jude tried to smile again, and this time managed a halfway one. "I asked you first. Except I already have a nickname for you. It's Mr. Pretty."

Daruss snorted. "Accurate."

Mr. Pretty grinned. "You're charming. Has anyone ever told you that?"

Jude shook his head.

"I'm Raylee. Now answer my question. I need you to." Even his name was pretty.

"Why? Are you a doctor or something?"

"Just finished nursing school. And it's because you have a concussion. I want to make sure it hasn't affected your memory."

"I can't remember some things." He had gaps.

Daruss turned toward them, opening his eyes and frowning, but he didn't say anything.

"Like what?"

Jude shook his head. "I don't know. I don't remember. If I did, we wouldn't be having this conversation."

Instead of taking offense, Raylee smiled again. "Good point. Why don't you tell me what you can remember?"

"I remember Daruss holding me against my will." Jude smirked.

Daruss growled. "Answer him, Jude."

"I am." Jude met Raylee's gaze. "I remember escaping. I didn't know Stanley was watching the house. But he was in the forest. Dummy me ran right to him."

"So you didn't meet him there?" When would Daruss believe him? When would trust become a part of the equation?

Jude sighed. "I wouldn't have escaped when I did if I'd known he was there."

When Daruss started asking him about Stanley, Raylee held up his hand. "His health comes first, Daruss."

Daruss's gaze softened when he looked at Raylee. That was when Jude knew Raylee was someone to Daruss. Whatever it was, there was something romantic going on. Jude was sure of it.

Daruss's eyes were reptilian, and he had fangs. And none of it was directed at Jude like it had been the last time they'd fucked.

Shit.

Jude hadn't realized he'd had a little hope where Daruss was concerned until it went out of his body as he exhaled. Emotion balled in his throat. He averted his gaze. Jude shut his eyes. He wished he could keep the tears at bay. He really didn't want to give Daruss the satisfaction of knowing he'd made Jude cry. But he couldn't stop them.

It was Daruss who spoke in that soft tone he sometimes got when he wanted to soothe Jude. Gods, Jude wished he could trust it. He wished it meant something. Knowing it didn't hurt even more. "You don't have to talk about the beating, baby."

Jude shook his head, dismissing Daruss's comment. "The first time Terrell...he just wanted to cause pain. Keep me from figuring out how to get away from him. The second time he was angry. He went too far. I think he knew it."

Raylee wiped a tissue across his cheeks in the gentlest of ways. "What happened next?"

"Don't remember anything until Samson came into my room."

Raylee let his hand go and stood. He pressed the call button on the bed. "I'm going to have a conversation with the nurse in the hall."

"Can you..." Jude shook his head. He wanted to ask Raylee if he could ask about Jude going home but he didn't have a home anymore. He didn't have anywhere to go after he got out of the hospital.

Raylee took his hand again. "How can I help you, honey?"

"My name is Jude."

"All right. How can I help you, *Jude*?" Raylee misunderstood why he'd given his name.

"You asked me before."

"Oh." Raylee relaxed his shoulders as if in relief. "You don't mind being called honey?"

"Not as long as you don't mind being called Pretty."

Raylee blushed, which somehow elevated him from pretty to beautiful. "What were you going to ask me?"

"Nothing. It doesn't matter."

Raylee squeezed his hand right before letting go. He met Daruss's gaze. "I'll be right outside."

It seemed as if he were giving them privacy, but Jude didn't know why he'd do that. Maybe Daruss wanted closer.

When Raylee stepped outside, he left the door open. A woman in scrubs seemed as if she were just getting ready to enter. Whatever they talked about, it was said in hushed tones.

"What were you going to ask him?" Daruss put his hand on Jude's arm and patted him.

Jude pulled away, which tugged on the IV a bit too hard. "I wanted to know when I could go home."

"Do you want me to find out, baby?"

The endearment made the tears flow faster. He shook his head.

Daruss brushed away his tears with his thumb. "It's okay. I've got you."

Yeah, Daruss *having him* was part of the problem. "It's not okay."

Jude sniffled and then reached for a tissue, plucking one out of the box. He wiped his nose. Daruss handed him another one before he could grab it on his own. "Are you afraid Terrell will get to you?"

Jude shrugged. He hadn't thought about it, but he could thank Daruss for putting it in his head. "I guess."

"I won't let him get to you."

Jude shook his head. "Like you're any better."

As soon as he said it, he knew it was the wrong thing to say. After the beatings from Terrell, a part of him expected violence, even from Daruss. But all Daruss did was growl. He stood and went over to the window, staring out of it. "You make me fucking crazy and piss me off faster than anyone can."

"Take your new boy and get out of my life." Maybe if Jude didn't see Daruss ever again, the ache in his chest would go away.

"Why did you come to me? To give Terrell intel?" Daruss didn't turn from the window when he asked.

"Fuck you."

Daruss growled. "I want the truth once and for all."

"I've never lied to you, Daruss. Never once. I just didn't tell you who I was right away. But eventually I did." Fatigue washed over Jude. He couldn't keep his eyes open. "The guns were supposed to be Terrell's big payday. But they got to be too high profile. He can't sell them. Not right away anyway."

"So he's turning to human trafficking."

"And trying to piss you off so you won't focus on it. Everyone knows you don't put up with that sort of thing." Jude sighed. "Mitch was afraid for me. He thought I'd be safe with you until he figures out what to do about the guns."

"He's right."

Jude didn't respond right away. And when he did, he didn't open his eyes. Emotions lodged in his throat. "You're breaking me into pieces."

Daruss took his hand. "I'm not, baby. I swear."

Jude hoped Daruss wouldn't be there when he woke.

Chapter Seventeen

When Raylee entered the room, he could feel the tension in the air. Daruss stood at the window. Jude was sleeping.

Raylee stopped inside the door. "Should I go?"

"No." Daruss never turned from the window. "He actually likes you."

Raylee glanced at the machine. "Did he fall asleep or pass out again?"

"It was more like last time." Jude had been in and out. The fact he didn't remember coming to was what concerned Raylee the most. But his vitals were normal beyond the occasional spike when Daruss had made him angry.

Raylee stepped up to Jude's bedside, pulling the covers around him. Jude seemed peaceful as he slept. It hadn't been the case when he'd been under before. It was a welcome change.

His blond hair was messy. Raylee smoothed it out, but it didn't seem to make a difference. Jude's hair was thick and the color of sunshine-kissed gold.

"He's gorgeous." Raylee could see why Daruss was attracted to him. Raylee was too.

Jude had a softness about him when he slept that wasn't there when he was awake. He had been through a lot. The beating was the latest thing. His hard shell had taken years to form. Maybe it had always been difficult for Jude. Things didn't come easy for everyone. Raylee understood that in theory. But he'd never met anyone like Jude before.

"Yes, he is." Daruss turned from the window, folding his arms across his chest and leaning against it. "You like him back, I take it."

Raylee smiled and nodded. "I'd like to be his friend."

Daruss raised his eyebrows. "Just his friend?"

Raylee frowned. "I know he flirted with me, but it was harmless. I won't come between you."

"Jude meant to flirt. He's deliberate in most things he does." Daruss shook his head. "I don't know where I stand with him."

Raylee didn't like the dynamic. He wasn't sure where he fit in and that left him feeling a little insecure. It wasn't something he was used to. But if he took himself out of the equation, at least for the time being, he thought maybe he'd be able to help.

"I think you do know where you stand with him. You just don't like where that is." Raylee suspected Daruss was very good at complicating things. He needed someone to untangle the mess he'd made. If that had to be Raylee, then so be it.

Daruss had an expression he seemed to reserve just for Raylee. It was unclear what it meant but Raylee thought it might be a mix of admiration and surprise. "You're a smart boy, aren't you?"

Raylee shrugged and sat on the side of the bed next to Jude. "Maybe you're not that complicated. You just like to think you are."

Daruss unfolded his arms and crooked a finger at Raylee.

When Raylee closed the distance between them, Daruss wrapped an arm around his waist. "Here's what's going to happen. I'm going to kiss you and then you're going to help me figure out how to fix things with Jude."

Raylee took a step back, crossing his arms over his chest. "I'm not as naïve as you seem to think."

Daruss smiled. "All right. Why don't you tell me what you're not naïve about."

"Jude called you Daddy, which I take to mean you're bossy. I don't know if you should be right now though. I mean, Jude's basically telling you no. Maybe you should listen."

Daruss winced. "I don't like that word."

"Yeah, I kind of got that. You like control." Raylee smirked.

"I like taking care of people. There's a difference." Daruss pulled on Raylee's arm but in a gentle way, coaxing Raylee into his embrace again. This time Raylee returned the hug. Daruss kissed the top of his head. "You're saying I should pick my moments."

"Read the room." Raylee closed his eyes. Being in Daruss's arms felt good. He felt so secure. All his stress melted away.

"That leads me right back to where we started."

Raylee met Daruss's gaze. "I'll agree to a kiss."

The kiss was exactly what Raylee expected. It was sensual and made demands all at the same time. Daruss cupped Raylee's cheek before taking it to a deeper level. The hint of a tongue made Raylee want to climb Daruss. It had been a long time since he'd felt a kiss in every fiber of his being.

Daruss was very good at letting Raylee know what he wanted too. And Raylee was just about to give it to him, when someone cleared their throat.

The sound startled Raylee and he stiffened. Daruss ended the kiss and tightened his hold on Raylee as if protecting him from whoever had entered.

And then the nurse spoke. She cleared her throat again. "Sorry for interrupting. I'm just checking on him."

Raylee was a little embarrassed, especially because Daruss still held him close even though it was clear Raylee needed to have a conversation with the nurse.

"His vitals are normal, but he passed out again."

"I'll let the doctor know but keep us informed of how he acts when he wakes again."

"Thank you."

The nurse did whatever she thought was needed and then left.

As much as Raylee didn't want to watch Jude and Daruss go at each other with verbal guns drawn, Raylee hoped Jude remembered everything from the last time he'd been awake. That would be a step in the right direction.

Chapter Eighteen

It was daylight outside when Jude woke. The sunlight filtered through the window. Daruss sat looking out with Raylee on his lap. They looked perfect together, with the light streaming around them. Raylee was beautiful with his open innocence and the way he always seemed to smile even when he didn't want to. Jude could tell Raylee had had a good life. He'd had people who loved him. Probably more than just an older brother.

Jude remembered what that was like, before it had all fallen apart. It had been him and Mitch after that. Mitch was six years older than Jude. He'd been the only parent Jude had, protecting him and providing for him the best he could. It had been a lot of responsibility for someone so young.

Jude watched Daruss.

Daruss held Raylee as if he were fundamental to Daruss's existence. Even when he was quiet and trying to enjoy the view, Daruss still seemed wound tight. As if he were a spring ready to go off. He always worried about something.

Jude would like to know what went on in Daruss's mind. What did he worry about?

Daruss oozed danger and his willingness to kill was legendary. But it seemed each time Daruss took a life, that life was etched on his face. How was Daruss going to make a relationship work with someone as innocent as Raylee? If Daruss wasn't asking himself that question, he needed to be.

He liked Raylee enough to have mixed feelings about him being with someone like Daruss, and not because Jude was in love with Daruss. A part of him wanted to be selfish and hope it didn't work out. But Jude knew whatever he had with Daruss was over. Raylee was too nice of a person for someone like Daruss. While that was fact, Jude knew Daruss very well. He knew how protective he was.

Jude picked up the cup of water and drank through the straw. He tried not to think about how his heart ached seeing them together. It was a hazard of his current condition. Just like the bruises and concussion. Same thing but with a different cause.

He must have made enough noise because Daruss and Raylee turned in his direction.

Raylee came over to him, taking his hand when Jude put the cup on the table again. "You're awake. How are you feeling?"

"Like I had the crap beat out of me." That was the understatement of the century. Jude wondered how close he'd been to death. One more beating? Two? Or would Terrell have let him heal so he could sell Jude to that woman, making Jude wish for death.

Despite how bad it could have gotten, Jude preferred that existence or lack of, to watching Daruss and Raylee fall in love. That would shatter him into a million pieces. Maybe that was why Daruss had stayed when Jude had told him to go. Maybe Daruss wanted to torture him with heartbreak.

Daruss growled but didn't speak. His eyes were reptilian. He appeared even more dangerous than normal, and that was saying a lot.

Jude stiffened and would have moved away if he could have. But the fact remained, Daruss could tear him apart if he'd wanted to and Jude couldn't stop it. Not in his current condition. Not even if he had his full health back.

Raylee pressed the button for the nurse before meeting Jude's gaze. "We'll get you some pain medication."

Jude nodded. He wouldn't turn them down. "Thanks."

"I'm Raylee."

Jude smiled. He had a headache unlike any he'd ever had before. If his brain fluid leaked out of his ears, it wouldn't have surprised him. But he had to try for Raylee, even though he didn't feel like smiling. It was impossible not to make an effort for him. And how weird was that.

"I remember your name. Still pretty too." Jude didn't know which part made Raylee sigh in relief but something did.

"You remember." Raylee squeezed his hand.

"You're hard to forget." Jude darted his gaze to Daruss. His smile faded and his eyes narrowed. "So are you. Just in a different way."

Daruss rolled his eyes. "Don't start, boy."

Jude wrinkled his nose and pursed his lips at Daruss before turning to Raylee again.

It made Raylee chuckle. "You're feeling better."

"Like I got run over by a truck three times instead of four." Jude smirked.

When the nurse came in, Raylee went back to Daruss's lap. He faced Jude and smiled before addressing the nurse. "He remembered waking up last time."

"I'll let the doctor know." The nurse met Jude's gaze. "How's your pain level? On a scale of one to ten. Ten being the worst pain you've ever had."

"What do you mean, I remembered? Has that been a problem?"

Instead of the nurse asking him, Raylee did. "This is the third time you've woken up. Not the second."

"Oh." Jude wondered what he'd said and done.

"Answer the question about your pain level, Jude." Of course, Daruss had to boss him around. Maybe it was habit that had made Daruss demanding. It was either that or Daruss did it because Jude was his prisoner again. He didn't do it because he wanted what they'd had. Jude knew that much.

Jude held up his middle finger without taking his gaze off the nurse. "I'm at about a five. Mostly I have a bad headache. But my stomach area hurts a lot too."

The nurse raised her eyebrows at the way Jude flipped Daruss off, but she didn't comment on it. "I'll give you some pain meds."

"Do you have something to eliminate the pain in my ass?" Jude pointed to Daruss and smirked.

Someone took his hand. Jude turned to see that it was Daruss. Instead of tightening his grip, making it painful, Daruss held on to him with gentleness. Daruss raised his eyebrows, his expression saying he was done with arguing and Jude needed to be done too. Even his voice was gentle when he said, "stop."

Jude nodded.

He met Raylee's gaze. Raylee winked. His smile stayed in place.

Raylee addressed the nurse. "Can he go home soon?"

"I think it will be later today or possibly tomorrow. We'll send pain meds with you."

Raylee nodded and put his hand over the top of Daruss's and Jude's as if wanting to be included. It seemed too good to be true. For that reason, Jude pulled his hand out of Daruss's grasp.

The nurse pressed a button on the machine taking his vital signs. And then made sure his IV meds were still in place. She left the room a few minutes later.

Being alone with the two of them made the ache in his chest worse so he pressed the button to turn on the television.

He knew gold-hungry miners wouldn't do the trick, so he changed the channel. Reruns of a nineties sitcom came on, so he stopped and put the remote beside him again.

"What's wrong? Is it something I can help with?" Raylee asked.

Jude shrugged. "I doubt it."

"Are you worried about where you'll go when they let you leave?" He thought he was Daruss's prisoner, but it was more Daruss's tone than his words that made Jude question Daruss's intentions. Daruss sounded as though he cared about what bothered Jude. His tone was gentle, as if he wanted to caress Jude's soul with them.

"Yeah. A little."

"You can go home with me." Daruss had an arm around Raylee, but he held out his free hand, inviting Jude to take it.

Jude shook his head.

Raylee broke the tension. "I can help with your care."

Jude met Daruss's gaze. "Do I have a choice?"

"I don't know, Jude. Do you?" The muscles in Daruss's jaw ticced.

"When I find Mitch, I'll have a place to stay." Mitch was home. He always had been.

"Your brother is going to get you killed."

The statement while probably true, put Jude on the defense. "He's the only one who has my back." Which was also true. Mitch's involvement with Terrell had put them both at risk. He hadn't meant for any of it to happen. One bad choice had led to another and before they knew it, Mitch was Terrell's puppet and Jude was his punching bag.

Daruss's scowl was menacing, but Jude knew he didn't mean for it to be. That was just his face eighty percent of the time. Jude knew it meant he was considering what Jude had said. "He's the only family you've got?"

Jude rolled his eyes. "Do you want to hear about my shitty childhood?"

"No. I want to know if your brother is loyal to you."

Jude sighed. "It's been the two of us for a long time. When our dad died, Mitch did the best he could for me. Mitch got caught up with the Devils. He made a bad choice. And he's not a good person. Neither of us are, but he's not a complete shit either, Daruss. I can promise that."

Daruss pulled out his phone. He patted Raylee on his hip. "I need to make a call."

Raylee stood and then took the chair Daruss had vacated.

Jude called after him. "What are you going to do, Daruss?"

Daruss turned to Jude, meeting his gaze. "I'm going to see if I have an update on your brother."

"'An update'?"

Daruss shook his head. "I have people looking."

Jude sucked in a breath. "When?"

"Day one of you telling me he's in trouble."

Jude shut his eyes to the suddenness of the emotions. They clogged his throat. When he spoke, he couldn't get out more than a whisper. "Thank you."

Daruss exited the room, leaving the door open.

Jude watched him dial the phone and then put it up to his ear. And then he spoke into it. Jude couldn't hear the conversation.

He met Raylee's gaze. Raylee smiled. It put Jude at ease. Raylee had a way of making him feel as if everything was going to be okay, even when everything had always turned to shit for Jude. He didn't know why he was willing to trust Raylee's smile when his past had taught him the exact opposite.

Jude held out his hand, inviting Raylee to take it. Of course, Raylee did. He was too trusting.

Jude watched television for a few minutes, but he wasn't focused on it. Instead, he thought about the shitshow Raylee was in for with Daruss.

"Do you know what type of person Daruss is?"

"I've been told." Raylee shook his head. "Is this where you tell me to back off?"

"No. This is where I say you need someone to help you navigate a relationship with him. You'll end up traumatized by all the shit he does if you don't find someone."

Raylee winked at him. "Are you volunteering for the job?"

Jude couldn't help but smile. He shouldn't even contemplate a positive response. Saying yes to Raylee would give him another broken heart.

Jude knew what he should have said but he never did what he was supposed to. "Maybe."

Raylee tightened his hold on Jude's hand. "I'll take care of you. When you leave the hospital, I mean."

"Really? That would be great." Then he wouldn't have to deal with Daruss as much.

Daruss was right about one thing. Jude didn't have anywhere else to go.

Chapter Nineteen

The closer they came to Daruss's road the more he didn't like the idea of Jude being at his place. Or Raylee for that matter. Jude getting snatched feet from the house proved it wasn't safe. Daruss might be able to make it safer if he had the guys help with bodyguard duty, but it wouldn't last forever. Eventually Daruss would let his guard down and that was when Terrell would take Jude again.

He had to come up with another plan. One that would keep Jude safe in the long run. And for that he had to call the gang in. It would be best to get their input.

When he turned toward Wingspan instead, Jude took notice. Daruss saw him scowl through the rearview mirror.

Raylee had never been to Daruss's house, so he was oblivious.

Daruss answered the question Jude hadn't spoken aloud. "I'm worried about making you an easy target."

"Because Stan grabbed me in the woods." Jude bit his lip. "Nothing's stopping him from doing it again."

"I'll see what the rest of the gang says."

"So we're going to the club?" Jude raised his eyebrows.

"Yeah. If you can physically handle it." Daruss knew why Jude had asked.

"If I can lie down, I'll be okay." Daruss darted his gaze at them in time to see Jude putting his arm around Raylee. "You'll stick to me like glue. Okay, Pretty?"

Raylee's smile was sweet when he addressed Jude. "All right."

Their conversation warmed Daruss. It made his chest ache. He'd never cared about someone the way he did Jude. His heart made a beeline toward Raylee. It wouldn't take long before he was all in with him too. So the fact they seemed to connect with each other was a big step in the right direction.

"Just keep your eyes on me. Okay? And don't take anything liquid or in pill or powder form. No matter who offers it to you. And don't let Izzy flirt with you. Daruss will kill him." Jude knew Daruss better than anyone, but he didn't understand everything about mates.

Daruss chuckled. "Izzy won't flirt with either one of you."

"He flirted with me, Daruss." That was true but Izzy had stopped when Daruss had caught feelings for Jude.

"When was the last time?" Daruss knew it had been months, which had been well before things had fallen apart with Jude.

"Well, it's been a while." Jude met Raylee's gaze again. "Just... I'll help you navigate the club."

"Jude's worried the club will taint your pure soul." Daruss grinned. It was very cute the way Jude protected Raylee.

Jude pulled Raylee closer. "Someone has to. He's too good for the life you lead, Daruss. As long as I'm with you, I'll make sure he stays that way."

Raylee sighed. "Thank you, but I'm a flawed person. Just like everyone else."

"Not to the level Daruss and I are. But that's what makes you so great. You're like an angel." Jude had a clear view of the kind of person he thought Raylee was and he wasn't wrong. Raylee was innocent in a way Daruss hadn't encountered in a person in a long time. And maybe Jude was right. They'd need to make sure Raylee never got jaded. Daruss would have to shield him from a lot. But with Jude's help, they might just be able to keep Raylee's innocence intact.

Raylee chuckled. "I'm not but thank you for saying so."

Jude smiled. He hadn't very often since Daruss had rescued him. It was nice to see it.

"Jude." When Jude met his gaze in the mirror, Daruss said, "You have a new job. Do you understand what it is?"

Jude nodded. For the first time in a long time, he turned his smile on Daruss. It felt like a gift.

****

"Eyes on me, Raylee." Jude was clearly in pain. The way he held his breath and took slow steps gave it away. Jude winced and clutched his abdomen.

"That's it." Daruss lifted Jude into his arms.

Jude settled against Daruss, burying his face against his chest. "Raylee shouldn't see what's going on in there."

"I'll take care of it." Daruss met Raylee's gaze. "Get behind me but stay close."

Daruss kicked the door to the club and waited for someone to open it for him.

Raylee nodded but his eyebrows drew together. "This is ridiculous. You both know that, right?"

"No, it's not." Jude couldn't seem to get his voice above a whisper. "Have you ever seen strangers fuck?"

"Yes. I went to a college party once." Raylee rolled his eyes.

So Daruss's innocent little mate wasn't so innocent after all. That was good to know. "And what did you think when you saw it?"

"It was two women, so I didn't spectate." Raylee shook his head. "I can't imagine seeing that all the time."

"You should probably get used to it if you don't want me to shield you from it." So Jude planned on giving Raylee a choice as to whether he'd protect him or not. Giving choices was good, but Daruss agreed with Jude. Raylee needed their protection.

Raylee sighed. "I don't want to get used to it. No one should be used to that."

Daruss kicked the door again and was just about ready to yell when it opened.

Izzy scowled. His eyes were reptilian. He growled but stopped making menacing noises when he saw Daruss. He never lost his scowl though.

He stepped aside, letting them in. As Daruss passed, he said, "Thought you were taking him to your house."

"Changed my mind." Daruss didn't need to explain himself. Izzy would get why. "Is the bedroom free?"

"Yep."

"Is it clean?"

"Casper and Skippy cleaned up this morning. No one used the room yet." Izzy gazed at Raylee. He smiled. "I suppose Daruss will make us be on our best behavior around you."

Raylee gripped the back of Daruss's cut. Instead of answering Izzy, he pressed himself against Daruss.

It was awkward to walk with Raylee so close, but he managed to make it across the room and to the bedroom. Raylee came around and turned down the covers for Jude. Daruss placed him on the bed.

He knew he had to talk to the guys. It was an important conversation. But he could take the time to make sure Jude was okay.

Daruss pulled the covers over him before sitting on the side of the bed.

Raylee went around to the other side and sat cross-legged. He took Jude's hand, playing with his fingers.

Daruss winked at him, getting a blush for his efforts. "You can stay in here while I talk to my guys."

Raylee nodded. "So many naked people."

Jude snorted. "Told you. You're not ready, Raylee."

No. Raylee probably wasn't. And Daruss would have to make sure his lifestyle didn't scare him away.

Daruss focused on Jude, cupping Jude's cheek. Gods, he missed touching him. More than anything, he wanted the easiness they'd had before. He was afraid of never getting it back.

He hoped for a polyamorous relationship between the three of them. That was the best-case scenario. But there were factors working against that. One was Raylee's exposure to Daruss's way of life. How much could the boy handle? His history with Jude also made it hard to know if he'd get what he wanted. Not to mention, whether or not Jude and Raylee wanted that type of relationship. Daruss and Jude had played together with other people. Most notably, with Jonik. But that hadn't been working toward a relationship with him and with each other. It hadn't been anything serious. Not even to Jude before things turned to shit. But he couldn't look at Jude and Raylee and want anything else.

"Are you in any pain? Do you need anything?"

Jude shook his head.

Daruss kissed him. It was the first real one they'd shared, and it was sort of risky because Daruss wasn't sure how Jude would react. He kept it to just a press of the lips. It was light, designed to comfort, but it made a promise as well. Jude was a perceptive person. He knew Daruss was promising him more than protection. But it would be up to Jude if he wanted to accept the commitment Daruss was ready to make.

Jude sucked in a breath.

"The three of us will talk later."

Raylee had only raised his eyebrows. He didn't seem jealous about the kiss. His expression hinted at being intrigued more than anything else.

Daruss crooked his finger. Raylee smiled and then leaned over Jude. And then Daruss kissed him, making the same promise. Raylee didn't have to be surprised.

And there was one other thing Daruss needed to fill Raylee in on. The Daddy/Boy sexual play Daruss liked had extended to everyday life with Jude. He'd like it with Raylee as well. But Raylee might not be into it. Even worse was if he were turned off by it.

"I'll be just on the other side of that door. If you need anything, ask me. I'll hear you." Daruss made sure he met both of their gazes.

Jude nodded but still watched Daruss as if he were seeing him for the first time. He also seemed skeptical, as if he didn't know whether or not to trust the kiss. Raylee had a knowing sparkle in his eyes.

"What if we need more kisses?" Raylee's teasing took Daruss by surprise. Raylee might be an angel, but his teasing proved he had a couple black feathers in his wings.

"You can ask me. Or you can kiss each other. Entirely up to you." Daruss's answer seemed to be what Raylee expected because he smiled and held onto Jude's hand a little tighter.

Jude's eyes widened and he stiffened. He opened his mouth as if to speak but closed it again. And then he frowned as if he didn't know how he felt about it.

Daruss left the door ajar when he exited.

Chapter Twenty

Raylee questioned his own sanity. He'd never thought about dating two people at once before. Hell, he hadn't ever thought he'd date someone like Daruss. Daruss was dangerous and he'd be possessive. Most dragon shifter fated mates were. And he did illegal things, half of which Raylee didn't even want to know. And Daruss was in love with Jude.

Raylee understood why. Jude was sexy and vulnerable, even though he'd tried not to show it. And he was smart, although not in the same way Raylee was. Raylee had graduated with a 4.0 GPA. School had never been difficult for him. But Jude was right about Raylee being out of his depth when it came to Daruss. Raylee was scared he'd get caught up in Daruss's lifestyle choices and it would put him in danger. Maybe he'd even get beaten up like Jude.

But Raylee already felt a connection to Daruss. Not only that but they were mates. He could reject Daruss, but he already knew in his heart he wouldn't. And Jude. Jude needed him as much as Raylee needed Jude. That much was clear.

Maybe Raylee was understanding the situation wrong, but it seemed to him Jude was right in the middle of Daruss's gang and the gang of the guy who had beaten him up.

Jude turned toward Raylee, meeting his gaze. "You're okay with this?"

Raylee nodded and scooted closer. "It sounds crazy. Dating two guys at once. One of them being my mate."

Jude scowled. "Mate? I know a little about mates, but not much. What do you know about them?"

Raylee smiled. "I was raised by a dragon shifter, so quite a bit. My mom's a doctor. She travels to other countries a lot and stays for months sometimes. So my dad had me a lot of the time."

"So you and Daruss are mates."

"Yes. Daruss has been honest with me from the first day we met. He's made me aware of you and his feelings for you. I even knew about his motorcycle club and that he did some...unsavory things. Seeing it was a bit of a shock. I'll admit that. But overall, I'm not surprised by what Daruss is proposing. And I'm willing to see where this thing between the three of us goes." As speeches went, it didn't get more open than that.

"What are his feelings for me? Exactly." Oh, Jude was fishing.

"It's not my place to say."

Jude sighed. "You're taking a risk."

Raylee was aware of that. But he was in too deep to turn back now. "I care about you and Daruss. I won't turn my back on that."

"And what happens when I break your heart?" Wow, Jude was trying very hard to get rid of him.

Raylee let his hand go and averted his gaze to his lap. "Do you only want Daruss?"

Raylee could see why Jude might not be attracted to him. If Daruss was his type then Raylee was the exact opposite. Daruss was rugged and built as if he ate nails for breakfast.

Maybe it wasn't about the attraction at all. Maybe it was about the love he had for Daruss and wanting the relationship to move forward as it had been before. If that was the case, Raylee didn't fit into that.

Jude tried to take his hand, but Raylee pulled away. "I should say yes to that. You're in over your head. But I wouldn't be saying it because it was true."

Raylee scowled. "Then what is the truth, Jude?"

"I'm trying to protect you from us. You're going to get caught up in this war between the Dragon Skulls and the Chained Devils. Just like me." Jude shut his eyes and seemed to curl in on himself. "I don't know if I can save you from it."

Raylee stood and pulled back the covers, getting into the bed. After he adjusted the blankets, he scooted closer to Jude, facing him. "I don't know the details of how you got to where you are, but I know Daruss didn't put you there. The reason I know is because he did everything he could to rescue you. I think he did it thinking you were working against him. Now why would he go through the trouble of rescuing you if he also thought you'd turned on him?"

Jude shrugged. He closed his eyes. It wasn't long before tears gathered on his lashes. "No one has ever cared about me except for my brother."

"Daruss does. A lot, Jude." Raylee wiped the tears from Jude's face with the top sheet. "I care too."

Jude met his gaze. "I don't know how to trust him. Or you."

Trust was the hardest part of the whole thing. And somehow Raylee was caught in the middle of Daruss and Jude's past. If Jude had wanted to warn him away from a relationship with the two of them, he should have started off his argument in that way. It would have been a lot more effective.

"You're here, with us. You might as well learn how." Raylee leaned forward, getting inches from Jude's face. "I'll teach you to trust. You can teach me to protect myself. Deal?"

Jude smiled and closed the distance between them. Raylee was expecting the kiss, but he didn't factor in how sensual it would be. There was something about Jude that drew Raylee to him. At first, he thought it was because Jude needed medical care. Raylee was a natural caregiver in that way. And there was an attraction, but Raylee wouldn't have acted on it without a push from Daruss. He hadn't expected Jude to blow his mind.

Part of it was the way Jude had urged Raylee to open for him. He worked his way into Raylee's mouth with gentle licks. And Raylee gave him what he wanted.

Daruss had tasted dark, like whiskey. He'd had the ability to burn Raylee up with a kiss. Jude tasted like hot honey. Sweet and spicy at the same time. Jude would make it burn so good Raylee wouldn't understand what hit him until it was too late.

He knew Daruss would be able to charm the pants off him, but he didn't think Jude had the same ability. Of the two of them, Jude was far more dangerous. With Daruss, Raylee knew what to expect. But Jude would break his heart before Raylee even realized how he'd fallen so fast and so far.

Raylee ended the kiss and stood, backing away from Jude before he realized his fight or flight response had kicked in. Raylee covered his lips as if they were the thing that betrayed him.

He was hard. Not just halfway, but full-on able to pound nails. He'd never gotten that way from a kiss before.

"Did I do something wrong?" Jude looked as though Raylee had punched him.

Raylee shook his head.

Jude's lips were rosy and wet from the kiss. When Raylee left the bed, he'd pulled the covers away from Jude. So half his body was exposed. Even though he wore clothing, Raylee found the way he lay all vulnerable and open sexy.

When Raylee climbed back onto the bed, he cupped Jude's cheek. He'd never wanted someone so much in his life but he was scared of the feeling too.

Raylee initiated the second kiss. He took control, making demands. He wanted to straddle Jude's lap and rub their cocks together. He would have if it wasn't for Jude's injury.

Jude took over the kiss. Before Raylee knew it, Jude nearly lay on him.

The move must have hurt because Jude ended the kiss. He groaned and settled onto his side again. He laid his head on Raylee's shoulder and buried his face in the crook of his neck.

"Are you okay?" Raylee held him close.

"Just hurt my stomach. It's still tender where Terrell kicked me." Jude worked his hand under Raylee's shirt, resting it there as if he needed to touch warm skin.

"We got carried away." That was an understatement.

"You liked the kiss?" Was Jude uncertain?

"Yes. It surprised me how much."

"As in you didn't think I was going to be such a good kisser, or you were surprised that I made you hard?"

Raylee chuckled. "Something like that."

Jude smiled and kissed the underside of Raylee's jaw. "I wonder if Daruss will let us do more than just kiss."

It was an odd statement to make, and Raylee didn't know how to take it. But he was all for taking the kiss further. "He doesn't seem like he'd be jealous if we did more."

Jude chuckled. "No. Not jealous. But we'll need his permission. Unless we want to get punished."

"'Punished'?" What did that entail?

Jude yawned. "We're his boys. He's our Daddy. Have you ever heard of a Daddy/boy relationship?"

Raylee ran those words through his mind for a moment. He'd picked up on it at the hospital, but Daruss hadn't elaborated. "I've heard of it, but I've never been in one before."

"You are now, if you want to be."

"I don't know. I think we should talk about it a little more."

Jude didn't respond. His breathing evened out. Jude's pain meds made him fall asleep easily, which was a good thing. He needed to sleep so he could continue to heal.

Raylee held him close and decided to shut his eyes too. A nap sounded like a good idea.

Chapter Twenty-One

Daruss wanted revenge. His anger churned inside him, ready to react. Daruss glanced at each one of his guys. They were ready to go too.

His guys were itching for a fight. Nash was already half-shifted. He'd seen what Terrell was capable of because he'd been at the Devils' clubhouse a lot. Skippy was always spoiling for a fight. Most of the time he waited for an excuse to start shit with someone but not always. And Skippy was big even by dragon shifter standards. More times than not his opponent ran in the other direction upon seeing him.

And then there was Gavin. Daruss might have had his doubts Gavin would exact revenge, but after he'd looked in on Jude and saw his bruises and cuts, he was on board. The rest of him didn't need to be visible. Jude winced and groaned in his sleep. Even after a couple of days, that hadn't changed very much unless he was doped up.

Gavin was the deadliest in their gang. In more ways than one. Daruss had seen him in a fight. When he targeted someone, he never relented, but he always needed a good reason. The last fight they'd had involved Gavin's mate. Daruss saw Gavin differently after that day. He respected Gavin's ability more. And not only to fight but to also lead.

But it was Izzy who Daruss counted on the most. No one ever saw him coming. He seemed as if he were easygoing, always teasing and flirting with the prettiest, unattached boy in any room. But underneath was a dragon ready to strike. It was as if he were a snake buried beneath fallen leaves in a forest. He had the patience of a saint and the willingness to strike when the timing was right. Daruss needed that particular skill the most.

Every one of his guys had shown up. One call was all it had taken. The members who hadn't were the two assigned to infiltrate the Devils clubhouse.

In all the years he'd been Alpha of the Dragon Skulls, he'd never taken their loyalty for granted and he never would again.

"Let me look in on my boys and then we'll get started." That one statement from Daruss made everyone turn to him. They quieted but not for long, although the music stayed off.

Daruss went into the bedroom. Jude was still lying with Raylee, curled around him as if Raylee was a body pillow. Seeing them cuddle made Daruss half-hard. They were so pretty together. His boys were getting along better than he'd expected.

Raylee was awake but Jude was still sleeping.

Raylee smiled. "I'm trapped."

Daruss chuckled. "Got yourself into a predicament, huh?"

"Yeah. But he seems to groan less than when he was in the hospital. I'm not sure if he's in less pain or if me being with him is keeping him calm."

"Maybe both." Daruss sat on the side of the bed. He kissed Raylee. "I haven't talked to the guys yet. I wanted to check on you before the meeting started."

"We're fine for now." Raylee turned into Daruss's touch when Daruss cupped his cheek.

"Do you need anything?"

"Not right now."

"Don't be afraid to ask. I'll be just on the other side of the door. You can interrupt. I won't be mad." Daruss's boys came first. Not even planning revenge mattered as much.

Raylee nodded. "You're talking to your guys about where Jude should stay, right?"

"And you. You're in danger too." Daruss didn't want to tell Raylee about the other order of business, but it would give him perspective. Besides that, Daruss wanted Raylee to have all the information about him. He needed to know what he was getting into. Jude had been right about that. "And we're talking about ways to take Terrell down."

Raylee scowled. "What does that mean?"

Why did Daruss feel as though he had to defend himself and what he was about to do? "He beat Jude nearly to death, Raylee."

Raylee sighed. "So you're going to try to kill him."

"Cripple him is what I was thinking. Make him feel what Jude felt."

"What about calling the cops?"

"Maybe."

"So that's an option?"

Daruss smiled at the way Raylee challenged him. "One of many. I know a good cop."

"Does that mean you have one on your payroll?" Did Raylee think Daruss was in the mob?

Daruss chuckled. "No one could bankroll Mercury into turning dirty. Least of all me."

Raylee raised his eyebrows. "But you trust him."

"I trust him to do his job. Yes." And calling Mercury about those guns Terrell had stolen wasn't a bad idea, but it would probably get Mitch Burke in trouble, which would put him out of reach. Daruss wanted to have a conversation with the guy first. If that conversation turned bloody, then so be it.

"Has he ever arrested you?" Raylee was trying to trap Daruss into confessing his sins. He could see it coming from a mile away. But Raylee wasn't good enough at that game. Given enough time with Jude, he might perfect the art.

"Like I said, Mercury is very good at his job."

"How many times were you arrested?" Raylee lifted his eyebrows.

Daruss shook his head and leaned down to kiss Raylee again. "A lot. I haven't kept track. And I don't have enough time to talk about each arrest."

"What's jail like?"

"It stinks and it sucks." Daruss stood. "Enough questions, boy."

"But I have more. Like what you got arrested for." At Raylee's knowing grin, Daruss bought a clue as to what he was really about.

Daruss raised his eyebrows. "Do you want to be punished? Is that what you're aiming for?"

Raylee bit his lip and nodded. "Jude mentioned it, and I want to see what it was like to get punished by you."

Raylee's willingness to give the lifestyle a try made Daruss's cock go from half-mast to full-on erection.

"There are rules."

"What rules?"

"Ones we set together." And Daruss needed to find out what Raylee liked in terms of sexual play. "One rule I have is for you to call me Daddy."

"During sex or always."

"That's your choice."

"Oh." Raylee might be inexperienced in a lot of ways, but he figured things out quicker than most would. "Okay, Daddy."

Daruss kissed Raylee. "We'll talk about it a little more but later."

Raylee nodded.

Daruss kissed Jude on the cheek before leaving.

When he came back into the main room, everyone turned toward him.

Casper bartended but he didn't offer anything to Daruss as he normally would. He knew Daruss wanted a clear mind for the conversation.

"About Jude. For those who don't know, Mitch Burke is his brother. Mitch is MIA at the moment."

Izzy spoke but it was for the benefit of the entire gang. "Seryn is on it. He's got a lead. That's all he's reported so far."

Daruss nodded. He didn't need to tell Izzy to update him. Izzy would anyway. "It's not that I don't trust him. It's that I don't trust anyone, including him."

"Can we trust Jude?" This question came from Landry. There was no one more skeptical than him. Daruss had blinders on, and everyone knew it. He needed Landry to give him perspective.

"Yes." Daruss made sure the conviction was evident in his tone. "He said Mitch sent him here for protection. Here's why I believe him. Mitch stole those guns that made national news. Jude never once denied that."

Gavin raised his eyebrows. "How do you know that?"

"Jude told me. He also said Terrell didn't expect the crime ending up being too big for Terrell to handle. Terrell knew he couldn't sell them without getting caught. He had been banking on them. Since that well ran dry, at least for the time being, he figures he'll starts another income stream."

"That's what we would do," Izzy said.

"Exactly. Except unlike us, he decides selling human beings is the way to go. And Jude makes the perfect commodity. He's gorgeous and young. Mitch picks up on what Terrell thinks and sends Jude our way because he knows our reputation." Daruss sat back. "All the dots connect. That's why I don't think he's lying."

"Terrell has to die, Daruss." MacIver held his mate close. The two were never separated. "The shit he's into is too much. And what he did to Jude can't fly, man."

Daruss narrowed his eyes. "That's what I was thinking too."

"So you're keeping Jude?" This came from Izzy. He'd be the one to take out a threat if he thought Jude was one. Nine times out of ten he'd follow orders but if he thought Daruss was wrong, he'd do what he wanted.

Daruss needed to let him and the others know Jude was off-limits. He'd kill any one of them if they posed a threat. He didn't care about them being Skull members.

"He's family. No matter what he's done. Everyone here better understand that." Daruss didn't care if he was the enemy, not that he thought he was anymore.

Izzy nodded. "Then he has my protection."

"Good. Because I need a place to put him. Somewhere Terrell can't find him. My mate will need it as well after we finish with the Devils."

The bedroom door squeaked when it opened. Raylee stood with his hand on the casing. His eyes were wide, and he was pale. He opened his mouth to speak but then shut it again.

Daruss softened his expression so he wouldn't scare him even more than he already had. "Come here, boy."

Raylee hesitated but closed the distance between them.

Daruss patted his thigh. He didn't expect Raylee to sit but he climbed into Daruss's lap as if he were a cat. He even wrapped his arms around Daruss and buried his face in the crook of Daruss's neck.

"I'm sorry for scaring you, baby."

Raylee didn't answer. Instead, he asked, "Can I have some water?"

Daruss pointed to Izzy who sat at the bar. The majority of the people in the room were dragon shifters who had excellent hearing.

Izzy grabbed a bottle from Casper and then threw it to Daruss who caught it one-handed. Daruss handed it over.

Raylee took it, clutching it to him as if it were his lifeline. "Thank you."

"I'll need to continue the meeting. You can stay if you want but it'll be more talks of killing and worse." He wouldn't apologize or pretend he was someone he wasn't. It wouldn't do either of them any good. But he worried about doing permanent damage to his relationship with Raylee before it really even started.

All Raylee did was nod and then settle against Daruss.

"All right. So I want to hit Terrell where it hurts the most. His income." Daruss met Ronin's gaze. "Cripple his moonshine business."

Ronin nodded. He knew Daruss didn't care how he did it.

"Find out more about the trafficking. That's the real moneymaker."

Jude stood in the doorway. He clutched his middle. "There's a woman. She's from the Grave Wolves club. She had a patch on her cut the last time I saw her. That's how I know. Terrell was going to sell me to her, but she didn't want me because Terrell marked me up to much."

Raylee scrambled to go to Jude. "I thought you were sleeping."

Jude leaned on Raylee as they made their way over to Daruss. Raylee guided Jude to sit next to Daruss before he sat on his lap again. Daruss wrapped an arm around Jude, pulling him closer and then his other arm around Raylee, holding him in place.

Jonik took his phone from his pocket. "That's a good lead. I'll see if my people can find out more about her. Maybe she's the mastermind behind Terrell's little operation."

Daruss met Izzy's gaze and then turned to Nash. "We'll get our people on it too."

Nash and Izzy nodded.

Daruss kissed Jude on his temple. "Good boy."

Jude smiled and leaned against him, shutting his eyes.

"The last issue is hiding my boys."

Gavin cleared his throat. "The internal connection will go a long way toward keeping them safe."

In other words, bond with them. The sooner the better. "Right."

"Jude can stay with me." Raylee took Jude's hand. "Dad will let him."

"Enzo can protect them. He has experience." Gavin wouldn't say what experience. He didn't make a habit of gossiping about other people, not even when the information was relevant. "We can move them to my house in a week or two."

"They can stay on the farm." MacIver's parents owned a working farm. No one would think to look for them there. "My house next. My neighbors are all clan. They'll protect the boys if it comes to that."

Daruss whispered in Raylee's ear. "I'm staying too. Make sure Enzo understands that."

Raylee handed the bottle of water to Jude. "I just need to call him."

Jude took it and opened it, taking a drink.

Daruss sighed in relief. His boys would be safe. And he had a plan to make sure they stayed that way. He'd still be worried until this thing with the Chained Devils was finished.

Chapter Twenty-Two

Jude had been around enough dragon shifters to know one when he saw one. They were tall people, even the females. And they all had green eyes of various shades. When an older Black man exited the house, his dark green eyes were the first thing Jude noticed. He was beautiful even though he scowled and folded his muscular arms over his chest.

"That's your dad?" Jude didn't want to make it seem like he was doubting Raylee. It was just that there were two factors that made Jude question the biological possibility for there being any connection at all. Raylee didn't appear as if he had Black ancestors, and he was as human as Jude. "You must take after your mother."

Raylee chuckled. "He's my older sister's father. We have the same mom. Dad adopted me when I was a baby."

"That explains a lot." It didn't explain the finer details of their family dynamics. But one thing Jude understood was Raylee's parental situation wasn't typical.

"Speaking of explaining." Raylee opened the back passenger door. He turned to Daruss, meeting his gaze. "Let me talk to him before you get out."

"He agreed to have us here, didn't he?" Daruss scowled.

"Yes. But he's not happy about it." When Raylee exited the vehicle, Daruss rolled down all the windows in the truck, including the ones in the back.

As soon as Raylee grew close enough, his dad pulled him into a hug. He spoke, although Jude couldn't make out what he'd said. Whatever it was Raylee nodded and pointed to the truck. Raylee seemed to make his dad's scowl deepen.

His dad tucked Raylee against his side and made his way over to Daruss. "I'll buy you trying to stop a human trafficking ring. But that's not why you're here. So what the hell are you getting my boy into?"

Raylee seemed to meet Daruss's gaze. "Don't make it worse, please?"

"He couldn't possibly," his dad said.

Raylee and Jude spoke at the same time. "Oh, yes, he could."

Raylee met Jude's gaze through the window and grinned.

Daruss snorted. "Little smartasses."

Enzo's scowl was a little less prominent. But he seemed to blame everything on Daruss, which would suit Jude just fine if he were still mad at him. But Jude had started to forgive Daruss when he had said he sent someone to search for Mitch. Couple that with Daruss not leaving him once since the rescue.

Terrell didn't even know who Raylee was. At least it wasn't likely. So staying with his family made the most sense. They might be able to stay in one place longer. Jude would heal faster if he wasn't always uprooted, although he understood why Daruss had wanted to move them all the time. Terrell would get revenge on Daruss for rescuing Jude from him. Revenge seemed to be the law of the land for clubs like the Skulls and the Devils.

"Daruss is trying to keep me safe," Jude answered before Daruss could. "He's afraid the man who hurt me will find me. Raylee might get caught in the crossfire."

"Raylee already explained that." Enzo sighed and peered into the back of the truck, meeting Jude's gaze. "Tell me what he left out."

"Daruss wants to make Terrell leave me alone." Jude bit his lip and scowled, not wanting to reveal Daruss's plan in its entirety. Not that he knew it anyway. He'd been asleep for a lot of the discussion, but he knew how Daruss worked. "He wants to punish Terrell for hurting me."

Daruss growled. "Jude."

No one told an outsider gang business. Yeah, yeah. Jude rolled his eyes. "It's Raylee's dad, Daruss."

"How are you planning on punishing this guy?" That was a good question. Enzo probably didn't want the answer as much as he thought he did. Or maybe he had a shady past. Maybe he'd done stuff that made him identify with Daruss. His reaction to Daruss's answer would tell his story.

Daruss grinned. "Very slowly. Now can I get out of the truck, or should I take my boys and head to Gavin's house?"

Enzo raised his eyebrows. "Both of them, huh?"

Yep, the guy had a story to tell.

Raylee turned a pretty shade of pink. The color started at his neck and went all the way to his cheeks.

Jude chuckled but covered his mouth when Raylee glanced at him.

Enzo relaxed and took a step back. "You're welcome here."

Daruss opened the door and exited the car. He pulled open the back door. "I'm gonna help you out. Okay, baby?"

Jude knew the movement would hurt but he nodded anyway. Daruss would try to minimize the pain as best as he could, but it would still cause him pain.

Daruss wrapped his arms around Jude, holding him close as he slid Jude across the seat. The next thing Jude knew, he was in Daruss's arms.

Jude wrapped his arms around Daruss and lay his head on his shoulder. Daruss always smelled like cinnamon and dragonshine. The scent comforted Jude in ways he probably shouldn't have let it.

Raylee rubbed Jude's back as they walked into the house together.

When they entered, stairs were in front of them with a living room on the left and a hall on the right. On the other side of the hall was what appeared to be a dining room. Jude could make out a part of the table and a chair tucked under it.

Raylee took the lead, heading through the dining room and kitchen to the hall. "This way."

They followed.

The walls had a plethora of pictures. Most were of Raylee as a boy with an older curly-haired girl. The girl was clearly Enzo's biological daughter. It wasn't only the green eyes and dark skin giving it away. She resembled him in several ways, even as a child. Raylee and the girl seemed happy and well-adjusted. Not at all like him and Mitch when they were kids.

Enzo stood in the hall, watching them. "We eat dinner together. Not in our rooms."

Raylee sighed but raised his hand as if in acknowledgement. "I know, Dad."

Wow. They even ate dinner as a family. Jude couldn't remember the last time he'd sat at a table with other people to eat.

The room they entered had it all. It was a separate apartment with a bedroom off to the right. The living room reminded Jude of Raylee. It was well-lit with natural light and a navy couch with pillows that matched. The bookshelves definitely were Raylee's style. He struck Jude as the bookish type.

They made their way into the bedroom. It had a bigger bed but wasn't made for three people in a polyamorous relationship. And a dresser with a backpack leaning against it.

Daruss laid Jude on the bed and crawled in behind him. "Are you okay? Any pain?"

Raylee lay in front of Jude and took his hand, smiling.

"None. I'm fine." But he was overwhelmed by the tactile response he got from them. It felt as though it were an affectionate assault. And what made it worse was Jude was starting to feel a little better. He still probably couldn't walk without his abdomen hurting, but he'd felt fine while lying down.

Instead of telling this to Raylee and Daruss, and hurting their feelings, he shut his eyes, even though he didn't feel tired. He kind of liked all the touching and the attention anyway.

The longer he lay there with them surrounding him, the more he relaxed. And before he knew it he yawned.

Maybe he was a little tired after all.

Chapter Twenty-Three

It felt as if it had been years since Daruss had held Jude while they slept. In reality it had only been a couple of weeks. He knew it wasn't over. They had a lot to prove to each other.

Love wasn't the issue but trust...yeah, they didn't have that. Daruss wasn't sure how to build it. He wasn't sure how he'd earned it before everything had turned to shit. But he knew how he'd lost it. Not believing Jude had done some damage. He'd been honest with Jude. Jude could count on that at least. But was it good enough to get them to a better place?

Raylee had managed to move away from them. He'd even turned so he slept in the fetal position.

Daruss hooked an arm around Raylee's middle, pulling him closer. He tried not to wake either of his boys but didn't succeed with Raylee.

Raylee stiffened as if he wasn't sure what was happening.

"You're safe, boy."

At the sound of Daruss's voice, Raylee relaxed again. He grabbed Daruss's hand, holding it to his chest.

Jude wiggled between them but put an arm around Raylee. He sighed as if content and settled again.

Raylee and Jude taking to each other could have gone the opposite way, or they might not have had any chemistry between them. The fact they did, and it was so recognizable, made Daruss feel good about his choice. He stopped questioning whether he was doing right by them. He could be pushy sometimes. The situation made it difficult to tell if they'd been attracted to each other or if they'd gone along with what Daruss wanted. But it seemed they gravitated toward each other all on their own. They hadn't needed him to do anything. Jude turned so his cheek rested on the back of Raylee's head. "Smells good," he mumbled.

Daruss smiled. "Yeah, he does."

"Coconut shampoo." Raylee seemed content to lie there.

"Maybe. It's also you. Something unique to you. Smells like hot sand." It was hard to describe scents to a human. Their senses weren't as sharp as a shifter's. But Raylee smelled like the sunlight when it hit a sandy beach.

"I'm not sure that's a compliment." Raylee didn't seem to mind if it wasn't because he giggled.

"It's a good thing, baby. You're my sunshine boy."

Jude kissed Raylee on his shoulder. "Mine too."

"Are you even awake, Jude?" Raylee giggled again. It was a cute sound and one he hadn't made before. Daruss had to wonder if maybe Raylee hid behind a smiling face. Were there dark clouds blocking some of his light? If so, Daruss would find it and kill whatever made Raylee unhappy.

"Sort of. I'm sweaty. You guys are like furnaces." Jude kissed Raylee again, so Daruss kissed Jude. "I feel gross."

"You're not gross." Daruss sniffed Jude's hair.

"Do you want to shower? Dad's bathroom is bigger than mine. He won't care if we use it." Raylee had a great idea. Daruss would love to get naked with his boys. It hadn't happened with the three of them yet and it felt as if it were another step in the right direction. "There's a bathtub in my bathroom if you'd rather."

"I would love a shower, but I don't know if I can stand that long." Jude's hand rested on Raylee's hip.

"We can help you." Raylee squeezed Daruss's hand as if wanting him to agree. "Right, Daruss."

Daruss smiled. "That's right. Do you remember what else you can call me if you want."

"Daddy."

Daruss loved the way it sounded.

"I just want to make sure you're sure about this...about me." Maybe it was good Jude wanted to talk about it. They needed to get everything out in the open. "You guys are mates. I know that's important to dragon shifters."

"It's important to all paranormals." Raylee might be human, but he'd been raised by Enzo. He probably knew as much about mates as Daruss did. "I'm still willing to see how this will work between the three of us."

Daruss kissed Jude's neck. "We need to work on trusting each other again."

Jude sucked in a breath as if he hadn't expected Daruss to have a conversation about that. "Yeah."

"I'm sorry for not believing you. I made a mistake." He hoped an apology was a step in the right direction. It was a good restart.

"I'm sorry too. I should have told you who I was sooner."

"I lied when I said it was nothing more than fucking. I've had feelings for you for a while." That was the last thing Daruss had left to confess.

"Don't lie about that again, okay?"

"Never, sweetheart. I promise." Daruss kissed his cheek.

Jude bit his lip and then said, "I'd like to take a shower, Daddy."

Raylee squeezed Daruss's hand. He had as much to lose if Jude had said no because Daruss and Raylee were mates. It had to be them asking Jude to try. Not just Daruss.

Raylee let Daruss's hand go and climbed off the bed. "So, shower?"

Jude nodded and started to scoot across the bed, but Daruss stopped him. "I'll carry you, boy."

Daruss winked at Raylee, bringing out a blush.

He tried to be as gentle as possible when he lifted Jude from the bed, but Jude still winced.

"I'm fine. Not much pain." Any at all was too much but Daruss tried to be as gentle as possible. "I can probably walk."

"Would you like to try?" Daruss asked.

"It's just down the hall. Not far." Raylee pointed toward the door.

Jude nodded. "It doesn't hurt as bad."

"Where does it hurt the most?" Daruss put Jude on his feet, but he made sure to go slow and keep a firm hold.

"My stomach."

Raylee put his arm around Jude from his other side. "Your chart said you have extensive internal bruising. You'll heal but it'll take a few days. Lots of rest and stuff. That's all you need."

Daruss winked at Raylee over Jude's head. Jude was too focused on each step to pay attention.

Jude stopped and met Raylee's gaze. His expression was flirtatious. "You'll take care of me?"

Raylee nodded. "Of course."

Jude glanced at Daruss. The flirtation was gone. They had too much of a history for flirting, but he smiled. "Will you?"

"It's my job as your mate."

"We're not mates."

"Not yet." Daruss and Raylee spoke at the same time. Raylee grinned, which made Daruss smile. It was Daruss who continued. "It's not as simple as saying words. I'll have to bite you while we fuck. And then I'll do the same thing to Raylee. It has to be in that order if we're going to complete the bond."

"Oh." Jude scowled. "We've done it like a thousand times, Daruss. You never wanted to bond with me then?"

"Raylee and I had to meet first. Right, baby?" Daruss met Raylee's gaze.

"That's right. The three of us forming a relationship would have been a lot more difficult. And it doesn't work without me." Raylee met Daruss's gaze as if daring him to contradict the statement. While it was a bold one to make, it was also true.

Raylee brought something to the mix they hadn't had before. He brought sunshine and light whenever he entered a room, including Daruss's relationship with Jude. But he also required Daruss to commit to a relationship with them. Raylee wouldn't accept anything less. Not that Daruss wanted anything less either. They were on the same page with the seriousness of their relationship. But if it had been Daruss and Jude, it would have taken a lot longer for Daruss to commit to exclusivity. Even love wouldn't have been enough for that.

Loving Jude before meeting Raylee had opened him up to the possibility of accepting the love he felt. He'd closed himself off to it, doing everything he could not to feel it with anyone. If it weren't for Jude, Daruss might not have been so open to accepting Raylee as his mate.

Things happened the way they were supposed to.

He didn't know how to explain all of that to Jude. He wasn't sure if Jude would understand. But he knew what Jude would get. He wanted to get it across to Raylee too. For that reason he met both of their gazes. "We all have to be sure about bonding. Because it will only ever be the three of us after that. We're exclusive."

Raylee blinked as if Daruss had said something shocking. "I've never even had a one-night stand. Not to mention two guys at once. I'm a little excited and freaked at the same time about that part, if I'm being honest. But it would have never crossed my mind to sleep around."

Jude chuckled and kissed Raylee's cheek. "Of course, it wouldn't."

Raylee sighed. "I'm just saying. You guys don't have anything to worry about with me."

Jude started walking again. He winced. "Daruss is worried about me. Not you, Pretty."

Daruss's chest ached at the nickname Jude gave Raylee. "I'm not worried about you either. I'm saying you need to be sure because it's permanent. Til death do us part and everything that goes along with it."

Jude met his gaze. "It's been permanent for a long time for me, Daruss."

Daruss hadn't known Jude felt that way about him. Daruss had to clear the emotion from his throat before he spoke. "And Raylee?"

Instead of answering Daruss, Jude met Raylee's gaze. "You're easy to love. Has anyone ever told you that?"

Jude was a little charmer and a flirt when he wanted something. But he'd meant what he'd said. Maybe it wasn't love yet, but he was in step with Daruss. They would fall for Raylee easily.

Raylee's cheeks turned a pretty shade of pink. "My sister teases me by saying that. And then she'll pinch my cheeks. It's annoying. But I like when you say it."

Jude smiled. "Good. Because I'll probably say it a lot."

"Me too."

Raylee's blush deepened. "What if I don't say it back right away?"

"You can say it whenever you want. When you're ready." Daruss wouldn't pressure Raylee into anything. The mating pull was growing along with their connection. Daruss's dragon wanted Raylee with a ferocity he'd never felt for anyone. The love would slam into him as soon as Daruss had his arms around Raylee.

"You get a choice too, Ray-Ray. Whether you want to do this mating thing or not. You can say no. So can Daruss. It's not a done deal yet just because we're already talking about our feelings." Jude was right. As much as Daruss's dragon wanted to make them his, they had a choice.

Raylee pushed a door open at the end of the hall. A bed sat in the center of the room, but they didn't stop to linger. Instead, Raylee led them to a door left ajar.

The bathroom was lavish. Maybe Enzo really liked his shower time.

"Wow. I'm glad I made this choice."

Raylee chuckled. "Yeah. Dad has a thing for his bathroom."

"I have a thing for his bathroom too." Jude grinned, meeting Daruss's gaze. "He has the good body wash. That same one you use."

Daruss didn't use anything special. It was a brand he bought at the supermarket, but for some reason Jude had always thought it came from somewhere special and Daruss had never corrected him. "He's got good taste."

Raylee snorted. "No, he doesn't. Jazlyn buys it for him. She says it makes him smell less like a grumpy dragon."

Jude chuckled. "That's it exactly."

Daruss guided Jude to the toilet and had him sit on the closed lid. "I'm going to start the shower. Raylee can help you undress."

Jude nodded but bit his lip. He seemed worried about something.

"What's wrong? Are you in pain?"

Jude shook his head and then met Raylee's gaze. Raylee stood behind Daruss so he couldn't see Raylee's expression but must have smiled. "I don't know if you'll like my body. I'm not that thin."

Daruss growled. "I've seen you lots of times. You're fucking gorgeous."

Daruss realized almost as soon as the words left his mouth that it wasn't about what he thought, because Jude rolled his eyes. "I know you think so, Daruss. I'm not worried about you."

Daruss growled again and stood. As soon as he turned toward the shower, intending to turn it on and adjust the spray, he met Raylee's gaze. Whatever was running through the boy's head made him as insecure as Jude. "You too?"

Daruss sighed and closed the distance to take Raylee into his arms. Raylee stopped him by shaking his head. "You know how I told you my mom's a doctor who travels overseas."

"Yeah."

"Well, I used to visit her sometimes. Jaz too. If the place wasn't a war zone or whatever. When I was seven, the medical buildings was bombed. "I'm fine. It's just that I have a couple of scars. And they, um, look pretty bad."

Jude smiled. "We're both a mess, aren't we?"

Raylee returned the smile. "Yeah."

"No. What you are is mine." Daruss pulled his shirt over his head and set it on the sink. He met Raylee's gaze. "I'll help Jude while you take off your shirt. Just your shirt, boy."

Raylee blinked at Daruss, staring at him as if he hadn't seen a naked chest before. His gaze seemed frozen on Daruss. Raylee licked his lips "One of these things is not like the others."

Jude snorted. "I know, right."

"Do what I say, boy?" Daruss tried to put some level of authority into his tone, but he couldn't help but grin. "And don't call me a 'thing'."

"Sorry. One of us is ripped beyond belief." Raylee met his gaze. "Is that better?"

"Take off your shirt. Sassy boy." Daruss didn't wait for Raylee to do as he was told. Eventually the boy would understand when Daruss gave him an order he needed to follow it or there would be consequences.

Daruss kneeled in front of Jude and lifted the bottom of his shirt. "Lift your arms."

Jude complied and Daruss pulled his shirt over his head. He set it next to his own on the sink.

When Daruss turned toward Raylee again, he had his shirt off but held it in front of him.

Daruss closed the distance, taking Raylee into his arms. He took the shirt from him in the process. "The scars won't matter."

"Do you promise?" Raylee scowled as if he didn't believe Daruss.

"Yes. You're beautiful. Nothing will change that." Daruss turned them toward Jude and then released Raylee, letting them look at each other.

Doing so gave Daruss an opportunity to take in the scars on Raylee's chest. He had one near his upper shoulder and the other ran across his abdomen. They were faint and a darker pink than the rest of him. Beyond ramping up his protective instincts by about a thousand, Daruss didn't think they detracted from Raylee's sexiness.

Jude didn't seem to have an issue with them either. He licked his lips like he did when he was turned on. "You guys are hot together."

Daruss grinned. The wheels in his mind were spinning, coming up with ideas to make his boys crazy with need. He wanted to fuck them, but he had to find out what Raylee liked first. Daruss already knew Jude was up for almost anything. He had an appetite for sex that had kept Daruss on his toes.

Daruss kissed Raylee's cheek before whispering in his ear. "I want you to take off your clothes. When you're done, you can help Jude with his."

"What will you do?" Raylee turned toward him, touching his chest to Daruss's abdomen as if in a bid to get skin-on-skin contact.

Daruss wrapped his arm around Raylee's waist and then trailed his hand to his ass, getting a feel. The move also gave Jude the show he wanted since Raylee's ass was inches from Jude's face. "I'm going to turn on the shower."

"But you're getting in with us, right?"

Daruss smiled. "Of course."

Raylee held on to Daruss and then laid his cheek on his chest. He sighed as if with contentment. "Just a couple of more seconds to feel your warmth."

Raylee's skin felt chilled to the touch.

He patted Raylee on the ass. "Okay, let's speed this up."

Raylee turned toward Jude, kneeling on the floor beside him. The first thing he did was cup Jude's face and kiss him. It was sensual and also made demands. There wasn't any doubt they were into each other.

Jude drew Raylee closer and of course Raylee went. One of them moaned. Daruss couldn't tell which one.

Daruss wasn't sure how long he should let it go on. They'd be fucking in under ten minutes. Of that Daruss had no doubt. And while he would love to witness that, he also worried about Jude being in pain and Raylee being too cold.

Daruss leaned down, whispering in Raylee's ear again. "Do what I told you, boy."

Raylee moaned as if he couldn't bring himself to end the kiss. Maybe he needed the intimacy more than he needed the actual fucking. He seemed to like hugs and soft touches. Daruss would have to test the theory.

If he needed a gentler approach, he would be different from Jude. Jude wanted to fuck. All. The. Time. Jude liked it rough. And he liked the spankings that came from being a very bad boy. He'd even been a bad boy on purpose a few times to receive the punishments.

Daruss could already tell Raylee would be more of a challenge. He'd need to take care of Raylee in a different way, which meant he might have to get creative with his punishments. He'd need to think about what Raylee would like but he had something in mind to get him to listen.

"Stop, boy. Or you won't be allowed to come for the rest of the day." Daruss put enough authority in his voice to get Raylee's attention. He didn't want to have to follow through with that punishment. He could find ways for Raylee to earn back the right to come and Raylee probably wouldn't be able to help it anyway, but he needed Raylee to comply if they were going to get him warm.

Raylee pulled away. His cheeks were about as red as his lips. He focused on Jude's lap before lying against him. He shut his eyes.

Jude rubbed his back. "That's the worst punishment, Ray-Ray. Spanking is fun, though."

"I don't know about punishments." Raylee's sounded as if he were uncomfortable. Daruss hadn't noticed at first, but Raylee pressed the palm of his hand against his jeans-covered cock.

So his little mate was hard. That could work in his favor if Raylee played his cards right. "I won't tell you again, boy."

Raylee moved off Jude. He went for Jude's sweats first.

"What did I tell you?" Daruss turned on the shower and waited for the water to get hot. When he turned back to Raylee and Jude, Raylee seemed confused, and Jude smiled as if he knew exactly what Daruss was up to.

"I don't remember."

"What do you call me?" Daruss adjusted the water temperature before folding his arms over his chest and giving his attention to Raylee and Jude.

Raylee's scowl deepened. "What?"

Jude whispered in Raylee's ears. "Call him Daddy."

Raylee met his gaze. "I don't remember, Daddy."

Oh gods. The way he said it made Daruss hard. He'd already been halfway there from the kiss. Raylee softened his tone as if all he wanted was be a good boy. So unlike Jude who could be a brat on purpose sometimes.

"I told you to take off your clothes first." Daruss scowled as if in disappointment, but in reality, he couldn't have been happier.

Raylee's response was perfect. His cheeks had pretty pink blotches and he focused on the floor. "But I'm...I don't want to yet."

"Do you want to come later?"

Raylee nodded. "Yes, Daddy."

"Then do what I say." Daruss unbuttoned his own pants and slid them along with his underwear down. He took his socks off right after because they were less than flattering.

Raylee stared as if he'd never seen a naked dragon shifter before. Maybe he hadn't. Genetically speaking, Daruss was average for a dragon shifter. Raylee must know about dragon shifters, considering he had a father and a sister who were.

"He's serious about the coming thing, Ray." Jude licked his lips, and took in Daruss's naked form. It had been a long time since they'd been on good enough terms to be naked together.

Raylee stood. His hands shook when he tried to unbutton his pants.

Daruss took pity on him and did it for him. Daruss pushed his pants down. His skin was smooth except where the scars were. "Step out of them, baby."

Raylee braced himself with hands on Daruss's shoulders and did what Daruss said. Daruss helped him with his socks next. He wore bikini style underwear. They were yellow and hugged his little ass to perfection. They also outlined his hard cock. Daruss grabbed a handful of cheek before helping him take them off.

His cock brushed Daruss's face as it sprang free.

Daruss took it in hand and kissed the tip while meeting Raylee's gaze.

Raylee moaned. "Oh gods."

"Don't come." They would all have fun watching Raylee squirm.

Daruss kissed the tip again and then licked across the head before taking it into his mouth. Raylee tasted like he smelled. He was a breath of fresh air. It didn't matter what they were doing. Raylee would always be sunshine and smiles.

Daruss wanted to linger but he knew Raylee would come soon.

Raylee tightened his hold on Daruss's shoulders to the point he'd leave marks. Not that Daruss was complaining. He loved Raylee's responsiveness.

The second Raylee began to thrust, Daruss pulled off. Raylee whimpered. "No, please. Please."

Jude undid his pants and managed to fish his cock out somehow. He jacked himself off but stopped when he noticed Daruss watching him.

Raylee tried to thrust, but Daruss made him stay still. His hold was gentle which made Raylee whimper even more. "Please."

"What do you call me?"

"You're my Daddy. Please, Daddy."

"You know exactly what you need to do."

Raylee fell to his knees. His hands shook when he grabbed the bottom of Jude's sweatpants. As needy as Raylee was, he made sure he went slow, sliding Jude's clothing underneath his bottom. But the whole time Raylee's gaze was on Jude's cock as if he were hungry for it.

He handed Jude's pants and underwear to Daruss.

Daruss took his time gathering their clothing from the floor and putting them on the sink. He did it on purpose just to hear Jude and Raylee whimper. As soon as they did, Daruss turned to them.

"You were a very good boy. Do you know what good boys get?"

Raylee shook his head.

"Yes, you do. Say it."

"I get to come."

"That's right." Daruss softened his expression. "And because you were so good, I'll let you suck Jude's cock, but only if you want to."

Jude panted at Daruss's words as if the thought got him off a little.

"I want to." Raylee licked his lips. "Can I right now or do I have to wait?"

"Whenever you want." Daruss smiled. Raylee's eagerness was sexy.

Raylee was careful when he took Jude's cock in hand. He licked the pre-cum off the head before taking it in his mouth.

Jude cursed and ran his fingers through Raylee's hair.

Daruss could tell when Raylee took Jude to the back of his throat. It wasn't so much Raylee's reaction and the way his cheeks hollowed but the way Jude's eyes widened and then closed.

Daruss stepped close enough to whisper in Jude's ear. "Watch him."

Jude's eyes snapped open. He glanced at Daruss right before he focused on Raylee.

"He's hungry for you. He wanted a taste so bad." Daruss knew how much Jude loved dirty talk. He wanted to give his boy what he wanted.

Raylee moaned around Jude's cock as if expressing the truth behind Daruss's words. He cupped Jude's balls with one hand and held onto Jude's hip with the other.

Jude glanced at Daruss's cock.

"If you want to touch it, you'll have to earn it." Daruss would tell him how after the shower.

Jude nodded, knowing he wouldn't get what he wanted. He didn't argue unless he wanted to be punished. The kind of punishments Jude liked wouldn't happen until after he was well again. He'd have to be completely pain-free.

"Can I come?" Jude asked. Each syllable came out breathy and needy.

"Not yet."

Jude whimpered. "Please, Daddy."

"Tell me you're going to be a good boy and I'll think about letting you."

Jude bit his lip. The need built in him. He held his breath. But when he let it out again, he said, "I'll be good."

"Come. Now."

The command was all Jude needed. Jude stiffened right before he cried out.

Raylee sucked as if it were his most favorite job in the world. He didn't stop sucking until Jude shivered and then relaxed. He took every drop too.

Jude was so blissed out Daruss thought he'd fall over, so Daruss put an arm around him.

Raylee let Jude's cock fall from his mouth, kissing it as if he were saying goodbye. Raylee met Daruss's gaze. "Can I come now, too?"

"You want me to finish what I started? Or Jude?"

Raylee shrugged. "Can I choose both?"

Jude was the one who answered. "Yes."

Daruss chuckled. "Stand up though, boy. Jude can kiss it first."

Daruss knelt beside Jude.

As soon as Raylee made his cock accessible, Jude took it in his hand. Raylee cried out. He'd been ready to come when Daruss had pulled off. It wouldn't take much.

"Go slow. Don't let him come too quickly." Daruss watched as Jude made love to Raylee's cock as if it were the best thing he'd ever tasted. But he only licked it. He didn't take Raylee in his mouth yet.

Raylee was ready to beg again. Daruss could tell.

Daruss added to the sensation by licking him along with Jude.

Jude moaned, which sent a vibration through the entire experience. And then he took in the tip. Daruss licked where he could reach and decided to keep going along Raylee's abdomen.

Daruss kissed Raylee's nipple, tweaking it with his teeth. Gods, Raylee tasted good. "Sunshine Boy."

Raylee unraveled. He clung to them when he came. The sounds he made spoke of what waiting to come did to him. When his legs seemed to give out, Daruss stood in time to catch him.

Jude let go of Raylee's cock and leaned against them. Daruss put an arm around him too, making sure he was steady.

Raylee managed to cling to him and Jude at the same time, but he was boneless. So was Jude but Daruss knew that wouldn't last long. If he was well enough to come, he'd want it all the time.

"When can we do that again?" Raylee seemed as insatiable as Jude.

Daruss smiled. "Soon."

Daruss was still hard. His dick ached. But he had been planning on having a talk before getting to the fucking part. It was a little too late to reverse things. They could take a shower, talk, and then get to the bonding. Daruss wanted inside his boys before coming.

He lifted Jude before moving them all to the shower. He'd make sure they didn't linger too long. Bonding had to take priority but so did making sure his boys were comfortable and satisfied. It was his job to take care of them and he intended to do his best.

Chapter Twenty-Four

Raylee didn't know sex could feel so good. It never had before.

Not that Raylee had had much experience. The little he did have was with his college roommate and also with a guy he dated a few times. He'd been friends with his roommate, and it had been the first sexual experience for both of them. That was probably why it hadn't gone well. Raylee's dating experience hadn't gone well either. They'd gone out a half-dozen times and had sex once. The guy wanted to fuck on the first date. When Raylee wouldn't, he'd backed off but that didn't stop him from dropping hints all the time—like on every date. It got annoying. When they finally had sex, it had been less than mediocre. The jerk came and then left Raylee to take care of himself.

He wasn't sure how he'd feel about being Daruss's boy. He thought it would feel a lot like being bossed around but it was more about Daruss taking care of him and Jude. Daruss was demanding but he also knew what Raylee needed. He paid attention to Raylee's needs better than Raylee paid attention to them.

Since the shower, Raylee felt clingy. He needed closeness as well as praise. He'd never been like that before. Raylee sat on the bed with the blanket around his bottom half and Daruss's T-shirt on. Jude was between Raylee and Daruss. Too far away for Raylee's liking but he felt too insecure to say anything. Daruss lay naked on his side next to Jude who lay next to him.

The bruises on Jude's skin were turning darker. It meant he was healing but they appeared even worse than they had been. The caregiver in Raylee fretted over it. But Raylee also liked Jude. Affection would turn into love in no time at all. He also felt protective of him in a way he never had with anyone else. He was protective of Daruss too. Just in different ways.

They were his mates. He felt it in every cell of his body. The emotional turmoil seemed to seal the deal almost as much as bonding would.

Raylee pulled the covers further around Jude, making sure he wasn't cold and then worked his hand underneath. He had smooth skin and he felt warm. Raylee loved that about him, but it was his softness that made Raylee want to touch him all the time. He was so different from Daruss, who had hard muscles and ridges on top of ridges. They were different but equally appealing.

"I didn't mean to take things so far before talking first." Daruss covered Raylee's hand where he rested it on Jude's abdomen. He seemed to direct the conversation toward Raylee more than Jude for reasons Raylee didn't understand.

Raylee knew he blushed. He could feel the warmth creep into his face.

"I'm glad it happened. It was amazing." Understatement of the century.

Jude smiled. "Me too."

"My point is we need to talk before we go any further."

"Okay, Daddy." Jude had an impish way of saying things sometimes. He was very good at turning all that playfulness onto Daruss.

Daruss growled but it was teasing. When he met Raylee's gaze, his eyebrows drew together, making his expression severe.

Raylee stiffened although he tried not to. Since the daddy thing took center stage during the bathroom thing, he had some sort of weird psychosis going on where he didn't want to disappoint Daruss. And he felt as if he had already.

"I have a few questions for you and then we'll go over the rules. But first tell me what's wrong. And be honest." Daruss had the alpha thing down to a science. The fact that he could have that much authority in his tone while lying naked with his cock still hard said a lot.

"I don't want to disappoint you." That was true but not the main thing.

"And?" Daruss raised his eyebrows.

Raylee shut his and sighed. "And I feel like I'm going to come out of my skin if I'm not close to you."

Daruss's expression softened. He scooted back and patted the mattress beside him. "Come here, baby."

"You should take off the shirt first." Jude smiled.

Raylee pulled it over his head and moved around Jude until he was lying beside him.

"On your side, boy. Back to me." As soon as Raylee complied, Daruss tucked Raylee into him. Daruss rested his arm on Jude, as if needing to include him. His skin was warm even though he wasn't under the covers. His hard length settled against Raylee's ass. "Do you feel better?"

Raylee nodded. "Lots. Thank you."

"Here's a new rule for both of you. If you need something, tell me. I want to take care of you, but I might miss things. It helps me be a good Daddy to you."

"In every situation or just during sex?" It was a good rule regardless of their Daddy/boy relationship, but Raylee wanted clarification.

"Every situation, baby."

Raylee worked his hand under the covers again and touched Jude chest. He felt his nipple pebble under his fingers and liked the sensation, so he kept rubbing across it.

Jude moaned and moved into his touch. "Ray-Ray."

Raylee smiled and did it some more.

And then Daruss put his hand over Raylee's, stopping him. "We're not done talking."

Jude groaned and shut his eyes. "Can you say whatever you need to already, so we can do it again? Please."

Daruss growled. "Are you talking back to me, boy?"

"No, Daddy."

"Try again."

Jude sighed. "Fine. Yes. I'm sorry. I only meant that I like the way Ray touches me. And I want him to keep doing it."

"I like touching you too. You're so soft." Raylee ran his hand along Jude's abdomen. He made sure he was gentle, not wanting to cause him pain where he was injured.

"No more touching unless I say."

"Is that a rule?" Jude smirked.

Daruss kissed him. "I can't spank you until you're all healed, baby. So stop fishing for a punishment."

"You like to get spanked?" Raylee didn't think he would, but he would like to see Daruss do it to Jude.

"Yeah. When Daddy does it, it makes me hard." Judd bit his lip as if thinking about it made him hot.

"You're not going to spank me, are you?" Raylee was afraid it was a requirement.

"Not unless you want me to."

"I don't think I do." Raylee wasn't sure if he should say anything, but he figured since they were talking about it he might as well let Daruss know what he did like about what they'd done. "I really liked it when you told me not to come. Well, I didn't. But holding back made my orgasm so much better."

The memory of it made Raylee hard again.

"I know, baby. But I'm glad you told me." Daruss kissed Raylee's shoulder. "If there's something you don't like, what will you do?"

"Tell you."

Daruss trailed his fingers along Raylee's hip and then down to his cock, cupping it through his underwear. "Good boy."

Jude turned toward them, pushing the covers off himself. His gaze was hungry. He traced Raylee's scar with his finger and then cupped his cheek.

"I promise to do my very best to take care of you." Daruss kissed Raylee again. He must have met Jude's gaze because Jude's expression changed to one of hope. And maybe there was a little affection mixed in too. "That's a promise for you too, Jude."

"Thank you, Daddy," they said at the same time.

"These are the rules. Call me Daddy during sexy time. You get to choose every other time but know that I'm always your Daddy. That means I'll take care of you just like I promised. And you have to help me keep you safe."

"What does taking care of us mean in practical terms? Financially? Emotionally? Physically is a given, I think." Raylee needed to know what the parameters were. He might need a little help financially right now since he was starting out. He wasn't worried about that. Hell, he'd make a good living working for his sister if he wanted that. He didn't waste four years of his life in college not to be a nurse. But it seemed Raylee needed Daruss's affection sometimes.

Daruss squeezed his cock. Pleasure flowed through him. "I'll take care of you in every way, including your pleasure." He must have met Jude's gaze again because Jude bit his lip. "And you'll take care of each other."

"Any time we want?" Jude asked.

"Yeah. Any time. It's different with Raylee. Not like the other boys we fucked around with. He's your mate as much as mine." Daruss said it as if Raylee wasn't there, which added to Raylee's upset.

Raylee's cock deflated in an instant and he stiffened. He started to get off the bed, but Daruss tightened his hold. "Let me up."

"We have a rule about telling each other when we're upset, boy." Daruss could shove the rules up his ass.

"Did you tell that to all the other boys you guys fucked around with too?" Raylee wiggled until Daruss released him.

Raylee was off the bed in seconds. He went to his dresser and pulled out a pair of sweatpants and a T-shirt. He didn't bother putting on socks. The house was warm enough without them.

As soon as Daruss realized Raylee intended to leave the room, he growled. "Do not leave this room, Raylee Oyen."

Raylee's chest ached at the last name Daruss gave him. It almost made him forget about being one of many boys they'd fucked. He was a number for them. His gut churned when he thought about how many notches they had on their bedpost.

Raylee turned and met Daruss's gaze. "I need space."

"No. You need to come here so I can reassure you." Daruss wasn't wrong. Raylee did need his reassurance, but he wasn't ready for it yet.

"I'm telling you what I need, just like you said I should, and you're shitting all over it." Raylee shook his head and left the room. His last parting words were, "Keep your promises, Daruss. Or shove them up your ass."

Chapter Twenty-Five

Jude couldn't help his response to Raylee's grand exit. He didn't want to find Raylee's green monster cute, but there it was. It made Jude chuckle as soon as he left.

Raylee's jealousy was so huge he upset the beast that was Daruss because one thing was for sure, Daruss didn't find it funny even a little.

Since he was already digging his own hole right alongside Raylee by laughing, he figured he might as well keep shoveling. "Wow. And you thought I was the one with sass."

Daruss growled and started to get off the bed. "I pegged him wrong."

"Not entirely." Jude grabbed hold of Daruss's hand. "He was right about you not listening to him. Give him what he needs."

"Space." Daruss rolled his eyes and laid back down, drawing Jude closer. "Fuck."

They were still getting to know Raylee. "You and I have history. It probably makes him feel like the odd man out."

"He's not." Daruss could be so dense sometimes. He went at problems like a bull ready to use his horns. No thought. Just *"come here because I said so"*. He might be able to get away with that with Jude. Jude knew how to finesse Daruss into calming down. It was clear Raylee wouldn't even try, which meant Jude would have to work his magic on both of his men.

Jude sighed. "I'll talk to him. I think you should stay here for a few extra minutes."

Daruss kissed Jude and drew him closer. "Think you can fix it, boy?"

Jude bit his lip and smiled. "Will I get a reward if I do?"

Daruss smiled and snaked his hand down to Jude's cock. Jude sucked in a breath when Daruss rubbed his palm over his hard length. "Yes. And I'll let you pick what it is."

"I already know." Jude wanted to fuck. He wanted it so bad it made his cock ache.

As if Daruss read his mind, he said, "We'll get to the fucking. I want to bond. That should go a long way to reassuring you and Raylee. There will be no doubt about who you belong to then."

Jude shivered at the thought. He wasn't sure how he felt about the biting part though. The thought scared him a little, but if it was the only way then he'd do it. He wanted a chance at something permanent with Daruss and Raylee.

"I'll have to think about it." He had a high sex drive. With Daruss and Raylee in his bed all the time, it would get higher. Coming up with something else would be difficult.

"I have some ideas if you want them." Of course Daruss did. He was always one step ahead of Jude. All he had to do was figure out how to get a step ahead of Raylee too. That was when they'd find some cohesion.

"Maybe after I talk to Raylee." Jude rolled onto his side and lifted himself up. He had to use his arms. He never realized how often he used the muscles in his stomach until he had to avoid doing so. Everything he did, he had to go slow, but he was less like a snail than he had been yesterday.

"Do you want me to carry you?" Daruss sat up. He was so comfortable being naked. Jude bet he'd stopped noticing his lack of clothing.

Jude had to force himself to stop focusing on Daruss's cock. It was so large and fantastic. He couldn't help but remember what it had felt like inside him. He needed that again. The sooner the better.

But first to eradicate Raylee's jealousy. "If we both go, we'll make him even angrier. Me first and then you."

"Fine. But if you need me, just say so. I'll hear you." Daruss grabbed his jeans from a chair in the corner.

Jude took a few deep breaths and then stood, grabbing Daruss's shirt from the floor. He went to the drawer Raylee had opened and stole some of Raylee's sweats too. They were a little tight on him, but the shirt was huge, falling to his thighs, so it was fine.

Each step was painful, but he managed to step out of the room. He turned when Daruss called his name. Daruss closed the distance between them and cupped his cheek before kissing him. "I love you, boy."

Jude's gaze widened. "Really. You say that now."

"No better time. Should have said it months ago. Maybe then you wouldn't have left, and that fucker wouldn't have hurt you." Daruss blamed himself. Or least, he partially did.

Jude couldn't let him think Jude had run away from him. "I would have still left. I went to find Mitch. Not to get away from you. And I love you too. But then, you already know, right?"

Daruss smiled. "Yeah."

"I'm most of the way there with Raylee too. Just so you know." He didn't want to leave Daruss questioning his feelings. Transparency went a long way when there were three people trying to find their balance with each other.

"Me too. Make sure he knows that." Daruss kissed him one last time and then stepped back, but he kept a hand on Jude's lower back.

"You should tell him that too. He shouldn't just hear it from me."

Daruss kissed his temple. "You're a good boy."

Jude snorted. "You think I'm sassy."

Daruss grabbed a handful full of ass. "Yes. And sexy. And still a good boy."

Jude turned into Daruss, wanting another hug. "Thank you, Daddy."

"And I believe you." Daruss tightened his hold. "I know I've said it already. But I want you to really understand."

Tears threatened to spill.

"I'll protect you with my life. And I'll never hurt you." Daruss patted his ass before letting him go.

Jude met Daruss's gaze. "I'll never hurt you either. I promise."

"That's more than love, isn't it?"

Jude smiled. "Full-on commitment. And I'm ready for it."

Daruss patted his ass again. "Go make sure our sunshine boy understands that."

Jude nodded and kissed Daruss before turning and walking down the hall. He had to think about each step, going slow. He was tired of being in pain and didn't want to cause himself any more than necessary. But there really wasn't any. His gut twinged a bit as if one wrong step would send knives into Jude, but so far so good.

He found Raylee in the kitchen. He hugged Enzo and rested his head on his chest. At first, they didn't sense his presence, so he heard Enzo say, "Everybody has a past, son."

"I know. But will I be just another guy they played around with?"

"You know that's not possible. At least not with Daruss. He's your true mate."

"Not with me either." Jude shuffled into the room like an old man.

Raylee closed the distance between them. He wrapped an arm around Jude's waist and walked him to a chair, making sure he sat before he gave him hell. "You should be in bed, Jude. You're going to hurt yourself."

"I can't do worse than Terrell already did." Jude kept his tone even, not wanting to give Raylee another reason to be mad at him.

"That's not the damn point." Raylee growled when he sighed. He sounded like a baby bear trying to make itself seem meaner than it actually was. It was cute. Raylee kneeled beside the chair. "Are you hurt?"

"I feel fine other than my heart." Jude met Enzo's gaze over Raylee's head when Enzo cleared his throat as if he wanted to chuckle but didn't want to piss off Raylee either. Enzo smiled at Jude before turning toward the coffeepot, which gave them some semblance of privacy.

Raylee frowned. "Do you have pain in your chest?"

"Yes."

Raylee lifted his shirt. "Let me see."

"It's internal." Jude couldn't help the smile, but he tried to stay serious.

Raylee blinked once and then rolled his eyes. He sat back on his heels before standing. "That's not funny, Jude. I thought something was really wrong with you."

Jude grew serious. "Something is. Your jealousy is hurtful."

Jude knew the second the words were out of his mouth he'd put Raylee on the defense. The problem was he didn't know what to expect from him. He was about to find out how Raylee reacted when someone really pissed him off.

Raylee got inches from his face. "Am I going to be another boy you messed around with once?"

Jude straightened in his chair. "I'm half in love with you, Ray-Ray."

Raylee blinked as if Jude had slapped him. He took a step back. "How many people have you said that to?"

"One."

"When did you say it?" Raylee put a hand to his chest as if his heart ached.

"Five minutes ago in the hallway." Jude smiled. "Looks like your heart hurts too, huh?"

Raylee fell to his knees again and then rested his head on Jude's legs. "Yeah."

"You're the only one now, Ray-Ray. That's what being mates means. That's what you guys said earlier. It's what I want. I know it's what Daruss wants." Jude moved Raylee's hair off his face. "We're yours. I promise."

Raylee shut his eyes and moved until he was hugging Jude around his middle. They probably looked strange with Raylee on his knees lying across Jude's lap and Jude with his fingers buried in Raylee's hair.

It wasn't until Daruss walked in that Jude glanced up.

Daruss's expression appeared worried but hopeful.

Jude smiled and nodded, letting him know it was all right.

"I really care about you, Jude. I want this thing with the three of us to work. I want it so bad and I know you guys have history. It's obvious in the way Daruss knows what you like. And it makes me feel...as if maybe I'm a third wheel during sex."

Jude cleared his throat. "Your dad is still in the room, Ray."

Enzo chuckled and grabbed his mug. "Not anymore."

Jude nodded in thanks. They needed privacy. But it seemed as if they were taking over Enzo's house and that didn't seem very fair to him. So Jude would much rather have had their conversation inside Raylee's little apartment. It was what it was, though.

"You're not the third wheel." Daruss looked at Raylee as if he were the most precious person in the whole world. Jude recognized it because he did the same with Jude.

Raylee jumped in Jude's lap. He sat up and met Daruss's gaze.

"You're the missing piece." Daruss held out his arms. When Raylee went to him, Daruss lifted him off his feet and held him. "You're ours. Our mate. Our love. Our baby."

Raylee laid his head on Daruss's shoulder. "I'm sorry."

"That's okay."

"I should have let you reassure me."

Daruss smiled. "Yes, you should have."

"I don't want to be punished."

Daruss winked at Jude. "Do you think you deserve one?"

Jude knew that question was loaded. No matter how Raylee answered, Daruss would make sure he was punished. What would matter the most was whether Raylee told the truth.

"Yes." Raylee whispered it. Jude barely heard his response.

"What do you think your punishment should be?"

Raylee's sister came through the back door as Raylee answered. "I want to come? Please."

She stopped inside the door. Her eyes were wide. She turned right back around and left the house.

"Do you think you deserve to come?" Daruss already had a plan. Jude could tell by his expression. But Jude would bet he would make Raylee believe he couldn't.

"No." Raylee seemed to tighten his hold.

Daruss rubbed Raylee's back. "I'll let you come."

Raylee sighed.

"But you'll only do it on my say so. Even if that's tomorrow or the next day."

Raylee groaned. "It's the same thing."

Jude chuckled. "You're good at whining. It's very cute."

Raylee mumbled something Jude couldn't hear but Daruss did because he rubbed his hand over Raylee's ass. "I'm hard too, baby. But I think we're all hungry, so you'll have to wait until after I make you something to eat."

"I can make it." Raylee wiggled as if he wanted Daruss to put him on his feet.

Daruss stopped him when Raylee started round the kitchen peninsula. "I'll do it, boy."

Raylee nodded. "Okay, Daddy."

Raylee fell to his knees again and went right back to where he'd been, lying in Jude's lap. Jude rubbed his back.

Enzo and Jazlyn came into the room together. She must have used another door to enter the house.

Almost everyone was afraid of Daruss. It was stupid not to be. He was ruthless and vengeful on a good day. He didn't seem to have any effect on Enzo though. "Make enough for everyone."

"I planned on it."

"Good." Enzo went to the table and sat across from Jude. "Did you get things straightened out?"

Jude wasn't sure if Enzo was talking to him or not, but he answered anyway. "Yes. Thanks for the privacy."

Enzo nodded.

Jazlyn sat in the chair next to Jude's. "Two, huh?"

Jude chuckled because she wasn't talking to him. She aimed her question at Raylee. Raylee must have known it because he mumbled out a "yes".

"Seems complicated."

Jude and Raylee answered at the same time. "It is."

"Not that complicated since this is the second time you two have answered at the same time and in the same way." Daruss pulled out chicken breasts from the freezer and stuck them in the microwave. He grabbed a couple of boxes of pasta next.

"We're practicing. Soon we'll be able to..." Jude tapped Raylee on the back, hoping he got the clue and spoke next.

"...finish each other's sentences," Raylee mumbled.

Enzo snorted and then turned toward Daruss. "You have your hands full."

Daruss shook his head. "Don't I know it."

Jude planned on keeping Daruss on his toes too. No way was he letting go of the chance to make Daruss a little crazier than he already was.

Chapter Twenty-Six

They needed to bond. The sooner Daruss could tie Raylee and Jude to him, the better it would be for everyone. What he didn't know was how he'd tie Raylee and Jude to each other. Or if him bonding with both of them would create an internal connection between Jude and Raylee too. He'd never met anyone who had bonded with two humans at the same time, so he wasn't sure what to expect. A dragon shifter in Wingspan had two mates. But one was some type of cat shifter, and the other was a vampire. They had been able to make the connection themselves. Jude and Raylee had already formed an emotional connection.

He had to bite Jude first because they weren't true mates. His bond with Jude wouldn't hold if he started with Raylee. But it wasn't his bond with them he was worried about. It was theirs with each other.

He'd managed to get Jude and Raylee back to the bedroom, but he thought maybe Enzo would know what to do.

Enzo was finishing up with the dishes.

Daruss leaned against the counter. "Do you know anything about human matings?"

"Other than they don't call it that, you mean?" Enzo smirked.

Daruss waved that off. "I know they don't. It still is though. At least some of the time, right? They fuck around with others before they get to the commitment part just like everyone else."

Enzo wiped his hands on a dish towel and turned. "You're asking because of Raylee and Jude."

"Yep. I want them to have an internal connection." Daruss shrugged. "Just don't know how it works for humans."

"Physiologically speaking, paranormals shouldn't have an internal connection either. The fact that most humans don't with each other should be scientific proof that a connection isn't possible. But one exists anyway. How? We don't know."

Daruss sighed and shook his head. "So you're saying science can't prove anything."

"I'm saying on a scientific front, we have a lot of work to do if we're going to answer questions. But I know some witches can read minds. It's somewhat similar, is it not?"

"You're asking me? I don't fucking know. What I do know is my boys need to have an internal link if I'm going to protect them. So how does it work with humans?"

Enzo smirked. "You're assuming it's different than with paranormals?"

"I'm not assuming anything. I'm admitting ignorance. Do you know or not?"

"Not entirely, but I do know humans bonding with shifters, and probably other paranormals creates a physiological response. Although unexplainable, they do develop an internal connection. Their life expectancy increases. Some heal faster. So my advice is for you to mate them first and then they mate with each other."

Daruss nodded. That was what he had planned all along. At least he knew his instincts were correct. "Thanks."

"I'll kill you where you stand if you hurt my son. It goes for Jude too. He needs someone to look out for him and I'm going to make it my job."

"Figured that was coming." If anyone else had threatened him, they would already be dead. But Enzo had the same objective as Daruss. He'd be an idiot not to align with him. It would keep his boys safe.

Enzo was a no-nonsense kind of guy, which Daruss liked. At least he knew where he stood. "Best way to protect them is to change a few things. I think you know what I'm talking about."

Daruss knew exactly what he meant. All the criminal shit Daruss did would have to come to an end at some point. Enzo was right about it being the best way to keep his boys safe. Selling shifter drugs had connected him with some bad people who weren't loyal to anyone. They'd cut Daruss down if they needed to and where would that leave Raylee and Jude?

But it wasn't just about that. The whole thing with the Chained Devils had started over territory and would end over it too. Their gangs were neighbors. And in terms of business, there was only enough for one of them. Moonshine was a big business. They sold the legal shit on the shelves in liquor stores, but everyone wanted to get away with a sin. They'd pay top dollar to be naughty. Daruss's gang made good money off it. The Devils did too. But they cut into each other's bottom-line too often.

He didn't know what the right answer was. All he did know was his boys would get caught in the middle. Jude already had. He couldn't let it happen again, but it seemed as if it were a fast-moving train. The future was set in stone as if it were buried in the bedrock beneath his feet. How did he break through it and change some parts while leaving others?

"I'm working on it." Daruss moved around the peninsula heading for the hallway.

Darus was almost out of sight when Enzo stopped him. "Daruss."

Darus met his gaze. "Yeah."

"Don't fuck in my bathroom anymore."

Daruss grinned. He was bad at following rules. Enzo knew Daruss's reputation well enough to know he'd find a loophole. "We didn't fuck. We made love."

Daruss headed down the hall, but he still heard Enzo say, "The whole damn house is going to smell like sex."

That was a great idea. Fucking his boys on every flat surface he could and even some that weren't flat sounded like the best way to spend the rest of his life. Pissing off Enzo was a bonus.

When he got into the bedroom, Raylee was on top of Jude, straddling his lap. Both boys were naked. They kissed as if there was no other purpose in life. Raylee's ass was on display.

Daruss shut the door behind him. He opened the drawer and hoped there was lube inside because it was the one thing he hadn't thought of.

The bottle was small, but it would do. He would buy more tomorrow.

He sat on the bed. They didn't stop kissing but when Daruss ran his hand down Raylee's back to his ass, Raylee moved into his touch. His responsiveness was so sexy.

Knowing they were so close to bonding brought his dragon to the forefront. As dominant as Daruss was, his dragon ruled almost everything he did. His protective instinct. Wanting submission from his boys. His willingness and ability to fight for what he wanted. Even the fact that he didn't like following the rules, including the ones imposed on him by society.

When it came to his boys, he felt almost feral, as if something had fractured. At the same time, he didn't want to scare them. Jude didn't understand that much about dragon shifters. He'd been scared of Daruss when his eyes turned reptilian, and his fangs had dropped.

They stopped kissing and met his gaze. Jude's eyes were wide as if he wasn't sure of Daruss's mood. Raylee appeared as if he wanted to climb Daruss like a tree.

Daruss patted his thighs and met Raylee's gaze. "Sit on Daddy's lap."

Raylee seemed relieved as if he were waiting for permission. When he moved off Jude, Daruss noticed how hard his cock was. Daruss would take care of Raylee, but first he needed to reassure Jude.

Raylee wanted to straddle his lap, but Daruss wouldn't let him. Instead, he made him sit so he was facing Jude. But he made sure to hold Raylee close. His sunshine boy liked to cuddle, and he seemed to need physical affection more than Jude did.

Raylee wrapped his arms around Daruss's neck and held on as if he needed Daruss to keep himself afloat. "Will you touch me?"

Daruss knew where he meant. Raylee wiggled in Daruss's lap. "Sit still, boy."

Raylee scowled but he obeyed. He pressed on his cock in a bid to get some type of friction.

"Who does that belong to?"

"You." Raylee whimpered when he took his hand away.

"And who am I?"

"My Daddy." Gods, he loved it when his boys called him that.

"You'll come. Eventually. But I need to talk to Jude first. And then we need to talk about your punishment."

Raylee laid his head on Daruss's chest and sighed. "Okay."

"Okay what?"

"Okay, Daddy."

Daruss winked at Jude when he smiled. Jude seemed relieved by Daruss's reaction. "I'm partially shifted because I'm excited to bond with you and Raylee. Not because I'm angry. Do you understand, boy?"

Jude nodded. "Sorry."

"You don't have to apologize. You don't know much about shifters. You're learning. It's okay to ask questions." Daruss wanted to educate him. He'd scared him enough in the past and had to work to make it right. "It happens when my emotions are high."

Jude bit his lip. "Oh."

"I don't mind telling you how and why I've shifted. So if you need to know even after we bond that's okay." Daruss cupped Jude's cheek at the same time he rubbed Raylee's back.

"Thank you, Daddy." Jude leaned into Daruss's touch. "Can I touch myself?"

"Yes. While I get undressed." Daruss kissed Raylee. "Do you want to touch him?"

"Yes, Daddy." Raylee leaned down and kissed Jude on his hip. He couldn't quite reach his cock from where he sat on Daruss. "Can he touch me?"

Daruss met Jude's gaze. "Bring him close to coming but don't push him over." Daruss patted Raylee's hip, wanting him to move away.

Raylee seemed excited when he moved off Daruss. "Is that my punishment?"

Daruss smiled at the way Raylee's eyes widened. "Yeah, sort of."

Raylee scowled but he trailed his fingers along Jude's stomach toward his cock in an almost absentminded way. "I thought it would be something I didn't like."

Daruss stood, taking his shirt off. "I'll never really punish you for having emotions, no matter how you feel. But I'll find any reason I can get to make you feel good."

Jude wrapped an arm around Raylee's waist and pulled him close, cuddling with him. "Punishments feel good. It's pleasure overload sometimes but Daddy still makes sure you like it."

Daruss loved Raylee's eagerness when it came to their sexual play. "It's all about taking care of you."

Raylee and Jude watched him as he unbuttoned his pants. He wondered if taking off his clothing would always feel a little as if he were giving a strip tease.

Raylee lay on Jude's side with his head on his chest and his hand around his cock. It was then that Daruss realized Raylee was their baby. He wanted to be held the most. He'd demand closeness as soon as he felt secure in their relationship. And Jude would either step aside so Daruss could take care of him or do so himself.

Daruss would have to make sure Jude wasn't ignoring his own needs. And he would have to make sure he hugged Jude too even when he didn't ask for it.

Daruss winked at them as he took off the rest of his clothes.

Jude licked his lips like he did whenever he was turned on and Raylee's eyes did that sparkling thing.

"Sit up so Jude can reach your cock, boy." Daruss came back to the bed and slid between Jude's legs. He pushed Jude's legs back, exposing his puckered opening. It had been so long since he'd been inside Jude. It felt as though it had been forever. Just seeing it made Daruss wanted to fuck into him with abandon, but it wasn't about his needs. His boys deserved the best sex of their lives. Daruss intended to do everything in his power to give it to them.

Daruss kissed Jude's thighs. "No coming."

Raylee whimpered as if getting denied was the thing he was looking forward to the most.

Jude moaned when Daruss licked from his pucker to his balls. "Oh gods. That's so good."

"I want to see." Raylee must have tried to move because the bed shifted.

"I want to kiss you on your cock, baby." Jude calling Raylee that became more appropriate the more Daruss and Jude got to know Raylee.

Daruss glanced at them. Raylee was on his knees. His hard cock jutted toward Jude's mouth. Jude held it, guiding it to his lips. He kissed the tip and then licked across it, tasting the pre-cum gathering there.

Raylee watched Jude as if he were the best movie he'd ever seen. His mouth was open, and his brows furrowed.

Daruss licked across Jude's pucker again. He wanted Jude to unravel. He needed to see it. Daruss would bond with him after, but he wanted Jude to beg for it first.

Daruss swirled his tongue around Jude's opening, loving how he whimpered and tried to move into Daruss's mouth as if he were begging for something inside him.

Raylee watched Daruss as if he wanted a taste too. But Jude had sucked him into his mouth, so Raylee panted as if he were going to come if Jude didn't stop. And Jude was trying to get him close to the edge. Daruss could tell by the way he hollowed his cheeks.

When Jude moaned around Raylee's cock, Daruss knew he was closer to his goal.

"Don't push him over, boy." Daruss wasn't sure if it was the command or his tone, but it made Jude stop sucking. It was as if the pleasure was so great it stole his breath.

Raylee whimpered and took himself in hand, pulling at his cock. "I'm so close. Please."

Daruss growled. "No touching yourself."

Raylee released his cock. The desperation was clear when he lay next to Jude and began rutting against him.

Raylee kissed Jude's nipple, licking across it. He was bent at what looked like an uncomfortable angle, but he didn't seem to care. His focus was chasing his own release.

Jude arched into Raylee even as he pulled his legs back further and lifted his hips.

Daruss reached between Raylee and Jude. And held him at the base of his cock. When Raylee scowled and met his gaze, Daruss growled. "No coming until I say."

Raylee shut his eyes and panted. "I need."

"Good." Daruss moved away from Jude. "Come here and get him ready."

He grabbed the lube and handed it to Raylee. When Raylee took it and focused on Jude, Daruss knew he had come down enough to follow orders.

"Get on your knees. Ass up." When Raylee did, Daruss had never seen anything better in his life. Jude, in the same position, rivaled it.

Daruss rubbed Raylee's cheeks before squeezing one. He was different than Jude. Jude had a bubble butt with more padding. He was fun to fuck because seeing his ass jiggle with each thrust was a little reward before the ultimate reward of coming. Raylee had enough muscle to have a pretty shape, but it still was perfectly round. Small but so tempting, Daruss couldn't help but want a taste.

Daruss loved rimming, but there was something about doing it to Raylee. Part of it was the mate pull. His scent drove Daruss crazy in ways he'd never experienced before. But most of it was Raylee's responsiveness. He moved into Daruss's tongue. The way his moan was muffled because he was kissing Jude. Daruss wasn't sure where Raylee's lips were, but he imagined them on Jude's balls.

Jude panted. "Another one. Please."

Daruss stopped what he was doing so he could watch his boys.

Raylee had a finger in Jude and was adding another one. He sucked Jude's balls into his mouth. With his other hand, he rubbed Jude's side and stomach, still trying to be careful of his injuries.

Jude lifted his hips and tried to fuck himself on Raylee's fingers. He begged Raylee for more. Jude was always hungry for something inside him. It made Daruss hot every time he got that way.

He wanted them so much.

Jude was eager for him. And Raylee was ready to be edged again. Daruss grabbed the lube and put a little on his palm. He settled above Raylee, so his cock rested between Raylee's cheeks. The pressure was what he needed.

He reached for Raylee's cock, kissing his nape at the same time. When he jacked him off, he made sure Raylee knew he wasn't messing around.

Raylee cried out, moving into Daruss. He fucked into Jude faster, matching Daruss's pace. When he started moaning and shaking, Daruss stopped, tightening his hold on Raylee's cock.

Raylee panted as if he'd run a million miles. "No. Please. Please, Daddy. Please."

Daruss whispered in Raylee's ear. "One more time. Then you can come."

Raylee whined.

The sound of it made Daruss even harder. He growled and fucked against Raylee's hole. He had to force himself to stop.

Daruss kissed Raylee on his shoulder. "When I fuck you, I'll bite you right here. But it's Jude's turn first."

"Please, Daddy." Raylee pressed his hips into Daruss and must have pressed into Jude too because Jude cried out. Raylee trembled beneath him. His cock jumped in Daruss's hand.

Jude moaned and lifted his hips. He panted a bit more. Raylee must have been massaging his prostate.

"Don't make him come, boy."

Gods, Daruss's hadn't ever been so in need. Holding back before the shower had been about him wanting to have stamina for the bonding. He needed to come twice. The way he felt, he didn't have to worry about it.

When Daruss let Raylee's cock go, he whimpered and tried to chase the touch.

"Lay next to Jude. On your back." Daruss wanted to see his expression when he touched him the next time.

Jude whimpered when Raylee pulled his fingers out and moved to lie beside him. The two of them kissed with abandon, as if that were the only lifeline they had.

Daruss had to remember to be gentle with Jude. He was still recovering. Hell, the poor boy couldn't even walk without measuring each step. But he seemed okay in his current position.

Daruss leaned over him but didn't put his weight on Jude. He kissed Jude's neck, taking in his scent. Daruss let Jude feel his fangs but didn't break the skin. He wanted to bite him in a bad way but he wanted them to be close to coming first.

And he still had another boy to edge. Daruss glanced at Raylee.

Daruss touched Raylee's cock with the tip of his finger and watched as he lost his mind. Raylee's cry forced him to end the kiss.

Raylee couldn't go one more time. He was so far gone already.

When Daruss took him in hand, Raylee began to beg. "Please, Daddy. Please."

Jude bit his lip and watched Raylee, as if he were the sexiest thing he'd ever seen. And he was. No doubt about that.

Raylee was flushed and panting. He moved into Daruss's touch.

All it took was Daruss whispering, "Come," and he let go.

Raylee gripped Daruss's hand in both of his as if he thought Daruss would let go and then curled around it. His cum landed on his chest and Jude's side.

"Don't stop. Don't stop." That seemed to be his mantra as he fucked into Daruss's fist. He slowed his movements, the tension leaving his body by degrees.

"Thank you." Raylee kissed Jude's shoulder as if he were the one letting him come. In truth he could reach Jude easier.

When Daruss leaned toward him to give him a kiss, Raylee latched onto him. He took over the kiss for a second. "What do you call me?"

"Thank you, Daddy." Raylee smiled, his body relaxing for the first time since Daruss had walked into the room.

Jude smiled. His cock was hard, but he wasn't as worked up as he'd been minutes ago.

"You're a good boy." Daruss kissed Jude's cheek and then his lips.

Jude cupped Daruss's cheek. When the kiss ended, he focused on Daruss's fangs. He must have been able to feel them when they kissed. "You think I'm good?"

"There are so many reasons why you've been a very good boy." Daruss smiled, revealing his fangs since Jude seemed so fascinated.

Raylee kissed Jude's cheek before settling again. The satisfaction was deep with that one. "You're the best, Jude."

Jude met Raylee's gaze and smiled. "Did you like your punishment?"

Raylee sighed and his smile widened. "More than. It made coming so much better when Daddy finally let me."

There was something satisfying about knowing he'd taken care of Raylee's needs. "You're a good boy too."

Raylee moved into his touch when Daruss cupped his cheek. "We're going to bond now, right?"

Daruss nodded. "First Jude and then you."

Daruss took Jude's hand and pressed his finger to his fang. "You can touch them, if it will make you more comfortable."

"I'm not scared of them." But Jude explored each fang. "It's just so fascinating. They look like the kind in vampire movies. Not the bad movies but the really good ones."

Daruss growled, keeping it playful. "I'm not a vampire."

Jude chuckled. "I want to see your dragon."

Daruss ran a finger down Jude's cheek. He'd avoided shifting in front of Jude because he hadn't wanted to scare him. "Are you sure?"

Jude nodded. "I'm sure."

"After we bond. I'll even take you for a ride when you're feeling better."

"What do you mean? Is that a euphemism?"

Raylee snorted.

Daruss chuckled. "I mean we'll fly together."

"Can I ride too?" Raylee asked as if he didn't know what the answer would be.

"Of course. It wouldn't be as much fun without our baby." Daruss kissed him before wiping some of the cum off Raylee's abdomen, using it as lube for Jude.

They'd talked long enough. It was time to get to the bonding. Gods, it felt as if he'd waited forever.

Daruss worked his finger inside Jude. His muscles were already loosened enough for Daruss to take him. Raylee did a good job. But Daruss wanted to get him worked up again. It was Jude's turn to be the center of attention.

Raylee's gaze sparkled with lust as he watched them, but he seemed content.

Daruss kissed Jude as he fucked him with his finger. "Hi."

Jude let out a breathless laugh. "Hi, Daddy."

"Do you want a little burn?" Daruss knew what his boy liked.

Jude nodded.

Raylee sat up, his cock wasn't hard yet, but it jumped as if it wanted to get that way again.

Daruss grabbed the lube, putting some on his cock. His control slipped, and he couldn't let it. Between Jude recovering and how quickly Raylee bounced back, Daruss had to put a leash on himself.

As soon as he pressed his cock to Jude's opening, he knew he had to stop for a second. If he didn't, he'd fuck into him with abandoned. The bruises on Jude's body were a visible reminder of why he couldn't.

And that little internal lecture was what he needed.

He pressed inside.

Jude panted. He knew not to take his gaze off Daruss, but it was obvious the pleasure was too great, making him want to close his eyes.

"Been too long." Far longer than Daruss would ever go without again.

Jude nodded.

"Missed you, baby."

Tears gathered on Jude's lashes. They didn't spill, though. He tried to speak but all that came out was a whisper. "Me too."

When Daruss bottomed out it was the best feeling in the world. He kept his thrust slow and careful, not wanting to hurt Jude.

"Tease his nipples." Daruss commanded Raylee as he held onto Jude's ankles. It was the right amount of leverage he needed to go deeper but still keep from slamming into him.

Raylee took it a step further when he not only licked across Jude's nipple, but he also took Jude's cock in hand.

Jude panted. His gaze grew desperate as if the attention would overload his system if they didn't stop soon. "Daddy."

Daruss grew even more feral, losing some of his control. He didn't lose his ability to take care of his mate like he thought he would. His dragon was careful, pressing in and pulling out in slow degrees.

"Mine. Say it." Daruss growled.

"Yours." Jude breathed out the words.

"Who are you?" Daruss's control slipped even more. His pace picked up but not by much.

"Your...boy." Jude moaned. "Oh gods."

"Mate. Say it." Gods, Daruss needed Jude to admit it. When he did then Daruss's dragon would be satisfied. It was the last thing before he bit him.

"Your...m-mate."

That was it. "Yes."

Daruss leaned down. Raylee seemed to know what Daruss intended because he moved, giving Daruss space.

Jude tilted his head to the side.

Daruss kissed the spot before biting down, breaking the skin.

Jude cried out and clung to Daruss, holding him tight. His ass muscles clamped around Daruss's cock and then warm wetness coated their abdomens.

Daruss worked on instinct when he shifted his hand and cut his neck. He pressed the cut to Jude's lips. Jude didn't hesitate to suck on it.

Daruss stilled, pressing inside Jude. But the white hot need took over. He came inside his boy. It was the best feeling in the world, right there next to bonding.

Daruss took a few more swallows before licking the wound closed. He kissed it and then further up his neck. Jude was done sucking on the wound Daruss had made so Daruss kissed his jaw. His cheek. And finally, his lips.

Jude had never been more blissed out. He had a smile on his face and his eyes were closed. *That was so good.*

Yeah, it was. Daruss kissed Jude again.

Jude's eyes snapped open. "What...you didn't speak, did you?"

We have an internal connection.

Jude's eyes were wide. And then he turned to Raylee. "I can hear him. In my mind."

Raylee smiled but then averted his gaze as if he felt left out. Poor baby. "I bet it's great."

Jude's eyes softened and he gripped Raylee's nape, pulling him down to him. "Daddy has to recover for a minute. But as soon as he does, he'll give it to you as good as he gave it to me."

"I know." Raylee sighed and rested his cheek against Jude's chest. "I'm sorry. I want Daddy inside me too. I got jealous again."

"What did I tell you about that?" Jude was so good at helping take care of Raylee. The dynamic between them couldn't have been better.

"That you love me and so does Daddy." Raylee played the part of being the baby to perfection. Daruss knew it wasn't calculated. It was who Raylee was. Eager to please. Wanting all the attention.

"That's right."

"I still need, though." Raylee was as insatiable as Jude.

In the long run it was a good thing, but they'd keep Daruss busy. No doubt about that. Maybe even too busy to continue all the shit he'd been doing. He needed to take the gang in a new direction. Enzo was right when he said the boys deserved to feel safe. And they deserved to have all their needs met.

It was a change for everyone in the club, not just him, but it also needed to happen.

Chapter Twenty-Seven

Raylee hadn't ever been so needy in his life, but Daruss and Jude seemed to bring it out in him. It seemed as if a switch had been flipped during their sexual play before their shower. He couldn't turn it off, not that he wanted to.

He couldn't believe how hard he was again. After the best orgasm of his life, he didn't think he'd be able to get it up anytime soon. But watching Daruss fuck Jude was the hottest thing he'd ever seen. It was as though he were watching live porn but there was love involved, which made it even hotter.

Daruss was so careful with Jude. And he'd used Raylee's cum as lube. So in a way, he'd been inside Jude too.

Raylee loved how cuddly Jude was. He kissed next to Jude's nipple and closed his eyes.

Daruss rubbed his ass cheek.

Raylee moved into his touch. He turned to face Daruss and opened his eyes, meeting his gaze. "Can I touch you?"

"You've been a very good boy." Something about Daruss saying that did it for Raylee. Daruss seemed to know it too. "You don't have to ask, baby."

Raylee straddled Daruss's lap and wrapped his arms around Daruss, laying his head against his chest. Daruss had the right amount of chest hair. It felt soft and crisp on his cheek. He had tattoos everywhere. Raylee laid against the head of a dragon. Its body wound down Daruss's chest around to his side. The tail ended on his hip. Raylee traced it with the tip of his finger.

Daruss reminded Raylee of an art gallery. The tattoos were beautiful and intense, like Daruss.

The one on Daruss's shoulder made Raylee shudder and he wasn't sure why. It was of a skull with a pretty dragon tail woven through the dark eye sockets. The dragon's mouth was open as if it were ready to crush the skull with its sharp teeth. The dragon had fangs like Daruss had in human form. They dripped blood.

Daruss tightened his hold as if he thought Raylee was cold.

"What's this one mean?" Raylee touched it and wondered if he really wanted to know the answer to his question.

"It's a dragon skull tattoo. All Dragon Skulls have one."

"Do Jude and I have to get a tattoo?" Raylee wasn't sure he wanted one that represented violence so well.

"Only if you want one." Daruss rubbed his back in slow circles.

"I'm not a Dragon Skull." Raylee wasn't sure he wanted to be. All he wanted to be a part of was their mating. He wanted to feel Jude and Daruss in his mind. He wanted to communicate internally like they had. The sooner, the better as far as he was concerned.

"My guys...they're loyal. They'll protect you with their life. The shit we do...you and Jude can't get mixed up in it. Ever." Daruss's tone was severe, as if the thought of Jude and Raylee getting caught up in the criminal stuff caused him stress.

"I already am, Daruss." Jude had turned onto his side, facing them. He looked so debauched with cum all over him and his nipples all pink and plump from when Raylee had teased them. Seeing him like that made Raylee's cock twitch with interest.

"I know. But I'm going to fix that, so you won't be ever again. And then you and Raylee will stay away from it for good. It won't be like it was before. Do you understand me, boy?"

Raylee traced another tattoo. This one was Jude's name. The letters were simple. But the tattoo was above his heart. The dragon tattoo surrounded it as if it were protecting Jude.

Raylee moved so Jude could see it. "It's your name."

Jude scowled in confusion. "What are you talking about, baby?"

"The tattoo."

Jude tried to sit up but winced. He laid down again. It amazed Raylee that Jude could get fucked so thoroughly and that didn't seem to hurt much but sitting up caused him pain. It was a sure sign of healing when certain activities didn't bother the injury. Thank the gods, sex was one of the things Jude could do.

Daruss lifted Raylee and moved so Jude could see it. The way Daruss did it made it seem as if he were gliding through water, as if Raylee was as light as a feather. The strength it took made Raylee hot as if he were burning up from the inside out.

Jude reached for Daruss, touching the tattoo before meeting Daruss's gaze. "When did you do this?"

"About an hour before your rescue."

"When you still thought I was a traitor?" Jude scowled again. "Why would you do that?"

"Because it didn't matter. I knew I loved you anyway." Daruss leaned forward and kissed Jude.

Jude cupped Daruss's cheek. He smiled and shook his head. "I can't believe I didn't see it before."

"They aren't easy to see." No, they weren't. They blended in so well with the dragon someone might miss them. Daruss straightened and Jude's hand fell away.

"I think it's sweet." Raylee kissed Daruss on the tattoo.

"Yeah. It is." Jude never lost his smile.

Daruss straightened and turned his attention to Raylee. "Move back just a little, baby."

Raylee did. It was then that he saw his name. It was in the same font as Jude's tattoo. Daruss had it tucked under the dragon next to Jude. The only reason Raylee hadn't seen it before was because he'd lain his cheek on it.

Raylee kissed it, keeping his lips in place.

"I got them at the same time." Daruss cupped the back of Raylee's head. He didn't hold him in place or provide any sort of pressure. It was a simple gesture of affection. "I love you as much as I love Jude, baby. You're our sunshine boy."

Raylee didn't feel so sunny sometimes. He had bad days too. But he didn't think it was about that. Their lives had been different than his. They'd been through so much. Maybe he was a light in their storm.

Raylee met Jude's gaze when he took his hand. Jude kissed his palm. "I'd get your name and Daddy's tattooed on my body."

Raylee smiled. "Where would you get them?"

"You can have my right ass cheek. Daddy can have the left one." Jude's eyes sparkled with mischief.

Raylee snorted and then full-on laughed when Daruss growled.

Daruss reached out and smacked Jude's ass. "The only thing you need on your ass cheeks are my handprints."

Jude laughed. It was one of the few times he'd sounded so carefree. "Promise, promise."

Daruss winked. He tried for a scowl, but a smile peeked through. "I already promised you, boy. After you heal, remember?"

Jude shivered. "You weren't just teasing?"

"Be naughty and see if I don't."

"Can I watch?" Another thought occurred to him. "Can we do more of what I like?"

Jude bit his lip and met Raylee's gaze. "We can be naughty together."

Raylee liked the sound of that.

Daruss chuckled. "Wait until we finish the bond before you test me."

It was Raylee's turn to have Daruss inside him. He was a little nervous because he'd never had anything as big as Daruss's cock before, but then he'd never done it with anyone he loved before either.

Raylee ran his free hand down Daruss's chest. He made sure to touch Daruss's nipples.

Daruss hissed but didn't protest. So Raylee went lower. He traced the ridges on his abdomen, liking the feel of them. Each one made his blood heat.

Daruss cupped his ass cheek. He rubbed his finger around Raylee's hole.

Raylee pushed into Daruss's finger.

"Are you ready, boy?"

Raylee didn't know but he nodded anyway.

He worked his way down Daruss's abdomen to his cock. Daruss was hard again. The weight of it made Raylee moan. He couldn't touch himself. Daruss already told him no, but he needed something touching him, so he pressed into Daruss's cock and his own fist.

Daruss stopped touching his ass and gripped his cock. He didn't jack him off but just held him in a firm grip. With his other hand he held him by the nape.

When Daruss kissed him, Raylee's world narrowed. No one else existed until he felt a slick finger at his opening. It had to be Jude. Raylee could feel Daruss's hands on him. It was confirmed when Jude said, "My cum is in you."

It felt right having Jude with them. It was as if Raylee could breathe again. He didn't even recognize the tension in his body until it all slipped away. And it wasn't that he didn't feel safe and secure in Daruss's arms because he did. The tension wasn't about any of those things. It was about feeling whole within the relationship. The only way he obtained that was if Jude was there too.

Raylee pressed into Jude's finger as he entered him. He'd always loved having something inside him. Not that he'd ever topped.

Raylee had never had anyone make so many demands with a kiss before. He fell into Daruss as if it were the most natural thing to do.

He touched Raylee, as if he were the most precious person in the world, while also promising safety and security.

Raylee could say no. He could reject Daruss and all his promises. Daruss knew it as well as Raylee. Raylee chose Daruss and everything that came with him. The protection, the demands, and the danger. He accepted it all because he knew his life would feel empty if he didn't.

Jude added another finger. "So tight. Such a pretty ass."

No one had ever called him pretty as much as Jude. And someone like Jude saying it made him believe it even more because Jude was beautiful with his baby face and would have appeared as if he were the sexy boy next door type if not for the hard living in his gaze.

Daruss ended the kiss, trailing little licks along his jaw to his neck. He growled when he got to the spot where he'd bite Raylee. And then he latched on, not breaking the skin but he commanded Raylee to stay still and let him bite.

Raylee knew the mating bite would feel good when they bonded but he hadn't expected teeth on his skin to make his blood heat. "Please, Daddy."

Jude added another finger.

Raylee moaned. Jude held still while Raylee fucked himself. He went slow, getting used to the fullness.

"He's ready, Daddy." Jude pulled out of him.

Raylee whimpered, wanting them again.

Daruss lifted Raylee. "Guide me in, boy."

Raylee positioned himself so Daruss's cock was at his opening. The head had barely breached him when Raylee stilled. He braced himself on Daruss's shoulders and met his gaze. "It's big."

Daruss breathed as if he were already worked up. He flashed his fangs. "Mine."

Raylee nodded and took a little more. "Yours."

Daruss growled and wrapped his arms around Raylee, holding him as if he couldn't get close enough.

"Daddy stretches you so good." Jude panted as if he were the one with a cock inside him.

Raylee took more, bottoming out. He stilled again, letting himself adjust. "So full."

"Yeah. That's exactly right." Raylee didn't turn to see what Jude was doing but he imagined him jacking off. The sound of it was unmistakable.

Raylee moved when he felt ready, lifting off and then sinking onto Daruss. He created a rhythm that wasn't as fast as he would like but it made his blood sing a little at a time.

Daruss seemed to know what he needed because he tightened his hold, stilling him and then fucked into him. He increased the pace until their skin slapped together.

Raylee cried out. He clung to Daruss and wasn't sure what made him do it but he bit Daruss where his neck and shoulder met. He hadn't meant to break the skin and wasn't aware he bit so hard until he tasted blood.

Daruss hissed, fucking into Raylee harder. "Come. Now."

That was all it took to send Raylee over the edge. His muscles clamped onto Daruss in an attempt at keeping him inside. He had to stop biting when the pleasure became overwhelming.

Daruss bit him as he was coming down from his orgasm. It sent him over the edge and felt as if the first orgasm had never ended.

Then Daruss growled around the bite right before he filled Raylee with his cum, staking his claim on Raylee's body. Or maybe it was his soul. The connection certainly went that deep. Maybe it went even deeper.

Daruss tightened his hold as his movement became shallow and then he stopped. He still held Raylee as if he was afraid Raylee would disappear. And he still drank from him.

It wasn't until Jude said, "Daddy. I need him" that Daruss let go.

He kissed Raylee's wound but didn't lick it closed. Instead, he shifted his hand and reached over, cutting Jude's shoulder. Jude didn't even flinch. He was on his back with his hard cock in his hand. It was slick with lube and angry with need. He panted as if he were close.

Raylee kissed Daruss and moved off his cock. He felt empty when it slipped away. "Thank you, Daddy."

"You're a good boy." Daruss patted Raylee's ass, sticking his finger inside him as if he couldn't get enough of feeling it.

Raylee never got tired of hearing that.

He kissed Daruss again and hugged him tight before climbing off his lap and going to Jude.

"Can you come again, boy?"

"I'll try really hard." Raylee wasn't sure but it didn't matter. The thought of having Jude inside him was exciting. He wanted more and he wanted it all the time.

Raylee kissed Jude. Jude's desperation was clear. He didn't need foreplay or for Raylee to linger.

"Be careful when you straddle his lap, baby."

"I will, Daddy." Raylee pushed Jude's hand away and positioned his cock at his opening. Since Daruss had already opened him, he slid inside. Raylee sighed in satisfaction. Gods, he loved having his mates inside him. He'd never have enough.

He fucked himself on Jude's cock, increasing his pace. It wasn't until Jude reached for Raylee that he faltered. He licked at the blood sliding down Raylee's chest first before latching on. Jude sucked at Raylee's mating mark.

That's it. My good boys. Daruss's dragon was there in his mind and so was Jude. The three of them were one unit. He wasn't sure where one of them started and the other stopped.

Thank you, Daddy. That was Jude! Gods, he had an internal link with Jude as well. How great was that?

Raylee continued to fuck himself on Jude's cock. The friction he'd created on his cock went a long way to getting him hard again. He didn't think it would happen so quickly but there he was, the need building almost as if it never really left him.

Thank you, Daddy. Raylee wasn't sure what he was even grateful for. He had a list of reasons. The praise. Fucking him so good. Letting him come. Allowing him to have a connection with him and with Jude. One was amazing. To have both made him the luckiest person in the world.

When Jude's blood stopped flowing, Raylee kissed the wound and pressed his cheek to Jude's.

Jude kissed from his wound along his neck to his jaw and then his mouth.

Daruss rubbed his ass cheeks and then pushed a finger alongside Jude's cock. Raylee moaned. "Come."

Raylee wasn't sure which one of them Daruss was talking to, but it didn't matter. The command went straight to his balls. He had to end the kiss when he couldn't contain his reaction. He cried out. His movements become stilted. He had to force himself to keep going so Jude could come too. But he didn't have to for very long. Jude was right there with him, obeying Daruss just as Raylee had.

Jude grunted and panted. When Jude pressed into him, Raylee helped by taking all of him inside and then stilling. Jude shivered and then went limp beneath him, so Raylee moved again.

It was Jude who slapped Raylee's ass and smiled. "Daddy, make him keep still."

Raylee grinned and did it again before settling on Jude, lying on him as if he were the best pillow.

Daruss chuckled and lay beside them. He rubbed Raylee's back.

Raylee yawned and shut his eyes.

"All right. Come here. You can't fall asleep on top of him."

Jude let his arms fall to his side as if he knew Daruss was about to pluck Raylee off him as if he were a rogue hair. But he kissed Raylee's cheek.

Daruss let him stay long enough for Jude's cock to grow soft inside him. And then he did indeed move Raylee, so he was between them. Daruss's back was to Raylee's front, and he wrapped his arm around Jude as well, including him.

Raylee kissed Jude's cheek. "Sleep so you can heal."

Jude smiled. He closed his eyes. "I think I did some sexual healing. Not in any pain at all."

Raylee had almost fallen asleep when Daruss's phone rang.

Daruss grabbed it. "Jon."

The volume wasn't loud, but Raylee still heard what was said because of how close he was to Daruss.

"There's an auction. Tomorrow night. My employer needs your people to shut it down."

"And who is that, Jon?"

"You don't need to know."

"Fuck off then." But Daruss had stiffened.

"The Devils are hosting it."

Daruss cursed. "Where?"

Jonik gave him the details.

"Meet me at the club tomorrow." Daruss ended the call without giving Jonik time to respond. And then he called someone else. "Tell all the guys to be at the clubhouse. Early afternoon."

"What's going down?"

"A fight. Tell everyone to bring their A-game."

Raylee didn't know what an A-game was, but he bet for dragon shifter that meant they would shift. Raylee pressed into Daruss even more when the worry set in.

Daruss ended the call and put the phone back on the nightstand.

He kissed Raylee's temple. "Shh. It's okay, baby."

Raylee wanted to believe it, but he couldn't help but think something bad would happen to Daruss.

Chapter Twenty-Eight

Jude held Raylee's hand when they entered the club. Daruss supported Jude as he walked, helping him. Jude felt better so he didn't need it but it made Daruss happy so he allowed it. He experienced twinges in his gut but nothing more than that. He still had to take slow steps but overall, he was fine.

All the sex they'd had in the last twenty-four hours probably helped more than anything. Taking in Daruss's blood seemed to speed his recovery time. Or at least that was what Raylee said he thought might be why he was feeling better.

As soon as they entered the clubhouse, Raylee squeezed his hand. His lily-white innocence took a nosedive. It was the very thing Jude didn't want to happen.

Jude sighed. "We really need to have rules for everyone when Raylee's here, Daddy."

Daruss chuckled. "We just got done debauching him six ways to Sunday and you're still worried about his delicate sensibilities."

"I'm right here and can hear you guys." Raylee rolled his eyes but his gaze went to a boy in the center of the dance floor who wore lacy panties and nothing else. Several people watched him with lust in their gazes but no one touched him. Everyone in the club knew the rule about unwanted advances. Even lustful looks were considered unwanted in some cases. But Patty loved the attention. He'd made his desires known when he'd first arrived at the club. That was the only reason Daruss didn't knock people's heads together for staring.

All except for Raylee.

Jude did a countdown in his mind for the exact second Daruss would reprimand him.

He hadn't even gotten to one before Daruss growled. *Look somewhere else, boy.*

Sorry. It's just that I can see his...you know what.

Jude tried to hide his amusement but couldn't manage it. He chuckled. "It's his cock, baby. That's what you can call it."

Raylee rolled his eyes. "I know. But if I said it, Daddy would be even more upset."

"That's not logical."

"Yes, it is."

"No it's not. Daddy knows where you looked. It doesn't matter what you call it."

Daruss couldn't hold on to his scowl. He chuckled. "Go sit on the couch, boys."

Daruss patted Jude's ass and then Raylee's before going to the bar.

Jude was the one who led Raylee to the couch. He pulled Raylee against his side.

Raylee's lips touched Jude's ear. "Why is it so hot in here?"

Jude grinned. "Izzy turns the heat up when some of the boys want to be in their underwear."

"So they'll be comfortable?" Raylee fanned himself with his shirt.

Jude chuckled. "Sort of."

Raylee grew quiet as he thought about that. "Does he do it on purpose?"

"Sort of." Jude pulled his shirt over his head. "Izzy's good at getting around the rules without breaking them."

"But he's not supposed to look at the people who don't want to be looked at? And he manages to follow that rule?" Raylee watched Jude with wide eyes as Jude stood and undid the button on his pants.

"I think his logic is that shedding their clothes also loosens their inhibitions. Everybody knows Izzy's always up for a good time." Jude pushed his pants down as he talked. He had on thongs. He knew Daruss liked them. He hoped Raylee would too.

Raylee sucked in a breath. "What are you doing?"

Jude grinned. "Getting comfortable."

He gathered his clothes and put them in the little cubbies against the far wall. Jude had to walk across the room to do it. He folded his clothes and put them in one of the empty boxes.

Two people watched him. He could feel the lust through their bond. He met Daruss's gaze on the way back to Raylee. Daruss's eyes shifted to his dragon, and he licked his lips.

Izzy and Nash were talking to Daruss. He might have been paying attention to the conversation, but Jude couldn't tell. When Jude had walked far enough to have his back to Daruss he slapped his own ass cheek just so Daruss could see it jiggle. When Jude met his gaze again, Daruss grinned.

He turned back in time to see Raylee's cheek turn a pretty shade of pink. There was lust in his eyes but also uncertainty and maybe a little jealousy.

Jude straddled Raylee's lap and boxed him in. He kissed Raylee on his mating mark as a reminder of who held his heart. "You should get comfortable too."

"I don't like it, Jude. People are looking at you." Raylee covered Jude's bare ass cheeks with his hands as if that made them less noticeable.

Jude rolled his eyes. "Daddy's the only one watching me. Now he's watching you touch me."

Raylee didn't take his eyes off Jude. "Do you promise?"

"Do I promise what?"

"That you won't let them look at your body."

Jude didn't know how he'd avoid being seen by people in the room. There was a difference between lustful glances and people seeing him.

"Almost everyone here is a dragon shifter. You know they don't view nakedness the same way humans do." It was one of the first things he'd learned about shifters upon meeting Daruss and the other Dragon Skulls. Shifters didn't seem to take nakedness as a license to treat him like a plaything the same way humans did. Feeling safe and secure, regardless of what he wore, allowed him to relax. All the tension disappeared whenever he was in the clubhouse.

Raylee sighed. "Yeah, okay. I still feel like your body is only for Daddy and me."

Jude licked Raylee's neck. "Mmm. Yeah. Just for you and Daddy."

Raylee wiggled underneath him. Jude felt his cock grow hard. He wanted the barrier of clothing gone but it was up to Raylee. He wouldn't push any further than he already had.

Raylee kneaded his ass cheeks. "You're sexy like this."

Jude kissed Raylee under his jaw. He was about to ask Raylee if he wanted to take it into the bedroom when Daruss let out an ear-piercing whistle.

Jude sat beside Raylee. He whispered in his ear. "Daddy's calling a meeting."

"Nonmembers get the fuck out." Daruss had two bottles of water and a glass of what was probably dragonshine as he closed the distance between them. He handed them each a water before sitting on the couch.

The music cut off in the middle of a song. The dancing boy stopped and went to one of the cubbies, pulling his clothing on. Several others also headed that way. And two clothed individuals left.

Raylee climbed into Daruss's lap, leaving Jude further away from them so he scooted over until he was plastered to Daruss's side.

Raylee leaned against Daruss, getting comfortable, as if he knew Daruss hadn't meant they had to leave.

Of course, Daruss had to tease him. "You're awful confident."

Raylee pulled Daruss's arm around his waist and played with his fingers. "About what?"

Jude covered their hands with his own, wondering what Raylee would do.

Raylee took it and put it in between their hands, as if Jude was the filling in their hand sandwich.

Everyone waited for Daruss to say something to them. Instead, Daruss kissed Raylee's cheek before kissing Jude. "About not leaving with the others."

Raylee shrugged. "I don't want to be away from you. Jude doesn't either. Right, Jude?"

Jude smiled and agreed even though he knew Daruss didn't have any intension of making them leave. He wouldn't be able to protect them if he did. And besides that, he knew he could trust them. He could feel their worthiness through the bond they shared.

Daruss wiped the hair off Raylee's forehead. A few of his strands were wet and clinging to his skin. "Izzy, turn down the heat. My mates are hot."

"Thank you. It was either that or shed clothing."

Izzy went to the thermostat and pressed a few buttons. "Since you made all my fuck buddies leave, I might as well."

Ulises was a member but didn't ride. Or he hadn't the last time Jude had talked to him. Maybe he'd taken the plunge and bought a bike. He didn't have a cut, but he sat on a bar stool. As soon as Izzy glanced his way, Ulises flipped him off.

Izzy's expression turned sheepish, and he tried to close the distance, but Ulises hopped off the stool and hid behind Gavin and his mate. Ulises was family to them.

Gavin scowled and shook his head at Izzy as if he knew what had transpired between them.

Jude didn't want to get involved but he would love to know the gossip. Not that he would ever ask. That was a good way to get on Daruss's bad side. Since he'd just gotten off it, he knew what a horrible ride it was.

Daruss leaned forward and whispered in his ear. "I'll tell you later."

Jude met his gaze. The surprise was probably clear in his expression.

Daruss winked and then addressed the room. His gaze went to Jonik who had his arm around Wren. They were the only nonmembers who were allowed to stay. They seemed to know they could.

"A birdy told me the Devils were holding an auction."

"What are they selling?" Skippy asked.

"Humans."

More than one person growled.

"Where the fuck did Terrell's humanity go?" Nash asked and shook his head.

Another member whose name was MacIver spoke up. "We're shutting it down, I take it?"

"We're making it our new mission." Daruss met Jonik's gaze when he said it.

Jonik nodded as if in gratitude.

"What's the fucking plan?" Daruss asked Jonik.

"For now, just show up where my employer says."

Daruss didn't like it. His scowl said as much but he nodded.

Jude had a bad feeling about the whole situation.

Daruss kissed his temple. He must have felt Jude's unease through their bond because he said, "I'll be okay, baby. I promise."

Jude scowled and wondered if Daruss would be able to keep that promise.

Chapter Twenty-Nine

All Daruss could picture was Jude being auctioned off. Daruss wouldn't have been able to protect him from the possibility of what came. It very well could have happened. If Daruss would have waited even one day longer to rescue Jude, Terrell would have beaten Jude to death. But there had been a small possibility of Terrell leaving him alone long enough to heal so he could sell him to the highest bidder.

Raylee wasn't any safer. Not with him walking around Wingspan, working at his sister's bookstore. And he was nice to everyone. Anyone could pluck him right off the damn sidewalk.

You boys will always have a bodyguard when I can't be with you. Daruss had left them in the hands of two capable gang members. And they were at MacIver's house in Wingspan, so they had the clan surrounding them. But his gut still churned with worry. *Tell MacIver and Landry if something happens to you, I'll kill them.*

Daruss already knew they wouldn't. He could practically see Jude rolling his eyes as if the thought of someone hurting them was ridiculous. Considering it had happened to Jude already, he was just being obstinate.

He pictured Raylee walking up to MacIver and turning those big brown eyes onto him. And his pretty smile. He'd say, "Excuse me, sir. But Daddy said to protect us, or he'd kill you." How could anyone take offense when he presented it that way?

We don't want to. Raylee spoke for them. They were smart enough to let Raylee do the talking when they had to tell him no. It was difficult to argue with Raylee even when he was angry. *They don't leave the room even though Jarrell keeps wanting to watch romantic comedies and MacIver keeps grumbling about watching too many of them.*

Daruss decided to let it go. *I want you boys to stay together. Don't even go to the bathroom without each other.*

Yes, Daddy. They projected it at the same time.

Daruss had to concentrate on his surroundings because they were pulling up to a strip club. The place was in a college town with two clubs in the same strip mall-type building with separate entrances.

The lot was dark with just a few lights scattered around and none near the back. But the club signs provided a neon glow. Each club had a cute name designed to draw men like Daruss in. *Lil Darlings* was the club they'd go into.

There were more bikes in the lot near one particular entrance, so he parked amongst them. He had most of his guys with him, leaving six guys to take care of the boys, including his own.

Almost everyone was inside already so they were alone in the lot except for three college-aged kids at the other end. Daruss heard them laughing.

"Why are so many bikers here? Is there some charity event happening or something?"

"At a titty bar." One of them smacked the other in the back of the head. "Stupid."

"Who fucking cares? Naked girls are inside. Focus, Eion."

And good for them. They'd stay alive longer if they didn't involve themselves with a bunch of bikers.

As soon as Daruss saw the set-up, he knew their plan wouldn't work. The area was too crowded. They'd expose themselves as shifters if they started a fight. They'd have to stay human.

Jonik seemed to have the same thought and so did Gavin because they walked up to him. "My employer has people inside already. They're incapacitating the buyers quietly and one at a time. But people are noticing. What he needs from us is to create a diversion. Samson has almost all of the victims in a safe location inside the building, but it won't stay safe for much longer."

Izzy scowled and glanced at Jonik before meeting Daruss's gaze. "Why are we trusting him?"

"Because whoever he works for is trying to shut down human trafficking, including the Chain Devils' little operation."

"Don't we want to know who this guy is, boss?" Izzy asked.

"Yes." Daruss met Jonik's gaze. "And Jon will tell me. But later, when this shit is over."

Jonik shook his head. "I can tell you some of it. Not everything."

Whatever the fuck that meant.

"We don't have time to argue about it." Daruss met Jonik's gaze. "We're making ourselves a bigger target."

The best thing to do was to go in fighting. They'd make it known they were after the Devils. It was the quickest way to give Jonik's employer what he needed. But doing so would piss Terrell off in a big way. He'd get revenge. Daruss had wanted to make Terrell suffer before he finally killed him. He'd accomplish that if he went in shouting about the Devils, but would that put a bigger target on his boys?

"The only way to end it is to stop the human trafficking in this area. It's not just about the territory war between your gang and Terrell's anymore."

Before bonding it wouldn't have mattered. Daruss would have thrown himself into the fight and damn the consequences, but he couldn't protect his mate if he were in prison or worse, dead.

He had to take the target off his boys first and to do that he had to get a little dirty.

"Let's show them a good time." Daruss headed for the front entrance. His guys fell in line.

As soon as they entered, he clocked the bouncer across the face. The bouncer was a big guy but not as big as Daruss. He was also human, which meant he wasn't as good at taking a punch, especially not one from a dragon shifter. He dropped like a stone.

Jonik climbed over the sound booth, which was stupidly close to the front entrance, the music came to a screeching halt. The DJ held up his hands, but Jonik did something to the guy's neck, touching it in some way that made the DJ lose consciousness.

"Who's a Chained Devil?" Daruss yelled, scanning the room. He grinned like a lunatic, which seemed effective for some because they headed out of the back entrance. "We've come to play."

Several people stood and headed their way. They all wore the Chained Devils cut. Others left with the people who didn't want to fight.

Daruss snapped his fingers, telling his guys to go after them. It wasn't a fight they were avoiding. They had a different reason, although Daruss wasn't sure what it was. Whatever they had in mind, it wouldn't bode well for the Dragon Skulls.

A guy sitting at the table nearest the entrance glanced at the booth, wanting to know why the music stopped. When he saw Jonik, he stood. He pulled out a knife so big it appeared as if he were about to flay Jonik's skin off his body.

Jonik saw him coming, jumping over the booth, and attacked him. Daruss wasn't sure how Jonik had done it, but he had possession of the knife. It was as if he snapped his fingers, and the knife came to him. Jonik plunged it into the guy's chest before the Knife Guy's friends could react.

His friends did come to his aid, although it was too late. Jonik pulled the knife out of Knife Guy's chest and threw it, with no small amount of skill, at a woman who came at him. Another guy grew closer, but Jonik had him on his back with a kick to his stomach.

That was what got everyone fired up. The sexual energy turned dark and violent as if a switch had been flipped inside everyone. It didn't take much to get a bunch of bikers to fight. Daruss hadn't thought twice about it either before bonding with his mates.

The club was all red velvet and black walls. Tables and booths gave people places to sit.

There was a stage with a half-naked girl on it. She screamed and ran behind a curtain.

A long bar was to the right with a female bartender who wore a tight, half-shirt showing a lot of under-boob. She didn't seem as scared as the girl on stage. She held a broken liquor bottle, wielding it as if it were a weapon. She didn't come out from behind the bar, so it wasn't as though she wanted to be a part of the action. She was still prepared for anything.

Daruss fought his way through the room. They were outnumbered, but it didn't matter because they already accomplished their goal. Everyone's attention was on them, even the people who didn't want to fight.

Everyone who posed a threat was human except for a couple of the guys who Daruss had encountered. They'd been wolf shifters. One guy sniffed the air, punched Daruss as if his heart wasn't in it but he had to put on a good show, and then made his way to the back.

As he searched for Terrell, he noticed a dark-haired guy in a trench coat. He had a dim gray light in his hand that he pushed into a woman who was also out of place amongst the bikers. She wore a red dress that hugged her curves, but she wasn't one of the dancers. While her dress left little to the imagination, she was still too covered to be anything but what she appeared. A buyer. She seemed frozen in place as if she couldn't move, but that didn't make sense. The panic in her expression grew the closer the guy came to her. When he pushed the gray ball into her, she crumpled to the floor.

The man stepped over her body, drew another ball from somewhere and moved on to the next person who wasn't dressed like a biker. He was taking out the buyers one at a time. That much was clear.

Daruss wasn't afraid of much but the man scared him. It seemed he was on their side, though. Daruss didn't want to know him.

Daruss's attention wavered when someone moved along the back wall. He recognized the Chained Devils cut before he realized who it was. He'd only ever seen Terrell when fighting broke out and it was always from a distance. Terrell let others fight for him and he slunk off like a little mouse.

If he didn't get to Terrell while he was in the club, there would be hell to pay later. Daruss felt the urgency in his bones.

Daruss tried to control himself, but his dragon came to the surface. And all he could think about was taking out Terrell before he got to Jude. Raylee wouldn't leave Jude, so he'd get caught in the crossfire.

He fought his way through the room, gaining a few cuts and bruises but shifting would heal them.

He knew his eyes had shifted when everything he saw became more vivid. Despite that and in his haste, he didn't notice the knife until it entered his gut.

He managed to get one thrust before Daruss grabbed his hand and broke it. He dropped the knife and clutched his hand. Daruss picked up the weapon and then grabbed his wrist. He held his hand on the table and stabbed the knife through the center of his palm.

Daruss flashed his fangs and growled. "Fucker."

Blood covered Daruss's shirt. The knife must have hit something important because he bled a lot in a few minutes. He couldn't do anything about it yet.

He had to get to Terrell. When he searched for him again, Terrell was nowhere to be seen.

Gavin closed the distance between them as if he sensed something was off. He punched two people who tried to slow him down. As soon as he saw the blood on Daruss's shirt, he cursed.

Gavin met his gaze. "Can you ride?"

Daruss nodded but he honestly didn't know if he could. All he did know was he needed to get to his mates.

They started out of the club. Izzy and Nash followed. Skippy saw them but he loved a good fight. He wouldn't stop until he was the last person standing. And since he could take care of himself, Daruss didn't worry about him very much. A few of the other guys left with them, including Jonik.

Jonik fell in line beside him. "The victims are safe. Samson and the others took them out the back. My employer is killing the last few buyers."

"The guy with the light, right?"

Jonik glanced at Daruss as if in surprise. "Yeah but keep your mouth shut."

Daruss shook his head. "Like I'd say anything."

"I know you wouldn't, but I still had to say it."

"Next time you see him, tell him I said that's a neat fucking trick." Daruss wanted to know who he was only so he could avoid him. No one should be able to kill as easily as Jonik's employer had.

Jonik didn't response. "He'll let us know if he needs us again."

"Of course." But will Daruss and his gang come running a second time? He didn't know.

The first thing he did was shut Raylee and Jude out, closing off their internal connection. He didn't want them to know how injured he was.

Chapter Thirty

Raylee knew the exact second Daruss had been injured. Daruss's surprise came first, as if he hadn't expected whatever happened. When the pain came through their bond, Raylee panicked.

He grabbed Jude's hand, holding it with both of his. Raylee's chest ached. *Something is wrong with Daddy.*

I know. I feel it. The panic wasn't as strong in Jude. It wasn't until Daruss disappeared that Jude's reaction grew desperate.

I don't know what to do.

Let me think.

Wren sat with them on the couch. Landry sat next to him. He was a tattoo artist who was tall like all dragon shifters, but he appeared as young as Raylee. He'd been through a lot in his life, if the shadows in his gaze were an indication. He reminded Raylee of Jude in that way. Landry was supposed to be there for their protection, but Raylee questioned whether he could do the job if it became necessary.

He drew in a sketch pad, not paying attention to the movie. But he showed Ulises what he'd sketched with a smirk on his face. Ulises sat on the floor at his feet.

"Accurate," he mumbled about the drawing. When Landry straightened, he tilted the pad just right for Raylee to see the sketch. It was a caricature of Izzy with his mouth around so many dicks Raylee couldn't count them.

Wren smiled with his eyes more than his mouth, but his lips twitched up.

Raylee would have too but for the fact Daruss was in pain.

MacIver held his mate in his lap. His eyes were closed, and he seemed content. Raylee wasn't sure if he was sleeping or not.

Maybe we should tell someone. They'll rescue him. Raylee didn't know what else to do. All he did know was Daruss needed someone to save him. He was ninety-nine percent sure of it. Raylee and Jude had been ordered to stay with Landry at MacIver's house. They couldn't disobey or they'd get in trouble.

Are we sure he's hurt?

He wouldn't shut us out otherwise. Raylee was sure of that. No way would Daruss hurt their feelings on purpose if he didn't have to.

You're right. He's probably doing it to keep us from worrying about him.

He's an idiot. I don't care if I get in trouble. I'm telling him that as soon as I know he's all right. Raylee would let Daruss know he'd crossed a line by shutting them out.

Jude smiled and kissed his cheek. "I'm with you, baby."

Good. Two against one was better odds.

Jarrell's brother sat at the kitchen island reading what appeared to be a textbook. Raylee wondered if he was in college. His name was Easton, and he was mated to the alpha of Wingspan.

As if he felt Raylee staring, he turned and met Raylee's gaze, and then Jude's. He drew his eyebrows together and asked, "Are you okay?"

Raylee shook his head, but it was Jude who answered. "Something's wrong with Daruss."

Raylee finished the explanation. "He was in pain and now we don't feel him."

MacIver tightened his hold on Jarrell. "Is he still alive?"

"He's shutting us out." The connection was still there. Daruss was present within their link. But it was as if he sat in a pitch-black room with nothing running through his head. Or maybe he'd put them there. Either way, Raylee felt the disconnection as if Daruss had severed his arm. He might as well have. It would have been less stressful.

The more he thought about it and sat there doing nothing to help Daruss, the more he worried. Then he was just pissed. But if Daruss was injured then that made Raylee feel guilty. And the emotional roller coaster went round and round.

MacIver relaxed again. "He's probably just doing some shady shit. He's protecting you."

Raylee was five seconds away from bursting. Instead, he turned to Landry. "He might be injured or worse. He might need someone to save him."

Easton met their gaze. His expression said he knew something, but he waited for Landry's response. His mate was with Daruss and the others. And maybe his mate hadn't shut him out the way Daruss had with Raylee and Jude.

Landry shook his head. "Our job is to protect everyone here. If the boss wanted us to rescue him, he would have told you to tell us that."

"It doesn't matter what Daruss wants. You need to do what will keep him alive." Raylee stood because he couldn't sit there any longer and argue with them.

Jude stood with him and put an arm around Raylee's shoulders. It turned into a hug when the tears started. *We'll save him ourselves. Just keep crying and follow my lead.*

It wasn't like Raylee was tearing up on purpose. If he had his choice, he wouldn't have started crying at all. He didn't know why he was when all he felt was frustration that no one took Daruss's safety seriously. He also had a sense of urgency to get to Daruss. He didn't know what to do but he knew standing around bawling about it wouldn't help.

What he did know was Jude had a plan. He'd escaped Daruss once and then the bastard who hurt him too. He was also a rule-breaker, which helped in this situation because Raylee wasn't one.

Sometimes breaking the rules was necessary.

"Come on. Let's splash water on your face so you can calm down. Then we'll see if Daddy will talk to us again." Jude led him down the hall toward the bathroom. They went inside and then Jude hugged him. "We need to sneak into the garage. I think there's a side door."

Raylee nodded. It helped to know they weren't just going to sit around doing nothing when Daruss was injured or worse. Maybe he was bleeding out somewhere.

Raylee took a few deep cleansing breaths before pulling out of Jude's arms and grabbing toilet paper to blow his nose. He threw it into the trash and met Jude's gaze. "I'm ready."

"We'll wait a couple of more minutes."

Raylee went into Jude's arms again. Daruss's absence made him insecure in ways he hadn't expected. To say he didn't like it was putting it mildly.

He pushed everything he was feeling at Daruss.

Of course, Jude felt it too. "You hit a wall, huh?"

Raylee shrugged. He wasn't sure what Jude meant. But Raylee would admit to having a bit of a temper sometimes. "I'm just really mad right now. At MacIver and Landry. And at Daruss. At the whole situation."

Jude kissed Raylee on his forehead. "It's up to us to save Daddy. Focus on that."

Raylee took another deep breath and let it out slowly. Before he could respond, someone knocked on the door.

Raylee stiffened.

Jude cursed. "We'll be out in a moment."

Instead of the person waiting, they opened the door. Easton stood in the doorway. He beckoned them into the hall.

Raylee met Jude's gaze, wanting to know what he thought. Jude shrugged as if to say they didn't have anything to lose by trusting Easton.

Jude held Raylee's hand as they followed Easton into the garage, which was across the hall and down a few steps.

Easton put his finger across his lips before turning the doorknob. He made a face when the door clicked open. They seemed to hold their breaths, and waited for a second, expecting MacIver to charge down the hall.

Nothing happened.

As soon as they entered the garage and Raylee shut the door behind them, Easton used the flashlight feature on his phone, lighting the way to the back door.

When they were outside in the backyard, Easton shut it off.

"We won't have a big head start." Jude took the lead, heading around to the front of the house. "MacIver or Landry will look for us eventually."

"My house isn't that far. We can take Gavin's truck. That will give us more distance." Easton headed down the sidewalk.

Jude grabbed the sleeve of Easton jacket, pulling him with them. "Let's stay out of sight."

"Right."

He followed them as they walked between houses. They made their way along the back of the properties. "Now lead the way."

Easton moved around them. "Gavin said they were going to some strip club. It's a thirty-minute drive from here."

"Let's take the same roads they would take. That way we're more apt to spot them." In some ways Jude was a natural leader. He took charge when it was needed, and he seemed to be good at it. Not only that but Raylee trusted him.

Easton's house was less than a mile away. He pulled a key out of his pocket and let himself in the front door, but he wasn't in there very long. When he came back out again, he held another set of keys.

He seemed embarrassed about something. The emotion was out of place until he explained himself. "I don't know how to drive. Gavin's teaching me but I'm not comfortable driving without him in the truck with me. It's also illegal to drive without a license."

Jude held out his hand. "I can drive."

Easton still seemed embarrassed. Not that he should be. People who lived in cities sometimes didn't bother learning how to drive. Why would they when traffic sucked most of the time and everything was either within walking distance or public transportation was available.

"I didn't get my license until I was eighteen." Raylee had been scared of other cars on the road and his own abilities. He'd been fine as soon as he'd gained confidence.

Easton smiled and bumped shoulders with him. "Thanks."

"I didn't either, but it's because my brother and I couldn't afford the drivers' education training when I was sixteen."

Easton handed the keys over and nodded to a truck in the driveway. "It's the older one. It runs great. I promise."

Jude pulled Raylee around to the driver's side and let him in first. Raylee scooted into the middle. He was just glad the truck had a bench seat.

Easton sat beside him in the passenger seat.

It didn't take long for them to get out of town, but he bet MacIver and Landry weren't far behind.

Chapter Thirty-One

Jude slowed to a crawl and then stopped when he saw motorcycles lining the sides of the road ahead. He turned off his headlights before pulling off.

"There's gotta be ten to fifteen of them." Easton leaned forward as if it would help him see the bikes better. "Do those belong to our guys?"

Jude's heart pounded as his nerves picked up. "No."

Raylee turned to him. "Why are they here? There are just forests on both sides of the road."

"And no houses nearby." Jude had been down the road before. The area was a mix of forest and farmland with few houses.

Jude remembered driving through a small town before they got to the bigger college town where the clubs were. They had about fifteen more miles to go before getting to the club.

Jude had been to the strip clubs before. He hadn't been there to party. He had to keep an eye on Terrell and the other Devils while Mitch stole whatever he could find from the cars in the parking lot.

Terrell would have wanted a cut even though he hadn't done any of the work.

Terrell had a connection with the owner of the clubs. The guy bought meth from Terrell and sometimes moonshine.

"What should we do?" Easton asked.

"Give me a second." Jude had to think like Terrell, which meant he needed to figure out what happened before Terrell ended up parked on the side of the road. "What game are you playing, Terrell?"

"Maybe they fought at the club and left after the fighting ended." He loved how having Raylee as a mate was like having an extra brain. Bouncing stuff off him was what Jude needed.

"Knowing Terrell, they left as soon as the fighting started." Which didn't explain why they were here. There was no reason to be. Terrell and his gang wouldn't have to go in this direction to get to their territory. But it did give them a timeline they could work with.

"What if..." Raylee and Easton said at the same time.

"They're waiting for the guys to come through this area." Jude opened the door to the truck and got out. "This road is on the top of a hill. There's another that parallels it at the bottom. I bet they have guns and stuff."

Easton's face turned white, and his hands seemed to shake when he opened the glovebox. He pulled out a pistol. "I don't really know how to shoot either."

Raylee scooted out of the seat and grabbed Jude's hand when he stood next to him. "I do. My dad taught me and my sister."

Jude hoped like hell they didn't have to use the gun. "Shut the door quietly and let's whisper from now on."

When Easton got out of the truck he handed the gun to Raylee.

Raylee let go of Jude's hand. The first thing he did was check to make sure the safety was on. "I've only shot at targets. I don't want to shoot anyone."

"They're going to try to kill Daruss, baby?" Jude hated to think about something happening to Daruss but it was a very real possibility.

Instead of panicking, Raylee scowled. "Good point. Does this Terrell guy know how hard it is to kill a dragon shifter? I'm just wondering because dragons can get shot and as long as the bullets go through their body, they can shift and heal quickly."

Easton nodded. "That's right but how do you know so much about shifters. You're human, right?"

"My family. I grew up around shifters and also hearing about the science part of being a shifter. My parents are doctors. My dad's a dragon shifter and retired. My mom is fascinated by their genetics."

"Which hospital do you work at?"

"I don't have a job in the medical field yet."

"Can we focus, please." Jude sighed and shook his head. Geeking out over medical shit sounded like the best way to gain unwanted attention. "To answer your question about Terrell's knowledge of paranormals. I'm not sure what Terrell knows. Probably very little. But as many times as the Dragon Skulls have fought with the Chained Devils, they should have figured it out by now."

Jude led the way into the trees, using them for cover as they grew closer to the bikes. He was pretty sure Terrell went into the forest on the other side of the road. That was where the hill sloped down. "Daruss would take the road below even though it's not a direct route because the road is maintained better and it's less travelled. If they're hurt, they might need to go slower."

"Do you think Terrell is smart enough to figure that out?" Easton asked a good question.

"No. But Stan is. He's the one who thinks about how to get Terrell and the rest of them out of their messes. In Stan's mind, that's all they're doing here." If something happened to Stan, it would be as good as killing Terrell too. Or putting him in prison. Either way, Terrell wouldn't figure out how to get himself out trouble on his own.

When they came to the first bike, Jude fished around in the saddle bag and came up with a flask and a switch blade. He didn't care about the flask, but he did take the knife. He opened it and stabbed the back tire. "See if you can find a knife in one of the other bags and slash their tires."

Easton and Raylee took off.

As Jude went to the next bike, he thought about Raylee getting hurt or worse. Terrell and the others could come out of the forest and see them. Or Raylee could cut himself with the knife. *Stay close to me, baby.*

I will. Raylee went to the bike next to Jude and looked in each bag before moving on. He eventually found one and began stabbing the tires as he made his way back to Jude.

Easton found one in the row across the road. Jude put a finger to his lips and then flattened his hand and moved it down, telling Easton to stay quiet and stay low.

Easton nodded and plunged the knife into one tire after another. He was the most efficient of the three of them, but it was because Raylee tried to stay close while still doing the work and Jude had to figure out which tires Raylee slashed. Jude ended up slashing them anyway.

No one saw them, which was somewhat of a miracle. It was as they entered the woods on the other side of road that Jude understood how many miracles had happened up to that point. Jude had never believed in them or any gods until Daruss had rescued him. But what took a close second was discovering how close Terrell and his men were to the road, yet they didn't discover Jude, Raylee, and especially Easton.

Jude had known the hillside sloped to the road below, although he'd never been in the forest that separated the two roads. The land leveled out for about twenty feet before declining.

Jude was the first to see them. He pulled Raylee and Easton to the ground, using a fallen log as cover.

Banjo kneeled, leaning against a tree. He hunched over a rifle. Banjo was aptly named because he played one all the time. It was his passion in life and the thing he did when he wasn't selling drugs and doing Terrell's bidding. He was good at it too. Banjo was a big guy with a lot of heft on top and around his middle with a little bottom half. The Chained Devils logo appeared bigger than normal with the red devil standing out amongst the natural surroundings.

Terrell, or maybe Stan, was smart enough to put distance between each guy. The spacing guaranteed someone would shoot every one of the Dragon Skulls as they passed along the road below.

The spacing also made it possible for Jude to take out each guy without getting caught right away. But Jude had never killed anyone. He didn't know if he could do it.

Jude glanced at Easton and then at Raylee. Jude didn't know what Easton was capable of, but he knew Raylee couldn't kill anyone. He'd already said as much.

Be my backup, baby. Jude would need one at some point because someone would discover him. There wasn't a way around it.

A backup for what? Raylee wouldn't like his answer.

Instead of answering, Jude stood. He took a step in Banjo's direction, but then a hand went over his mouth. He stiffened. His heart pounded and his chest tightened. All he could think about was keeping Raylee safe. Jude's mind raced a million miles an hour, trying to figure out how to get Raylee out of trouble.

It's MacIver and Landry. Raylee grabbed Jude's hand. Jude hadn't even realized he held his knife as if ready to strike.

Jude lowered the knife, but his adrenaline was still high. It wasn't until MacIver took his hand away and whispered in Jude's ear that he relaxed, as much as the situation would allow anyway. "Can you slit a throat?"

Jude nodded, although he didn't know. He'd never done it before.

"Can Raylee?"

Jude shook his head. "I'll do it. He doesn't need to."

If he could shield Raylee from having to kill someone, then he would.

Jude watched as Landry took out Banjo and moved on to the next guy.

"We don't have a lot of time. One of these fuckers will turn around and then the shit show starts." MacIver turned and walked away. He was a lot quieter than Jude thought he should be given his larger size.

He pointed at Easton. When he spoke, he kept his voice so low he mouthed the words, "Stay here."

Stay with Easton, baby. Use the gun if you have to. If Jude could glue Raylee to his side, he would, but he'd rather not have Raylee see him kill someone.

Jude followed MacIver to the road. They went around the bikes, using them as cover. MacIver reentered the forest. Jude stayed right behind him.

MacIver pointed to a guy straight in front of him and headed toward the one further away.

Before Jude could get to the guy he was supposed to kill, someone fired a shot.

MacIver closed the distance, pulling Jude to the ground and shielding him with his body.

It didn't take Jude long to figure out the shots hadn't come from Raylee. They'd come from the devils. And they weren't shooting at them but at someone at the bottom of the hill.

As soon as MacIver let him up, Jude made a beeline for the road. He'd never run so fast, but he wasn't running away like he had before. No. He ran straight for Raylee.

Landry was the first one to shift but MacIver wasn't far behind.

Jude got to Raylee just in time to see him pull the trigger. The link was unnecessary when it came to Raylee's emotions. His expression held more fear than any one person should ever experience. He aimed at one of Terrell's men who had somehow caught sight of Raylee and Easton. Blood poured from a wound in the guy's arm.

Stop, Raylee. Now. Jude didn't want him to kill the guy. Raylee wouldn't be able to live with it. The reason for the deed wouldn't matter after the fact.

Raylee met his gaze with wide eyes. His hands shook. He lowered the gun and put his arm around Easton in a protective gesture.

The wound kept the devil distracted long enough for Jude to grab him. What happened next came naturally. He didn't know how he could plunge the knife into the guy's neck or even how he knew he'd hit an artery, but it was clear he did when blood sprayed everywhere.

He wanted to puke. Instead, he glanced at Raylee and Easton. "Go to the truck."

Jude.

Go to the truck, Raylee.

He headed toward Terrell and his men, telling himself he could kill again. He had to if he wanted to keep his mates safe. But his body protested as if the violence made him ill.

Jude.

Jude turned, meeting Raylee's gaze.

I'm staying here to give you cover. He hoped Raylee didn't have to shoot anyone else. The only thing Jude could do was make sure he killed Terrell and his men himself so Raylee wouldn't have to.

Chapter Thirty-Two

Daruss knew he'd lost a lot of blood when he started to shiver. Winter set into his bones. At the same time, he sweated as if he'd been in the Sahara Desert too long. The extreme contrasts made for some serious discomfort, especially while riding.

He did his best to focus on the road, keeping his end goal of getting to Raylee and Jude in mind. He needed to keep them safe. They were in danger more than ever. Daruss pictured Terrell making a beeline straight for Jude and Raylee. He just needed to get to his boys before Terrell did, which shouldn't be difficult considering Jude and Raylee were hidden. The plan was to move them every few hours, so they weren't sitting ducks.

Protecting them was the top priority, but he also wouldn't mind some of his boys' tender loving care. Raylee would nurse him back to health. Not that shifting wouldn't do most of the work, but he'd love some of Raylee's attention. Jude would lie next to him, cuddling close and calling him Daddy every chance he could. Yeah, that sounded like the best medicine.

He would need to grovel a bit after shutting them out. He'd known it the second he'd done it. It was better to ask for forgiveness rather than permission.

He concentrated on breathing. The pain would steal the air from his lungs if he let it. But the longer he rode, the more he hunched over the handlebars. He slowed to a crawl when he couldn't give his attention to the road anymore.

His guys stayed with him.

Nothing like twenty-plus bikers riding like old men. Something about it struck him as funny.

When Izzy glanced at him as if he were crazy, Daruss knew he'd probably lost his marbles. Maybe they spilled out alongside the blood.

He was contemplating pulling over when he felt a sting on his lower back. When he began to lose control of his bike he stopped. He couldn't hold it up, so it landed on top of him, trapping his leg.

Daruss breathed through the pain and then took in his surroundings. He was pretty sure he knew what was happening. When he saw blood blossom across Izzy's chest, he was sure of it. Terrell hadn't been leaving to find Daruss's boys. He'd been setting up an ambush.

Daruss cursed. "Take cover!"

The shout came too late for some. Izzy wasn't the only one who'd taken a bullet. But everyone who could, dropped their bikes and headed for the ditch.

Gavin came to Daruss, handing him a gun. He lay beside him on the ground. "It's coming from on top of the hill."

Gunfire blasted through the forest. The foreignness of it made the birds stop chirping. Everything was quiet for several minutes and then more guns went off. But no one else was hit. No bullets bounced off the pavement or penetrated the trees around them. But it wasn't just the lack of bullets flying that made Daruss wonder what was happening on top of that hill.

Something whispered in his mind. It took him a moment to figure out what it was. Daruss could feel his boys' fear and unnatural amounts of stress. Raylee panicked. Jude was worried about Daruss the most but that changed to Raylee. At first Jude hadn't wanted Raylee to kill anyone. But then he worried about Raylee's safety.

And Raylee's panic grew to terror.

"Fuck!" Daruss didn't know or care how Jude and Raylee got on top of the hill. What he did care about was getting them down in one piece.

Gavin whispered, "Easton's up there."

"My boys are too. Help me get the bike off my leg." With Gavin's help, Daruss was out from under the bike.

Two dragon shifters flew overhead. One dipped down. A scream echoed through the trees.

MacIver. Daruss had fought with him and beside him enough times to know him in dragon form. The other dragon was Landry. A stream of fire shot from Landry's mouth. It was cold and wet enough for the trees not to catch fire for very long, but something else did. Two something by the way the flames separated from each other, becoming twin flames. The way the flames staggered told Daruss they were humans on fire. Fear and the will to survive took over their bodies, but nothing could save them from being burned alive. The fire didn't die much when they collapsed. One went a few seconds before the other.

Nash was the first from their group to shift. Several others shifted with him and joined the fight at the top of the hill.

Gavin checked Daruss's bullet wound, taking off his cut before lifting his shirt. "It went through. Shift."

Daruss let his dragon come to the surface. He'd only taken his shoes off before his body shifted. His clothing ripped as he changed into his dragon.

Daruss let go of his human senses. His dragon took over. The first thing he did was open the connection again. As soon as he did so, he got a glimpse at the damage he'd done.

Raylee was so relieved he was in tears. Daruss could almost feel the drops on his own cheeks. And Jude. Jude was scared and resigned all at the same time. Daruss had known some of it. They hadn't shut him out. It had been the other way around. But when Daruss had closed off his connection, it had made theirs with him weaker. As soon as Jude felt the connection fall into place, Jude's anger came through loud and clear.

I'm coming. Hang on. Daruss had to assess his pain level before he flew. It was still there but not as bad.

We thought you were dying. This came from Jude. And then Jude showed Daruss what he was doing, which was fighting to keep Terrell's gang away from Raylee. He held a knife in his hand and pointed it at a slim man with a calculating smile on his face. The guy had a gun, and it was pointed right at Raylee.

Raylee also had one too, but he was clearly scared. It was as if he questioned his aim. If he missed, the guy would turn on Jude.

Daruss roared and gave himself enough room to take off.

Gavin cursed and shook his head, going to Izzy to check on him. Izzy was awake but in a bad way. Daruss could tell he was in a lot of pain. Blood coated his abdomen. If he could get Raylee and maybe even Gavin's mate to help, maybe Izzy would pull through.

Daruss had to save his boys first.

Chapter Thirty-Three

Daruss flew to where MacIver hovered over the area. That had to be where Jude and Raylee were. Landry had created a barrier with fire. As wet as the forest floor was, the fire held long enough for him to keep it lit. When someone came too close, he blew fire at them.

Daruss looked at the scene from above. He could see why MacIver hesitated. All the guy had to do was change his aim and pull the trigger, shooting MacIver. What good would he be to Jude, Raylee, and Easton if he were dead?

But Daruss had an idea on how to distract him. He started making noise right before he landed and shifted.

The guy's eyes widened, and he seemed as if he would piss himself when he looked at Daruss.

That's Stan, by the way. Jude explained.

He won't make it out of the forest alive, baby. I promise. Daruss grinned at Stan when he pointed his gun at him instead of Raylee. As soon as he did, Daruss shifted again.

Stan took the shot but missed when MacIver dived onto Stan with his jaws open. Stan raised the gun, but it was too late. MacIver closed his teeth around Stan's body. It was over before it even began.

Daruss shifted again. He hadn't changed into his human body very long when Raylee barreled into him. *Oh my gods.*

Daruss hugged him, holding him close. *It's over now, baby.*

Daruss met Jude's gaze. He knew it would take more for him to come around than a simple promise. Daruss crooked a finger at Jude, beckoning him forward.

Jude shook his head. "It has to end, Daruss. One of us has to kill Terrell."

Daruss nodded. "I will. You, Raylee, and Easton go down the hill." Daruss held a shaking Raylee, kissing him on the top of his head. "It's okay, baby."

Raylee just clung as if he couldn't make himself let go. "I want to go home."

"We will but Izzy needs you. He's been shot. Gut wound. I don't think the bullet has come out yet." Daruss knew it would get Raylee's attention. Raylee was a natural caregiver. And he was probably the only one who could save Izzy's life.

Raylee pulled away and then handed the gun to Daruss. "I don't want it."

"All right." But Daruss didn't want the thing either. He didn't think he'd need it.

Raylee met his gaze. "Promise you won't shut us out again."

"I promise." That was easy to make. While Daruss didn't think it was a mistake, he wouldn't do it ever again. "I love you, baby."

"I love you too but that's never been the problem." Raylee was right. They had a lot of love. It wasn't a problem. The issue was Daruss's lifestyle. He couldn't continue putting himself in danger because it would always lead to jeopardizing his boys' safety.

"I hear what you're saying, baby."

"We'll talk about it later." And with that Raylee turned to Easton, holding out his hand. Together they trekked down the hill. Walking was the fastest way to get to Izzy unless Raylee and Easton let someone give them a ride on their back. He didn't think Raylee would fly with anyone but Daruss. Easton had the same issue. It was Gavin or no one for him.

Daruss met MacIver's gaze and pointed to the boys. MacIver made a chuffing sound and flew above them.

Daruss turned to Jude and raised his eyebrows. He closed the distance between them. The forest flood was cold and damp beneath his feet. The first thing he did was hold out the gun to him.

Jude shook his head. "I prefer the knife."

"Fair enough." Daruss cupped his cheek. He was surprised Jude let him. "Are you injured?"

Jude shook his head, averting his gaze. "We should get to Terrell before he takes off."

Landry had Terrell as well as three other Chained Devils members surrounded by a ring of fire. They weren't going anywhere.

"We?" He'd told Jude to go with Raylee and Easton, although he hadn't expected Jude to follow the order. He knew he wouldn't. Jude needed to see Terrell dead.

Jude met his gaze. His expression was pure defiance. "Do you even care about Mitch at all? Terrell has him stashed away somewhere, Daruss. I'm almost positive of that."

"No. I don't care about Mitchell Burke. But I care about you. And you care about him. That's why I have people searching. We'll find him." But that wasn't the most pressing issue.

"Terrell's the only one who knows." Jude's chin wobbled.

"I won't continue to put you or Raylee at risk, baby." All keeping Terrell alive would do was keep the fucking tit for tat game they had going.

Jude sobbed as if he were mourning the loss of his brother. Maybe he considered him dead already.

Daruss pulled Jude into his arms, holding him while he cried. "We could interrogate him, I guess."

When Jude spoke, it was after he'd calmed a bit. "Maybe we can rat him out to the cops about the guns, so he'll go to prison."

"There are two problems with that. Number one, biker code." The biker code said no ratting on anyone. Snitching got a biker a reputation that would get them killed. "Secondly, Mitch would probably go to jail too. He's the one who stole the guns, right?"

"Yeah."

"I'll get him to tell where Mitch is and then I'll kill him. Will that do?"

Jude nodded. "Thank you."

Daruss kissed him. "Do you want to help Raylee and Eston with the injured?"

"I killed three of these bastards and I need to see it through." Killing would eat at Jude if Daruss didn't do something to help.

Daruss made a mental note to find a therapist or someone for Jude to talk to.

Daruss held Jude's hand as he walked to the ring of fire. The flames were low enough for Daruss to see Terrell and the three other men inside.

Terrell wasn't the only one with a gun. Two others had one as well. No one shot at Landry though. Either they weren't sure if the bullets would pierce a dragon's scales, they feared Landry setting them on fire, or they were simply out of bullets. Daruss doubted it was the last one. There hadn't been enough gunfire for them to have run out.

"Ignorant human." Daruss grinned. A bullet would go through dragon scales, although it wouldn't penetrate very far. It was worse in some ways to get shot in dragon form rather than in human form because in human form the bullet had a better chance of going through. Of course, that was contingent on where the bullet entered the body. Some organs didn't heal. Like the brain and the heart. If a bullet pierced those, even a dragon shifter was as good as dead.

"I see your little whore ran straight back to you." Terrell sneered at Jude.

"For someone in such a precarious position, you sure think you have the right to speak about my mate in such a filthy way." Daruss's eyes and hands shifted. It was difficult to hold onto the gun, so he handed it to Jude.

"I was gonna make money off you. Then I found out your brother hid you. Fucking bastard cost me." It wasn't the fact that Terrell had called Jude a whore that pissed Daruss off. Or it wasn't *only* that. It was the fact he had the audacity to speak to him at all. And to say what he did, as if blaming Jude and Mitchell for his own sick nature, was a level of cruelty Daruss hadn't expected, although he should have.

"Where is he?" Jude asked.

"Don't talk to him." Daruss met Terrell's gaze and forced Terrell to hold it.

Sorry, Daddy. Jude moved so he was behind Daruss.

I wasn't talking to you, baby. Daruss tried to soften the way it came through their link but he was so pissed that, even though none of his anger was directed at Jude, he still couldn't keep it out of his tone.

Daruss shifted and moved away so he wouldn't hit Jude with his wings.

As soon as he was in the circle, one of Terrell's men was so scared he ran through the flames. He didn't even remember he had a gun in his hand still. Landry finished the job by blowing a stream of fire at him. He screamed and stumbled around for a few minutes before falling in a heap of burning flesh.

Terrell and the other two were almost kissing the fire. They screamed and huddled together as if it would save them.

Daruss shifted to his human form. Well, most of him shifted. His eyes and hands stayed. Terrell raised his gun, but his hands shook. Daruss shifted again and flew into the air as Terrell took the shot and missed by a mile.

Daruss landed, using his wing to knock Terrell away from the other two guys. Terrell fell, dropping his gun. When he shifted and said, "Light'em up", Landry did . Setting the two men on fire.

For all their guns, Landry had the best weapon and it had been forged by nature. Daruss was a little jealous but also grateful Landry was on his side.

Terrell's stunned fear was his downfall. By the time he came back to himself and fumbled to pick up his gun, Daruss had shifted and thrown it out of the ring of fire.

Daruss crouched in front of Terrell. "I promised Jude I'd keep you alive. He seems to think you'll tell him Mitch's location."

"If you let me go, I'll tell you."

Daruss chuckled. "You must be used to making deals with the Devil. You sold your soul the day you started selling people, didn't you? Or was it before that even?"

Terrell trembled. "I promise, man. I'll tell you exactly where he is. You can even have the guns."

Daruss grabbed Terrell around the neck, squeezing his airway closed enough to let the panic seep in, but not restricting his breathing all the way. Daruss wanted him alive for a few minutes longer. "You think I'd believe a human without a soul. Or that I care about Mitch Burke. I don't give a shit about him."

Terrell gasped and tried to pry Daruss's clawed hand from around his neck.

Daruss was careful to keep from piercing the skin, but he made sure to stay right on the edge of sinking in. "You beat on my boy. You called him a whore to his face. Hell, you said it to my face. And you tried to treat him as if he were nothing more than a slave."

Daruss pulled Terrell to his feet by his neck, which freaked Terrell out. Daruss's hand turned into a noose as he carried Terrell toward the flames. Landry didn't keep up with the flame so the damp ground ate the ring of fire until there wasn't much of a flame left. Daruss was able to walk over them without a problem, although they burned some of the hairs on his legs.

Landry shifted and stood to the right of Jude as if he were a sentry.

Daruss dropped Terrell at Jude's feet.

Jude was so startled he jumped back a step and held the gun on Terrell.

Terrell sucked in big pulls of air, clutching his throat.

Daruss crouched in front of him again, forcing Jude to lower the gun. "I'm far worse than the Devil. I don't want your soul. I just want to watch you burn."

Terrell shook his head, holding up his hands to Landry as if to ward him off. "No please. I'll do whatever you want. I swear. Please."

To Landry's credit, he appeared as bored and stoic as he was when not creating art of some kind. Landry wasn't a natural born killer the way Skippy was. He had limits. For Terrell and the Chained Devils, limits didn't exist when it came to killing them. And it was because he'd been on the shitty end of a sex trafficking ring. Daruss knew because he'd rescued him from it.

"I told you. I don't want anything. Only for you to fry." Daruss raised his eyebrows when Terrell blinked at him and tried to figure Daruss out.

"Underground tunnels. Mitch is in the underground tunnels." Terrell was near tears when Daruss turned to Landry as if he were going to give the order to burn him. He begged when Daruss stood as if to move out of the way of the flame when it came. "Please. I swear it. I'm not lying."

Before Daruss could give the order, Jude raised the gun, pointing it at Terrell's head.

Terrell sobbed. "I don't want to die."

Daruss turned to Jude. His hard expression didn't match what was in his heart. It didn't come close to it. Daruss was gentle when he took the gun from Jude.

Jude crumpled in Daruss's arms. Daruss lifted him off his feet, holding him in place with a hand under his ass. Jude wrapped himself around Daruss as if his life depended on it. Jude's tears came from a place of relief because he knew it was over. And they had Mitch's location.

Daruss didn't feel anything for Terrell when he raised the gun and shot him in the head. Well, maybe he felt a little relief too. He wouldn't hurt Jude ever again.

Daruss handed the gun to Landry and held Jude close. "It's over. All over, baby."

Landry scowled. "I don't want this thing."

"Hold on to it for a minute." Of all the jobs Landry had that day, taking the gun was the easiest one. "Whiny little shit."

"I'm not whiny. I fucking hate the smell of burning flesh. That's all." Landry got his attention and pointed to the upper road. "The boys took Gavin's truck. It's easier to carry him this way versus down the hill."

Jude laid his head on Daruss's shoulder. "We need to find Raylee. Make sure he doesn't have to kill anyone. He can't handle that."

Raylee wasn't the only one who couldn't.

"We're going to get our boy right now, baby. I promise. And there isn't anyone left to kill." The road was a few yards away. They walked toward the truck.

"You always keep your promises," Jude mumbled against his neck.

"I'll do my very best, baby." Daruss wasn't a nice person. He was cruel at times and did things society deemed wrong. But he would do anything for his boys. He made sure they knew that every single day.

"Can you promise to put on clothes as soon as possible?"

Daruss chuckled. "Yeah. As soon as, baby."

"Are you still injured?"

"Nope. I shifted enough times. Just little twitches. That's all."

"Good." Jude tightened his hold and then pushed all the anger at Daruss he had stored up.

"I know, baby. I'm sorry. You heard me make the promise to Raylee to never shut you out again. But I'll also think of ways to make it up to you."

"Well, how about moving us back home for starters. It's been forever." It had been a while since Jude had been to Daruss's house. It warmed Daruss's heart to know Jude thought of his house as home. That he longed to be in Daruss's space made it even better.

They got to the truck and Landry pulled the passenger side door open for Daruss.

Daruss managed to get in while still holding Jude. It was awkward but not impossible.

"Keys?"

"Driver's side. On the floor." Jude mumbled and then he lifted away from Daruss to meet his gaze. "Here's the thing. I'm not pissed you shut us out. I sort of get why you did. I would have too if we'd have been bonded while Terrell was beating me."

Daruss raised his eyebrows.

"I'm mad because you left me in charge."

"I left MacIver and Landry in charge, baby." Daruss glared at Landry when he got in. "Which they failed at, by the way."

Landry rolled his eyes as he fished around on the floor for the keys, coming up with them. "Jude's the sneakiest damn person in our entire family, man. He got away from you too."

They pulled onto the road, driving around to the other side and then cutting over to get off the hill. That was where the roads connected, but they would have to circle back to get to the guys and Raylee.

Daruss met Jude's gaze again. "I expected him to not run away again."

"I wasn't running away from you. I was running *toward* you. Because you shut us out. We thought you needed help, which you did. I'm just grateful Landry and MacIver followed us. They saved all of us. Not just Raylee and me." Jude was right about that. If it weren't for Landry and MacIver, they might have all been shot to death.

Landry just nodded. "You're welcome. You can pay me back by leaving me out of it. And with donuts. The jelly-filled kind."

Jude chuckled. "We'll do better than just a few donuts."

Landry parked the truck as soon as the bikes came into view. Some of the guys, who hadn't been hurt badly, had righted the bikes that had been laid over. They checked to make sure they weren't dinged up too bad.

"Just donuts." Landry left them in the truck.

Daruss saw Raylee working on Izzy. Raylee's hands were bloody, and he held a pocketknife. Izzy's face was distorted in pain as Raylee stuck the tip of the knife inside Izzy's wound and moved it around.

Jude turned to watch Raylee. "While what he's doing is turning my stomach, it's hot as hell watching him be all take charge and save lives."

Daruss chuckled. "Yeah, it is."

They watched as Raylee seemed to find what he was looking for. He dug around again, pulling a bullet from Izzy's body. Izzy cursed through the entire thing. He even called Raylee a little fucker. Getting called names didn't seem to bother Raylee. His attention was on the job at hand. But Izzy would apologize later and thank Raylee for saving his life. Daruss would make sure of it.

Jude turned back to Daruss. "Raylee lost it when you shut down the connection, Daruss. Like *really* lost it. Not like when he was jealous that time. But full-on crying and panic."

"I know it was your idea to come to me, baby. I would have come after you too."

Jude nodded. "I know because you did. But you're missing the point."

"I understand the situation as stressful for you. But you handled it perfectly. Now I know, if something happens to me, you and Raylee will be fine. But I'm fine." Daruss added that last bit because he could see the panic rise to Jude's face as if it had crawled up from his chest.

"It's not just about Terrell and the Chained Devils. Another gang will step on your toes. Raylee and I will be right back in the thick of it. With me trying to save both of you." Jude pressed his forehead against Daruss's chest and sighed. "I love you guys so much. I'd die for you, Daruss. For Raylee too. But I don't want to be put in a position where I'd have to."

Daruss swallowed the lump of emotion. "I don't want you to either."

He'd need to call a meeting sooner rather than later. But he wouldn't do it at the clubhouse. It was too public in a lot of ways. He'd call one at his house so his boys could settle in.

Taking the boys home would be the first step in creating their new normal.

Chapter Thirty-Four

Daruss moved a lock of hair off Raylee's forehead. He might need a haircut, but Daruss liked the way it curled at the ends. Raylee moved into his touch as if seeking out his presence. He rolled toward him and wrapped an arm around Daruss.

Daruss went onto his back. Raylee snuggled into him.

Jude came out of the bathroom. He wore baby blue briefs that hugged his package to perfection and his ass, not that Daruss could see it as he walked toward him, but he'd admired the view when he'd gone into the bathroom. Jude didn't wear anything else.

Daruss patted the bed on his other side, beckoning Jude to lie with them a little longer.

Jude smiled and crawled under the covers, cuddling in next to him. He used Daruss's chest as a pillow just as Raylee had. Before he settled in, he kissed Raylee on his cheek.

"Pretty Ray-Ray." Jude lay on Daruss.

"He is pretty. And so are you." Daruss ran a hand down Jude's back and then back up again.

Jude kissed Daruss on his chest. "Thank you, Daddy."

Daruss thought their hearts were even more beautiful.

"I'm proud of you and Raylee." Daruss might have told them already. He couldn't remember. But he thought it bore repeating.

Jude met his gaze. He knew what Daruss was proud of him for. "You're not going to punish us?"

"For being brave and saving not just my life but a lot of the guys in the club? You deserve a reward, boy." Daruss would brag about the boys' bravery as soon as he had the chance. Everyone in the club would know how proud he was. "And I'll punish you for putting yourselves at risk. The reward and punishment will be one and the same though."

"What kind of reward?" Leave it to Jude to pick out and isolate that one word. And out of everything Daruss said, too.

Daruss chuckled. "I don't know. What do you want?"

Jude's eyes sparkled with mischief. The little sparkle had drawn Daruss to Jude when they'd first met. He'd thought Jude had been reckless enough to give the likes of Daruss Oyen one night. One night hadn't been enough. Daruss should have known Jude would change his life forever.

Raylee stirred but snuggled closer. "I want to be able to sleep without you two talking and waking me up. And I want my punishment to be the usual."

Daruss lifted Raylee's hand to his lips, kissing his knuckles. "The guys will be here in an hour."

They'd slept through the night and all of the morning. They needed to get up. But yesterday had been a hard day. They'd needed the extra sleep, which was why Daruss hadn't woken Raylee sooner.

"Why are they coming here?" Raylee reached for Jude, wrapping an arm around him.

"I called a meeting. I'm letting them know the Skulls are turning legit." Saying it aloud made his stomach tighten. Daruss hadn't been nervous in a long time. But he knew some of the guys wouldn't like it.

Izzy was the only one he was sure of. He'd been with Daruss from day one. For Izzy it wasn't about trying to make a buck like it was for some of the other guys. In some clubs, being a member meant a person had connections in the not so legal ways of making money. That was how it had been for the Dragon Skulls. But Daruss wanted to either change that or leave the club. Izzy would be by his side no matter what.

Gavin and MacIver would too but for different reasons. They didn't give a shit about selling dragonshine and whatever drugs they could get hold of. They made money the legal way. They were in the club because they knew Daruss would stay loyal. And he expected it in return.

And they loved to ride.

Raylee sat up, crossing his legs. He met Daruss's gaze with wide eyes. He had a serious case of bedhead. "Meaning you're going to stop all the illegal stuff, right?"

"Yes." Why was Raylee so damn cute? It should be illegal.

"How do you think the guys are going to take it?"

"I don't know." Daruss knew he should be serious. Raylee asked some difficult questions. But Daruss couldn't think about anything but Raylee sitting there with his cheeks still rosy from sleep. He also didn't have anything on but his underwear and they were the bikini type. They were lavender and didn't cover his pretty little ass all the way.

"What are you going to say to them?"

"That my boys are the most important people in my life. That if one of them doesn't straddle my lap I might lose my mind." Daruss moved the blanket off him and patted his hard length. "Right here."

Raylee smirked. "I'm trying to be serious."

"No, you're trying to tease. Do you want to be punished for teasing?"

Raylee chuckled. "What's the punishment?"

"Not being able to come. All day."

Jude wiggled around, as if the idea of a punishment turned him on. Daruss knew what he wanted.

Raylee's cock grew hard. But he scrambled to do what Daruss asked. He even took off his underwear, getting naked.

Daruss met Jude's gaze. "If you continue to be a good boy, I'll give you a spanking."

Jude nodded. "I'll be good."

Daruss lifted Raylee so he could take his underwear off and then moved the covers so they wouldn't get in his way when he fucked Raylee. He picked Raylee up and placed him in his lap again.

Raylee even grabbed the lube and had the top opened, putting some onto his fingers and then he reached behind him to get himself ready.

"Fuck." Daruss's cock went from hard to hurting. He reached for Raylee, holding him at the waist.

"That's so fucking hot." Jude had his underwear off already.

He knee-walked over Daruss to Raylee, kissing him even as he seemed to touched Raylee's ass. When Raylee moaned, Daruss imagined Jude working his finger alongside Raylee's. Daruss wished he could see them. But he had a good view of Raylee fingering the crack of Jude's ass.

Daruss grabbed the bottle of lube and took Raylee's hand, giving him some.

Raylee slid two fingers between Jude's cheek, smearing the lube around his opening.

Jude ended the kiss. And then he pushed into Raylee's touch. "More, baby."

Raylee added another finger. "More, too."

Jude must have complied because Raylee sighed as if it was the best thing he'd ever felt.

Daruss could watch his boys make love all day. They were so beautiful together.

Daruss called a halt to it when the boys started panting and pushing against each other. "Pull out, boys."

Raylee whimpered and Jude bit his lip. But they did what Daruss said.

Daruss had a change of plans. One that would give both boys what they needed at the same time.

Daruss sat up and moved to the side of the bed. "Jude, lay across my lap. Face down."

Raylee panted. "You said I could ride you. Please, Daddy."

Jude hesitated, glancing at Raylee as if he wanted to give Raylee what he wanted.

"You will. But we're going to give Jude what he needs first. You'll wait. And watch. And not touch yourself." Daruss patted his lap when he met Jude's gaze. "Come here."

Jude scrambled to obey.

Daruss opened his legs just enough to allow Jude's cock between. Jude would want friction on it but wouldn't get it. While Jude didn't like delayed gratification, he would love getting to fuck Raylee after the spanking. It would be well worth waiting.

Jude lay across his lap. His ass crack glistened with lube.

Daruss pressed his finger inside for a moment before rubbing his cheek. "Are you ready?"

"Yes. Please, Daddy."

Daruss's hand came down on Jude's left cheek.

Jude cried out.

Raylee's eyes widened and he touched his own ass as if Daruss had slapped him instead.

Daruss brought his hand down on Jude's other cheek. He loved how pink Jude got.

Jude cried out again and tried to get some friction on his cock. When it didn't work, he whimpered.

Daruss brought his hand down again. And again.

Jude's ass turned a deeper pink.

Raylee climbed off the bed and kneeled near Jude's head. He lifted his chin. Their gazes met and held. "You like it?"

Jude nodded. "Touch my cock."

Daruss growled. "Looking. No touching."

Raylee moved so he could see Jude's cock between Daruss's legs. "It's dripping. Can I touch the tip?"

Jude moaned. "Please."

"Just the tip." He gave Jude another spanking.

When Raylee held his finger up, he had a drop of clear liquid on it. He met Daruss's gaze and then stuck the finger in his mouth.

Jude turned to watch him too. "Fuck."

Daruss brought his hand down three more times before he stopped.

"Daddy. Please." Jude tried to get something to rub against his cock.

Daruss met Raylee's gaze. "Get on the bed."

Raylee scrambled to obey, lying on his back. He spread his legs. "Inside. Please."

Raylee's cock was hard and angry with need.

Daruss rubbed Jude's hot ass cheeks. "You want to make love to Raylee?"

"Yes." Jude whimpered.

Daruss helped Jude stand. He rubbed a hand over Jude's ass again. "You're a good boy."

"Thanks, Daddy." Jude kissed him but he kept it brief.

He climbed on the bed and lay on Raylee, kissing him as he guided his cock inside Raylee.

Raylee gasped, which ended the kiss. He held onto Jude as if he expected him to disappear. "Fuck me."

Jude pressed his cheek against Raylee. His red ass flexed as he thrust inside. "You feel good."

Raylee wrapped his legs around Jude and held on as Jude moved inside him. Jude cradled Raylee. Each thrust was slow and sweet, designed for savoring the experience.

"Can I come?" Jude asked.

"Whenever you want." Daruss met Raylee's gaze. "Not you."

Raylee whimpered.

Jude picked up his pace. He moaned, stilling inside Raylee. When he moved again, his thrusts were shallow as if he didn't want it to end.

Daruss touched Jude's pretty red cheeks when he collapsed onto Raylee.

Jude kissed Raylee on his cheek and then his jaw and finally his lips. "Love you."

Raylee was almost at the point of tears. He was in so much need he couldn't even tell Jude he loved him back. He was so ready to come. Daruss knew because his whole body vibrated with need. It wouldn't take much to get him off.

Daruss patted Jude's ass cheek. "Time to give Raylee what he needs now."

Jude nodded and moved off Raylee. "So good."

Daruss winked. When he focused on Raylee, he growled and plucked him off the bed.

He sat with his back against the headboard.

He kept his arms around Raylee and entered him in one swift stroke.

Raylee held onto Daruss's shoulders.

Daruss held Raylee still. He didn't wait for Raylee to get adjusted, he thrust the way they both needed it.

Raylee panted and moaned. "I'm gonna come."

"Not yet." Daruss growled and pistoned into him. Skin slapped skin.

Raylee gripped Daruss's hair as he fell on his cock, giving as good as he got. "Daddy."

He fucked into him a few more times before he let Raylee get his way. "Come."

It was as if permission was all he needed. Raylee's release coated their abdomens. He tightened around his cock.

When Daruss's orgasm hit him, it was as if he'd been hit by a train. He lost his mind a little. He was pretty sure it went out his cock along with his cum. Raylee had taken his cum and his sanity. It mixed with Jude's.

Daruss held Raylee close.

"So good." Raylee clung to him.

"*Really* good." Jude curled into them. Daruss put an arm around him, holding him close.

Daruss sighed in contentment. "This is how every morning should go."

"Yeah. Except we should eat breakfast first. I'm starving." Jude didn't move despite what he'd said.

"Me too." Raylee kissed Daruss's chest before lying against him.

Yeah, everything was almost perfect.

He'd hit his mark as soon as he got himself out from under the pile of shit he'd spent years building. All Daruss really wanted to do for the rest of his life was take care of his boys. They came first, even above the club.

Chapter Thirty-Five

Raylee watched as Daruss made pancakes. They were his favorite. He hadn't been able to see much of Daruss's house when they'd arrived last night. In the light of day, Raylee was surprised by what he saw. It was clear Daruss intended for them to live there and while Raylee wasn't moved in yet and Jude hadn't had a lot of stuff to begin with, Raylee and Jude were on board.

The kitchen, living room, and dining room were in one big open area. There were a lot of windows and even sliding glass doors leading to a deck. From the windows and the glass door, Raylee could see the forest butt up to the yard.

The place must have cost a fortune.

Raylee sat at the kitchen island, sipping his coffee, and seeing Daruss in a new way.

Daruss knew he was watching. Raylee knew because he smirked. He probably could feel what Raylee was thinking like Raylee could with him and Jude. It wasn't like reading minds. None of the finer details of whatever he thought came through, but the vague feeling behind the thought did.

"I'll tell you everything you want to know. Just ask." Daruss put a plate of pancakes on the island.

Raylee felt Jude's arms come around him from behind. He kissed Raylee's cheek before grabbing his mug of coffee and sitting on the bar stool beside him. He took a sip and then slid it toward Raylee again.

"Thief." Raylee mumbled the word as if he were perturbed by it, but he didn't mind sharing with Jude. In fact, he rather liked it. He especially liked sharing clothes. They were of a similar size, so it worked out well. Jude was a little bigger, but it wasn't by a lot. They'd have double the amount of clothing once Raylee brought all his stuff over and Jude built up his wardrobe a bit.

"Sexy thief." Daruss put maple syrup on the table. Raylee notices it was the real kind. Not the fake stuff.

Raylee leaned into Jude. "Very sexy."

Raylee could still feel how good the morning sex was. The ache of his ass was a constant pleasant reminder.

Jude wrapped an arm around him. "You're thinking about sex again."

"It's hard not to when my butt aches. I want you guys inside me again."

Daruss put three plates and forks on the island and a bowl of fresh berries that seemed to come from nowhere. For a guy who hadn't been to his house in days, he could sure make magic happen in the kitchen. "It's a good thing you have two mates."

Raylee had to agree but he decided to change the subject. They'd be fucking on the kitchen counter in under five minutes if he didn't. While that sounded like a great way to spend a day, they were all hungry and Daruss's motorcycle club was coming over. "You have a nice house."

"We. The three of us share it now." Daruss put a plate in front of each one of them. And then grabbed a stool, sitting across from them.

He stacked their plates high with food, giving them way more than they'd be able to eat at one time. It was only after he had them settled that he served himself.

They were too hungry not to tuck into their food. Raylee had a million questions and probably wouldn't get them all out before people showed up. But food came first.

He took a few bites before continuing. "So your criminal enterprises paid for all this?"

Daruss smiled. "Not my current ones, but yes, this was paid for by illegal means."

"So you have a lot of money then?" Raylee hadn't given it much thought, mostly because it hadn't mattered. It still didn't.

"Is this going to be where you tell me you have a problem living off drug money because you wouldn't be. The Skulls don't make enough from drugs. A lot of the money comes from Dragonshine and even that's put back into the club. Or back into saving those in need. I made money a long time ago another way and then I invested that money. I've lived on it ever since."

Raylee thought about that. He knew he scowled the entire time, but he had so many more questions. "The only reason I asked was because you said you were going to quit all the criminal stuff. I was just wondering what you'll do for work but it seems you don't have to worry about it."

"No, I don't. You don't either, baby."

Raylee waved off Daruss's comment. "Oh, I'm not worried at all. I was just curious. And I want to help with the finances."

"I do too." Jude put down his fork. "I just don't know how yet."

Raylee met his gaze. "You want a job?"

Jude nodded. "I've never had one before. At least not a legitimate job. I helped Mitch steal stuff all the time. That's not exactly something you can put on your resume."

"I haven't ever had a real job either." Daruss shrugged as if he wasn't thinking about getting one. But maybe managing the investments was a real job. "I'll support whatever you want to do. I can cover your college tuition if you want to go to school."

"I don't know what I want. I just need to start somewhere."

"What about working at a small business selling books?" Raylee turned on the stool, facing Jude, ready to argue his point. "Hear me out."

"Okay."

"My sister really needs someone full-time. And then a part-time person. You'd be able to choose how many hours you'd get. And Jazlyn is a good boss—"

Jude covered Raylee's mouth. "I'll do it."

When Jude dropped his hand, Raylee said, "Really? Just like that?"

Jude shrugged. "I need to start somewhere. Your sister's bookstore sounds like a good place to me. And we'd be co-workers for a while, right?"

"Yeah, a few months. Until I decide where I want to work. I'm thinking somewhere local. I hadn't been before but Dad wanted me to stay close by anyway. And I don't want to have a long commute if I can help it." Raylee hadn't expected to find his mates and fall in love.

The front door opened without so much as a knock. Jonik and Wren walked in, taking off their shoes before coming into the room. Jonik nodded by way of greeting. "I heard the tail end of your conversation as I was walking up to the house."

Daruss rolled his eyes. "Of course, you did."

Jonik patted Jude's shoulder. "I miss our spa days. Wren and I would love to plan something with you and Raylee."

Jude met Raylee's gaze. "Do you want to go, baby?"

Raylee smiled. "I'd love to."

Jude met Daruss's gaze. "Is it okay, Daddy?"

Daruss growled as if being asked turned him on. Jude knew it would. That was why he'd done it. "You can go."

"Thank you, Daddy."

Daruss came around the island, scooting his plate across. He grabbed two stools and slid one over to Jonik and then nodded to the other side of the island. "Grab a plate and silverware if you're hungry. You know where they're at."

Jonik guided Wren to a stool, letting him sit. And then took a plate from the cupboard and two forks from the drawer.

Wren never said much. He always seemed terrified of everything and clung to Jonik as if his life depended on it. And he never made eye contact with anyone but Jonik. But he didn't seem worried about the history his mate had with Daruss and Jude. And it came down to trust.

Maybe Raylee had grown a little since mating with Daruss and Jude. Or maybe he was just content in his relationship with them. Either way, he'd learned to trust them too. It was a big part of what made their relationship work.

Chapter Thirty-Five

Jonik always had a reason for doing everything. Nothing was without calculation, even coming to the meeting twenty minutes early. Jude knew that about Jonik, so he stayed quiet and waited. Jonik would tell them what he wanted soon enough.

Daruss didn't have as much patience, though. "Get on with whatever it is, Jon."

Jude continued to eat.

Jonik prompted Wren to take another bite. It was as if he needed a reminder. It was a subtle tapping of his fork on the plate. Some sort of signal they'd agreed upon. "I heard your part of the conversation from outside, Raylee."

That got Raylee's attention. He glanced at Jonik as if startled and frowned. "You're a shifter? Not a dragon though, right?"

"Not only a dragon." Jonik smiled and tapped his ear. "I'm also a fox shifter. I have excellent hearing."

Jude could tell Raylee wasn't as intimidated by Jonik as the rest of the club. He didn't understand yet that Jonik pulled a lot of strings. In particular, Daruss's.

Daruss might be a lifelong criminal, but he was one with a heart. He'd saved a few people in the months Jude had known him. Not only that but Daruss had had a hand in rescuing a lot of people who later became Dragon Skulls. They were loyal to him because they owed him their life. That was why Jude didn't think Daruss would have an issue with the new direction he was taking the club.

But Jonik had his fingers in everything. Since Daruss was allowing it, Jude figured their goals aligned. Daruss would shut Jonik down when they were no longer on common ground.

"We were talking about jobs, I think, right?" Raylee took a bite and finished it before speaking again. "Why do you care?"

Jonik lifted his eyebrows at Raylee's tone. "My employer knows about what you did last night for Izzy."

"Were they there? I thought you worked for Daddy." It was getting easier for Raylee to refer to Daruss as Daddy in other people's presence. It was nice to see, and Jude knew it thrilled Daruss.

"I don't work for Daruss." Jonik seemed amused by Raylee more than anything, which was good. Jonik wasn't someone they wanted to make an enemy of. But Jude would kill him for even looking at Raylee wrong. Or he'd likely die trying but it was the sentiment that counted.

"What does your mob boss want with eradicating human trafficking? He's not doing it because he has a strong moral compass. I know that much."

"He has personal reasons."

"What are they?"

"Why have you saved people?" Most of the time answering a question with a question wasn't cool but Jonik wanted to know the answer.

"Because I could. Because I'm not a psychopath. Because I have a fucking heart. There are a lot of reasons, Jon."

"No one should live a life of abuse." Jonik pulled Wren into him.

Daruss nodded. "What does your employer want with my mate?"

Jonik addressed Raylee when he answered. "My employer wants to put him on the payroll."

Before Raylee could answer, Daruss lost it. He came off the stool and came around, getting in Jonik's face. "My mate is not working for your fucking crime boss."

Jonik raised his eyebrows. "Back off, Daruss."

Wren stiffened when Daruss grew closer instead. He was the reason Daruss moved away. Not because Jonik said too. "I didn't mean to scare you, Wren."

Wren nodded but moved closer to Jonik as if seeking protection.

Jonik held him and addressed Raylee again. "There are two things you should know. The first is that it's a request. Not an order."

Raylee smirked. "Good. Because I don't take orders from anyone but Daddy."

Jonik smiled as if amused. "The second thing is that you'd be caring for victims."

Daruss opened his mouth to speak but Raylee beat him to it. "I won't take money. But I'll help the people who need it."

"I'll let him know he has someone he can count on to care for the injured." Jonik met Daruss's gaze. "He wants to put you on the payroll too. It would be more of what you already have been doing."

"Just me or the club?"

"The club."

While Daruss was contemplating Jonik's offer, the door opened, and the guys walked in. Jude didn't think it was everyone. But it was most of the Dragon Skulls.

Daruss turned on his stool, addressing them. "I have two things to say."

Izzy chimed in. "You're getting all domesticated. We already know."

Daruss sighed. "Just let me say it."

Izzy waved his hand as if giving Daruss permission. "I gotta be done with all the criminal shit. It's a problem for my boys. So if you're still gonna do shit, I can't get involved. Which means I can't protect you when the shitshow starts, and it always does."

"How are we going to support the club?" This came from Nash.

"You know how the club gets crazy busy on the weekends." A lot of heads nodded. "I think we should charge for entry. But nonmembers only." Daruss nodded to Jonik. "And Jonik here wants to pay some of you to help with the human trafficking problem. If you want in on that, talk to him." Daruss stood and went around the island again. "Who wants pancakes?"

"We all do," Izzy said, and they all made themselves comfortable.

Daruss met Jonik's gaze. "I'm with my boy. I'll help, but I don't want the money. And my boys come first no matter what."

Daruss's phone rang. It sat on the counter, so Jude saw the name that popped up. It read *Seryn*.

Jude's heart beat a fast rhythm as he met Daruss's gaze.

Daruss answered without breaking eye contact. "Do you got him?... Good...Whatever you have to do. Just keep him safe..." Daruss smiled at something Seryn said. Whatever it was made his eyes soften. "Jude's worried about him too. Tell him Jude is safe and happy when he wakes up. And tell him that Jude said he loved him. Make sure he knows that part."

Jude burst into tears. Relief worked through his body like the sun's warmth.

Raylee hugged him. It was awkward but together they made their way over to Daruss. By then Daruss was off the phone.

Daruss held them both. "He's safe now. Seryn's tying up loose ends. As soon as he's done, they'll head our way."

Raylee kissed Jude's cheek. "Should we fix the room up across the hall from our bedroom or will that be too weird if he hears all our sex noises?"

Jude chuckled through his tears. "I really love you guys."

Daruss and Raylee were the most important people in Jude's life. He'd do anything for them. And maybe putting other people before himself was what love was really about.

****

Mitchell's in big trouble and he's not sure how to get out. Seryn is either an angel or he's a psychopath. Mitch isn't sure which. But one thing he knows, is Seryn's about to turn his life upside down. Click here to continue your journey with the Dragon Skull MC Daddies. Or Scan the QR Code.

****

Jonik is an assassin, not a savior. Finding his mate in the hands of his target means he has to be both at the same time. Jonik is yours FREE when you sign up for my newsletter. Or scan the QR code.

****

Honest reviews of my books help bring them to the attention of other readers. Leaving a review will help readers find the book. You can leave a review here: https://www.amazon.com/review/create-review/B01N5QOER2

About the Author

April Kelley writes LGBTQ+ Romance. Her works include *The Journey of Jimini Renn*, a Rainbow Awards finalist, *Whispers of Home*, the *Saint Lakes* series, and over thirty more. Since writing her first story at ten, the characters in her head still won't stop telling their stories. If April isn't reading or writing, you can find her playing with her cats. She also loves hiking. Her cats are leash trained so they go with her wherever she goes.

If you wish to contact her, emailauthoraprilkelley@gmail.com.

Made in the USA
Las Vegas, NV
07 April 2025

20631903R00163